Praise for Elena

Pack of Her Own

"There are a lot of subtle and not so subtle messages about a trans experience, and I really liked all of the metaphors being weaved around each other. All of the characters have a lot to wrestle with, between internal struggles and fears about society and physical dangers. Supernatural characters always have to deal with the matter of secrecy, but this author adds a couple more layers to give the story a deeper than normal feel."—*The Lesbian Review*

"There's big series potential here, so I'm curious to see where it goes!"—*The Lesbrary*

Mate of Her Own

"One thing that Abbott does really well here is establish both internal and external conflict for Heather and V to work through. I liked the way the author played around with shifter tropes to tell a queer story, and I look forward to reading more of her work."—*The Smut Report*

Hunt of Her Own

By the Author

Pack of Her Own

Mate of Her Own

Hunt of Her Own

Hunt of Her Own

by

Elena Abbott

2024

HUNT OF HER OWN

ISBN 13: 978-1-63679-685-7

This Trade Paperback Original Is Published By
Bold Strokes Books, Inc.
P.O. Box 249
Valley Falls, NY 12185

First Edition: September 2024

Credits
Editors: Jenny Harmon and Stacia Seaman
Production Design: Stacia Seaman
Cover Design by Tammy Seidick

Acknowledgments

As usual, my first acknowledgment goes to my wife, my Goddess, my love. You are my rock. You are my reason for being. But you already know all this, because I try to show you every day how much you mean to me. I love you.

There are amazing editors out there, and I'm lucky enough to work with someone who is absolutely up there with the rest. Jenny, you are an absolute blast to work with, and you're so good with figuring out what I'm trying to say and point out where I need to say more, or less, as the case may be. Thank you for being in my corner and for your amazing work. Here's to more projects together.

To my online friends, Chloe and TJ and Issy and everyone else who puts up with my sporadic posts. I'm not great at social media, but friends like you make things much easier. I appreciate the support and am grateful for the relationships we've cultivated. You all are awesome, amazing people.

And, of course, to my readers, my reviewers, everyone who has reached out and decided that one of my books might be for them. I appreciate you all so very much. I wouldn't be able to do what I love doing if it wasn't for you. Thank you, from the bottom of my heart.

To those who can't be with their loves right now.
May you one day be together and enjoy each other for good.

To my Goddess, who I could not be without.

Prologue

Rias

I bent over and started to draw the large chalk circle around the concrete pad that served as a back patio for my house. I kept my back to the werewolves and their human companion. There was no way I was going to show them just how panicked I was.

Sure, Wren, I can free Heather's wolf from its cursed cage, no problem. Hey, don't worry about it, just a walk in the fucking park for good old Rias! I shook my head and looked back at my work, trying to make it as perfect a circle as I could.

I didn't regret telling Natalie that I was a witch. I didn't regret offering my help. No, I didn't regret it. But damned if I didn't wish that I had at least considered keeping my mouth shut. They didn't know that I hadn't *really* used my magic since the day I was exiled. Sure, looking into Heather to figure out what was going on in there used a tiny bit of power, but that didn't count. I hadn't used my magic for anything big in almost forty years. I didn't have a fucking clue if I could actually pull this off.

If I'd been the one to curse Heather, I could get rid of it no problem. I could just draw the power out and have it return to its rightful place inside me. Of course, I wouldn't have cursed a person like that in the first place. I would never condemn someone to live half a life like that. Never knowing yourself fully because part of you was locked away, unable to be seen or felt? It sounded like torture to me.

And I knew what it was like to be tortured.

I finished the circle and let out a long breath. It was time to do this. Time to stop overthinking things and try my hardest to do what I told them I could. I was going to break another witch's curse. I only hoped my magic didn't end up getting me killed. Or worse, one of them.

"Wren." I glanced at the Alpha werewolf who seemed lost in her own thoughts. Her human mate, Natalie, stood off to the side, watching Wren with eyes that looked almost wounded. I didn't have time to worry about that. Whatever was going on between the two of them was their business. Unless they had play time in my kitchen again, I wasn't about to get involved.

"Are we ready?" Wren asked. I nodded and gestured at Heather, who sat in the middle of the circle.

I shot a quick look back at my magic circle. "We're ready." I beckoned Natalie toward the rest of us. "I can't just…delete the spell that is keeping her wolf locked up," I said. "It doesn't work that way. But what I can do is weaken it."

"What do you mean?" Wren asked.

"Think of this witch's spell like a cage inside Heather, and her wolf is trapped inside the cage, okay?" Nods all around. "I can't just unlock the cage without knowing how the witch did it in the first place. But I might be able to bend the bars enough to let the wolf out."

"Is this going to be dangerous?" Natalie asked.

"Potentially, yes." I caught Wren's eye and made sure she was looking at me before I continued. "That's where you come in, Wren. Her wolf has never known freedom. She's going to be scared, and that can be dangerous. I need you to help."

"How?"

I resisted the urge to yell at her. It wasn't entirely her fault she didn't know about what a werewolf Alpha could do for their pack members. The abilities of wolves were only one of the things I'd learned as a child, growing up in my coven.

"When I'm ready, I'll call for you. I want you to break the circle and do whatever Alpha magic you can to make sure her wolf comes out peacefully. Preferably before she rips my throat out."

"But I—"

I didn't bother with her excuses. I was honestly not even sure I was going to make this work, never mind make it out alive. I didn't need to listen to her blather. I knelt on the ground in front of Heather and reached deep inside myself to the pool of magic that had been sitting stagnant for all this time. It almost reached for me in its desire to be useful, and as I dipped a fingertip into the magic, it clung to me like a leech.

It wanted to be used, and I couldn't say I didn't want to use it. The magic was addictive, like most things in this world. We were taught moderation from a young age in the covens, and those who didn't abide by the rules of the covens were quick to find themselves in dire situations.

And by that, I mean literally burned at the stake. Some things never go out of style.

I took a deep breath and drew forth a trickle of my power. The magic reached forward and closed the distance between me and Heather. I began to hum under my breath but stayed focused on the magic and not the tune that was coming from my throat. My magic reached into Heather, and I guided it toward the disturbance I had sensed inside her earlier—the ball of magic that was the source of the curse.

I let out a small grunt, which interrupted my humming and my concentration. Whoever had placed this curse had done a damned good job. They knew exactly what they were doing, and more about the magic that gave werewolves their abilities than anyone I knew. I wouldn't even know where to begin to place a curse like this. But I knew where to start unravelling the damned thing. At least I hoped I did.

I started humming again and followed the flow of magic that moved with the tune as I wove it into the strands of the curse. I threaded it like the laces of a corset on either side of the weakest spot I could find. I drew on more of my magic and twisted more and more of it into the curse. My humming turned into words, and I sang lyrics from memory. I went through several different songs and was halfway through "She's Pretty" by Beth McCarthy when Heather gave out a pained gasp. I pulled back suddenly and searched for the cause.

Heather was snarling. Fur was growing in patches along her arms and face, and receding the next second, like her wolf had an idea of what was happening but couldn't quite make it. I stared as her teeth shifted and shifted back, and knew just how quickly she could rip out my jugular if I fucked this up, but I pressed on.

Wren took a step closer to the circle, and I shot her a look to make her stop. It was too soon. I needed more time.

I finished the song and searched my mind for the next. It was now or never. I reached for the magical laces and separated them, which forced the cursed magic apart and created a hole for the werewolf's power to slip through. The wolf took its chance immediately, and it was all I could do not to scream as the trapped power burst forth and engulfed Heather. I pulled my own magic back and noticed that the curse didn't try to close the opening I'd created. Clearly the original caster hadn't considered that someone else might come along and ruin their work.

"Wren!" I called out. "Now! Break the circle—draw out her wolf!"

I backed off as Wren charged in and knelt beside Heather, who had fallen sideways and was writhing on the ground. It wasn't the curse stopping her from shifting anymore. No, now it was only herself. And that was something I couldn't immediately help with, so I got up and ran to Natalie.

"Time to get to safety," I said as I grabbed her arm and led her back into the house with me. She pulled against me at first but seemed to think better of sticking around as Wren took Heather's face in her hands.

"Will they be okay?" she asked.

"I don't know. I did what I could for Heather, now the rest is up to Wren."

We retreated back into the kitchen. Natalie went to the window to watch whatever was happening, and after a few seconds I joined her. I kind of wanted to see the fruits of my labor too. Wren still knelt beside Heather. Her hand gripped the cursed wolf's neck, and she leaned in close to her face to speak. It looked almost intimate, and in a way, it was.

I glanced at Natalie. I knew she was Wren's mate, even if the Alpha refused to see it. But there wasn't the barest hint of jealousy on her face. Instead there were flashes of worry, of concentration, of pride. I smiled. She would make a good Lupa, if only Wren would get over herself.

It was slow, but Heather finally achieved her first shift, and in her place was a smaller, russet-furred wolf. Natalie let out a little whoop of delight as Wren shifted too, and together both wolves ran off toward the woods that lined the back of my property.

"It worked!"

I stared after the two wolves. Yeah, it had worked. Despite everything, it had worked. My magic had come through for me after all. I'd long given up on it being there for me, since I'd been exiled. I shook my head. Those were memories for another time. Today was a good day.

I raised my hand, palm up, and summoned a little of my magic. It jumped at my call, forming a tiny ball of light—witchlight—a few inches over my hand. A second later the light brightened until it flared and almost blinded me. The light disappeared as quickly as it appeared.

"What was that?"

I shook my head. "Just testing a theory." I let out a long sigh. Witchlight was one of the first spells a witch learned. If my magic was so rusty that I was screwing up things like that…I didn't even want to think about what that might have meant for Heather had something happened. "Sorry."

Natalie gave me a small smile. "Don't be sorry. You did something amazing tonight, you should be proud of yourself."

"I am." I was. I was proud of myself, but I also knew that using my magic like that was going to cause trouble. There was a good reason I was exiled from the covens, a good reason that I came to Terabend. "I just…don't know if I did the right thing."

"You just freed a werewolf from a curse that prevented her from shifting. How is that not the right thing?"

"Because there should have been someone else to do it. Someone who can control their magic better. Someone other than me."

She looked confused. "What do you mean? You looked like you had everything well in hand."

I laughed. "Really? Because I was flying by the seat of my pants." I let out another long breath. There was something about this girl, something that made me want to tell her everything. I felt like I could share my story with her, and she'd listen without judgment. "I'm…I'm not a very good witch."

"You helped Heather. That makes you a good witch in my books."

"And how many witches do you know?"

She paused for a moment, then smiled. "Touché."

I nodded toward the kitchen table and we sat down. We nursed whatever was left of our drinks from before the ritual. "You see, I'm not exactly supposed to use my magic for anything big. Anything at all, really, though small things would never be noticed."

"Why not?"

"Because I'm an exile. They kicked me out of the covens."

"Why on earth would they do that?"

Because I'm too powerful. The words died on my tongue. It was so stupid. I was born with a deeper wellspring of magic inside me than most witches. Add that to being able to draw on the magic of the world around me, like every witch was taught, and the coven had decided that I was too much of a liability to keep around.

"I just…the leadership and I didn't see eye to eye," I said. An understatement, to say the least, but in the end it was exile or being burned at the stake. I opted for the former, against the coven's wishes.

There was wonder in magic. It allowed us witches to do amazing, miraculous things, sometimes. But there was also power in that magic, and power corrupts. The covens were very strict about who learned what, and when an anomaly like me came around, they were quick to nip the problem in the bud. In my case, my parents managed to protect me until I was old enough to be on my own. Then they argued for exile over execution. It was only by the grace of the Goddess that I was still here. Something I thanked Her for every day.

"They exiled me," I said, my voice low and quiet. I didn't know if I was speaking more to Natalie or to myself. "They sent me away because they were afraid of me. Afraid of my magic. Afraid of what I'd do with it. So, they kicked me out, told me they'd hunt me down and kill me if I used my magic again. They were so afraid of me, and yet they threatened me? I was barely an adult and they made me fear for my life," I scoffed.

Natalie was quiet for a moment. "How long ago was that?"

I hesitated. I hadn't really thought about all this in so long. "About forty…ish years?"

"What? But you're—"

"I'm older than I look."

She looked curious. "Magic?"

"Yup. Magic."

"So why were they so afraid of you?"

I started to say *because I am*, but stopped before the words could come out. I didn't want her to know that. No one knew just how afraid of my own magic I was. No one else knew what kind of burden this was, having this kind of power, and having my entire life dictated. I missed out on my coven, my family, my life, because I was born more powerful than others. And with all I knew about my magic, the most important thing I'd learned was to be afraid of it.

"I don't know," I told her finally, knowing she was waiting for an answer. "They're stupid. I washed my hands of the covens a long time ago, before I came here."

I waited for the next prodding question, but it didn't come. Instead, Natalie looked almost sad.

"That sounds pretty lonely to me."

Ouch. Bull's-eye. Right in the heart.

"I'm okay."

She didn't look convinced.

"You know you can talk to me, right?"

"No offense, but you have problems of your own with Wren right now," I said, trying not to be unkind and failing slightly.

"Shit, don't I know it." She let out a long-suffering sigh. "Speaking of, I should probably head back to her cabin." I followed her out to the backyard to gather the clothing that the wolves had shifted out of, then around to the front where Wren's Jeep was waiting.

"It'll be okay. You know that, right?"

She laughed. "How do you know that?"

"I'm a witch, remember?"

I waited patiently as she climbed in the Jeep and drove away. When she was well and gone I returned to the house and went into the den, where I had set up my altar. It wasn't a grandiose thing, a small table with bric-a-brac scattered on it. The most precious part to me was the bowl with a set of bones in it. Some of them were given to me to start my set years ago, when I was a child. I'd added my own pieces to the collection, until it was a little handful of bones, some small seashells, some crystals, and a rare coin from somewhere I'd never been before.

I took the bowl in both hands and held it close. It was precious to me, something that no one had been able to take away from me. I took out the cloth to throw the bones on and placed it atop a soft mat on the altar to avoid them bouncing everywhere.

"Did I do the right thing? Did I help Heather and the others? How is this going to affect the future?"

I tossed the bones.

They landed splayed out across the cloth that had two circles carefully drawn upon it, one smaller and in the center of the larger one. I read the bones and took note of what had fallen outside of the circles and what had landed in the middle.

"Oh, fuck."

CHAPTER ONE

Rias

Three weeks later

My eyes snapped open as my heart beat a staccato rhythm in my chest. Then, to add insult to injury, the items that hovered around the room all crashed to the floor at the same damned time. It was a cacophony of crashes, clangs, bangs, and squelches—squelches?—that I couldn't ignore. I needed to give myself time to settle down. I glanced over the side of the bed, noted the mess, and took stock of what had fallen to the ground.

The worst of it had to be my laptop, now lying on its side with a nice long crack across the screen. I'd fallen asleep watching movies the night before.

I looked to the other side of the bed and found out what had gone *squelch.* "What the fuck?" I muttered. "Where the hell did that burrito come from?" I didn't remember having a burrito in bed recently. I pulled my knees up to me and covered my face in my hands, knowing that this was all preventable and cursing myself for letting it happen.

Inside me my magic roiled and twisted in a turbulent wave, urging me to draw it out and use it for whatever I could imagine. And I could've used it to clean the room, but instead I got out of bed and went hunting for the broom and dustpan.

This was not the first time this had happened in my sleep. I'd taken to sleeping inside a magic circle in my armchair some nights when I was really worried about it, but this time had caught me off guard.

Three weeks had passed since I'd released Heather, and my magic was not happy to be ignored anymore. It wanted to be used, to be refreshed, not to lie stagnant inside me as I eschewed it for mundane ways of doing things. The longer I let this go on, the worse it would become. I couldn't let the magic dictate my use of it. That was the first step down a slippery slope that would lead to using magic for everything—a dangerous proposition.

That's why the covens existed in the first place. To police the use of magic by witches. Because magic was addictive to a terrifying degree. So instead, they preached using magic in moderation and culled the herd when they felt like a witch was too powerful to resist the temptation.

I was lucky to get out of it with exile, with a promise never to use my magic again. My mother being the matriarch of the coven probably had something to do with it.

I rubbed my face and checked for my phone. It peeked out from under the bed where it landed. I needed to find someone who could help me figure out what was going on with my magic, someone who wouldn't go to the covens and narc me out for what I'd done in the first place. I didn't have a lot of contacts within the covens, but I thought I knew someone who might be able to help. Plus, she owed me a favor.

I could only hope that she had answers for me.

I took a sip of my chai latte and bit back a soft moan. That was one thing I couldn't find in Terabend, a damned good chai latte. Don't get me wrong, drip coffee was usually good enough for me, but once in a while I just wanted a little treat.

I settled into a chair on the patio of the small coffee shop in downtown Vancouver, a place I'd thought I'd never be again. My parents ran the coven outside the greater Vancouver area, and a lot of my past had been spent in the city, until the exile. Vancouver had changed a lot in that time, some for the better, some for the worse.

A few moments of savoring my latte later and a tall woman joined me in the chair across the table, her own coffee in hand. She stood almost a foot taller than me, with a short, dark Afro. She'd changed it since the last time I saw her. Back then her dreadlocks had fallen almost to her ass.

This new style was a good look on her.

"Danaan Rias," she said softly, "it's been some time."

"Too long, Brigid."

Brigid set her cup down and gave me a wide smile. "I'm surprised you came all this way just to see little old me."

"It would've been easier if you hadn't made me come all the way out here."

She shrugged. "I go where the work is, you know that. I've spent the last couple months here." She took a sip of her drink. "I know you don't like to come out here much. Too close to the coven for comfort and all."

"I haven't been around here for years. It…it's almost like it's itchy. Like something I can't scratch." I shook my head. "I don't like it."

"Then why make the trip?"

"Because I need your help."

"That's what you said on the phone. What's going on?"

"It's about…" I glanced around as if afraid that someone nearby might be eavesdropping. I trusted Brigid, but if another witch found out an exile was using their magic again, I wouldn't be long for this world. "My magic."

Brigid's eyes went wide. "What do you mean? You know you aren't supposed to be…to be using again."

I flinched at the way she said it, which insinuated it was like a drug. Not a terrible comparison, to be frank, but one that I didn't like.

"I had to. I had to help her."

"No, you were supposed to stop using your magic the moment you were exiled. And if you're having issues now, that means you did something big, not just a quick tidy of a room or cheating at poker or something. What did you do?"

"I did what I had to do. I couldn't let her live her life like that, not if I could help it."

"What do you mean?"

I sighed. "A werewolf friend of mine. She was cursed never to be able to shift. By a witch." Brigid gasped as her blue eyes widened in shock. "It wasn't fair for her to be stuck like that, so I helped her. And yes, I used my magic to free her."

"And now? What's the problem that brought you out here to me?"

"Now my magic won't shut up! It's like now that it's awakened, it wants me to use it all the time, to do everything with magic. Like it has a mind of its own."

"Shit." She shook her head. "How bad is it?"

"It's coming out at night," I admitted, "while I'm asleep. That's what happened the other night, when I called you. Not every night, but a couple times a week if I don't take precautions."

"Precautions?"

I nodded. "Like sleeping in a magic circle."

"That's not healthy, long term. Too much stagnant energy from inside the circle will dull your abilities."

I snorted. "Maybe that's not a terrible idea. Dull my powers, make them go back to sleep."

She shook her head again. "No, that's not what I mean. It'll dull your ability to control them, making the magic more likely to worm its way under your skin and tempt you."

I rubbed my face with my hands. "I know that. I know, I just don't know what to do now. I can't afford to let it…act out at an inopportune moment, and I don't want to give in to the temptation either. I was hoping maybe you knew something that could help."

We shared a comfortable silence for a few minutes. I sipped at my latte and grimaced a little at the now lukewarm drink. Brigid's eyes were closed, her face serene. She looked like she was ready to fall asleep, but I knew she was merely thinking.

Brigid knew more about magic than anyone else I'd ever met. More than my parents, more than my old coven. I'd met her shortly after my exile, and we'd become good friends. She too was without a coven, though that was by choice on her part. She was a nomad and traveled wherever she wished. She was on good terms with most of the covens in the country, and elsewhere. She knew what it was like to be alone, and had taken a liking to me, I supposed. We tried to meet up at least once a year or so, even if it was just to catch up.

She was the closest thing to family I had.

The longer the silence stretched, the more antsy I got. What if she didn't know? What was I going to do, allow the magic to ruin my life? I couldn't just ignore it. I'd tried that for the last three weeks and had gotten nowhere. I didn't want to hurt anyone, or myself. Magic like that…it was dangerous. If I let it leak out, the way it wanted, it would only be a matter of time before I hurt someone or someone got hurt because of me.

"I'm sorry," I said, finally needing to break the quiet between us. "I shouldn't have come down here to bother you with this. I know you're busy, that you don't really want anything to do with magic anymore—"

She held up a hand to interrupt me. "You know that's not what this is, sweetie. I'm not tossing you aside like the other witches did, you know that."

"I just don't know what to do."

"The problem is your magic. You have such a…such a wellspring of magic inside you that what I would normally suggest or advise to someone in your position might not work for you."

"Tell me anyways."

She let out a long breath. "The only thing I can think of, and I have no idea if it will work for you, is to start at the beginning."

"What?"

"Start from the beginning. As if you were learning to use your magic all over again. Small spells, moving things around, maybe, or practice with your witchlight. Things like that."

"What is that going to do?"

"It will hopefully satiate your magic and allow it and you to become accustomed to each other once again."

"I don't understand. You're telling me to start over? Like I was a kid again."

"Yes. Yes, that is exactly what I am saying." She gave me a smile like one you'd give a small child to placate them. "I know you remember your lessons. Hell, *I* remember my lessons, and I had them several decades before you."

I leaned back and took another sip of my latte, draining the cup of the last lukewarm dregs. It made sense. Start from scratch, get used to the magic again. It was going to be a lesson in patience, one I couldn't even be sure I was up for. "There has to be something different. Something else I can do. I can't just…forget everything I've learned."

"It's not a matter of forgetting, it's a matter of relearning how to function. And quietly. Because if a coven finds out what you're doing, they won't hesitate to try and drag you back for judgment."

"That's something I'd much rather avoid." I leaned forward over the table. "I spent years not using my magic at all, and it just…went into hibernation. I want that to happen again. I want it to just shut up and leave me alone."

She shook her head. "I don't think you'll get away with that again. Not with the kind of power you have. You need to find a balance within yourself. This is the only way to calm your magic so you can live with it once more. At least, the only way I can think of." She took a sip of her own drink, tipping it back. "I don't know how you managed to get your magic to sleep inside you for so long by just ignoring it the first time, but I'm certain that won't happen again. And honestly, Danaan, you have no one to blame but yourself."

"What?"

"It was you who decided to help this wolf." She held up a hand as if expecting my argument. "I know, I know, it was a great thing that you did, but the truth of the matter is that you did not *have* to do it, Danaan. You could have contacted me or tried to find another witch to help her. Or even have just said that you couldn't do it. You did, despite how noble your intentions, bring this on yourself."

I didn't have the words to argue with her because she was right. I had brought it all on myself. "It was the right thing to do," I said, crossing my arms and leaning back again.

"I'm certainly not denying that. I'd have done the same."

Was I regretting helping Heather? No. It wasn't her fault. I had spent the last few decades scared of my own magic because of my family, my coven. If the first good thing I did with it since then made me have to rethink everything I knew about my magic, then so be it. I'd do it again in a heartbeat.

"I couldn't let her live like that. It wasn't fair to her. I thought, maybe, if I put enough good in the world that something good would come back to me, I suppose."

"You know that's not exactly how it works."

"I know that. I just was hopeful. I mean, I threw the bones and everything afterward, hoping some good would come of it. But all I got was…nightmares."

She chuckled. "Well, there's your problem. You're still throwing bones. There are much better methods of divination out there that you could have used."

I shrugged. "I like the bones. They've never steered me wrong before, and I don't think they will now."

"What did they indicate?"

I hesitated. It wasn't the easiest thing, to interpret the bones as they fell, and even harder sometimes to explain to someone else what they showed. "Change. Big change. But about or regarding what is anyone's guess."

"That is a little vague. Are you sure you read them right?"

I glared at her. "I've been reading the bones since you were my age. I got it as right as it's gonna be."

She gave me a wry smile. "Then you better be ready to accept some change, no?"

The soft words were devoid of condemnation, but my face heated as I heard them. "I can handle change."

"But will you recognize it when it comes?"

The immediate response was of course I would, but something in me faltered before the words could come out. Wasn't that what I was doing here? Trying to avoid change. Wanting everything to go back to the way things were. The very definition of being anti-change.

"I'm scared," I admitted softly. "I'm scared to move forward, I'm scared to go back to the way things were. I don't know why I did what I did. It seemed like such a good idea at the time. Part of me wishes I could take the words back, has felt that way since I opened my mouth to Natalie in the first place. And another part of me is proud of the role I played in helping Heather. It's all so damned confusing!"

"The price of putting someone else first after so long of cutting yourself off from everything."

"I didn't cut myself off from everything."

"But you did, Danaan. And you had every right to. You were exiled, warned never to use your magic. What other choice did you have?" She gave me a wide smile. "Honestly, it's about time that you decided to take back your power."

"But they'll come for me. You know that."

She snorted. "And if you were doing terrible things with your magic, then they would be right to do so. Keep putting that good out into the world, and you will be fine."

"You speak like it's so damned simple."

"It is, in some ways. In others it will be the hardest thing you ever do." She glanced at her watch and frowned. "And that is where I must leave you, my friend. Apparently, I am a popular person today."

I shook my head. "I don't know if I can do this, Brigid."

She gave me that soft smile again, like she knew exactly what I was going through. "I believe that you can. You just have to do your best. That's all anyone can ask of you."

I stood up with her and we shared a long, pleasant hug. I almost shivered from the contact—something I hadn't had for a long time.

"Thank you," I said as we parted. "I don't know where I'd be without you."

"The pleasure is mine, dear. But don't let it be so long until next time. I enjoy our time together."

I nodded. "I'll do that. I'll try."

"That's all I can ask."

After another parting hug and a shy wave, she turned and walked away. I plopped back into my seat, my face in my hands, and let out a long groan. Start from the beginning, she'd said. Embrace change. If that was what I had to do to get control of my magic again, then I'd better damned well get started. I froze for a second, parsing her words again. What was I trying to do? Quell my magic so it didn't give me troubles like before, or learn to actually live with it instead of in spite of it? My first instinct was to go back to the way things were, when I barely knew my magic was there, drawing out the tiniest amounts once in a while to use for nothing important. But was that what I wanted? Or what my magic would allow of me?

"Fuck!" I snapped, loud enough that I got some looks from some passersby. I rubbed my face and grabbed my cup, then tossed it in a nearby trash can before wandering away from the coffee shop. My hotel was only a few blocks away, and it didn't take long to reach it, but I hesitated to go in.

I did not want to deal with another night of losing control. I did not want to deal with another night of being afraid of my magic. There was little I could do right now but try to keep my mind off things. A swim in the hotel's pool would do wonders, I decided. And then…well, then who knew where the night would lead.

Chapter Two

Ashly

I blinked back tears as I let out a massive yawn, trying to keep my focus on the road in front of me. In the passenger seat my father snored softly, reclined a little so he was barely noticeable from outside the car. But I noticed him. I had to live with him. Deal with him all the time. But I wasn't about to start getting mad at him for sleeping while I drove. I'd done enough of it while it was his turn, and honestly it was only a couple more hours until we got to Vancouver and our destination anyway.

Despite the exhaustion and the monotonous hours of highway driving, I couldn't keep a small smile from my face. I was finally getting to go on a hunt. No more waiting around for Dad to come back, no more cleaning the weapons or doing nothing as I worried whether or not either of my parents were going to return. Not this time. I was going to meet the other hunters, work with them, fight with them. I was going to get to do my duty to my family and to humanity as a whole.

I glanced at my dad out of the corner of my eye. He seemed so at peace, only ever looking like that when he was asleep. Awake, he was like a pent-up leopard, always stalking around, ready to pounce. He had to be like that. Our family were hunters of supernatural creatures. A hunter always had to be prepared for when the monsters decided to show their teeth. Even when most of humanity didn't believe in them. Hell, even I had trouble properly believing that these things were real, and I'd faced off with a freaking werewolf. That was the night when they told me what was real, when I learned that there was a whole other world out there that no one knew or believed in.

Doesn't help that the thing nearly killed me before I wounded it. My father finished it off and I walked away with a broken arm and hurt pride, but I was alive and I knew what was out there now. I knew how to fight them now. At least, I knew in theory. I hadn't been on a hunt since then, and that had been almost three years ago. But tonight, that was going to change. We were headed for Vancouver to help a couple of hunters there take out a nest of vampires.

"Keep your eyes on the road." My father's voice broke through my thoughts. I glanced to the side, but he hadn't moved at all or even bothered to open his eyes. But his presence seemed to grow inside the car, and I could feel him awakening. I turned my focus back to the road in front of us, fearing his displeasure. He could still take this away from me.

I drove the last two hours before we made it into Vancouver proper, plus a little longer before I pulled into the parking area for the hotel. My father was awake by then, staring out the car window. His eyes scanned everything that passed by. He didn't speak another word to me until I'd parked the car.

"Let's go."

I nodded and followed him without comment. Felt like I was dancing on fucking eggshells, and really in a way I was. I was ready to do pretty much whatever he wanted right now, to show him that I could be useful and obedient on hunts. Maybe then he would take me more often. Or better yet, let me have one of my own.

I was ready. I just needed him to realize it.

"Get some rest. You were driving for a while," he said as we let ourselves into the hotel room. He nodded to one of the two beds. "I'll wake you before anything happens."

"Are you sure? I mean, I'm okay to get started now."

He shook his head. "We're waiting on Dylan and Tony anyway. Might as well make use of the time."

I watched him for a few seconds as he tossed his duffel bag on the far bed and started to paw through it. It was full of clothes, cameras, and other paraphernalia to keep our cover as private investigators. Even the room was billed to an account that made it all seem legit. The only thing that didn't come with us was the majority of our weapons, which stayed in the trunk of the car. The gun laws in Canada were a lot stricter than those down south, which made carrying quite a bit harder. I had a small pistol at the small of my back and I knew my father had at least two on him, but we were careful not to let anyone see them. We didn't have permits for concealed carry—something that was nearly impossible to get here. Really, it wasn't like we could go to the RCMP and tell them that we needed the weapons because we hunted werewolves and vampires. They'd laugh us all the way out the damned door.

There was always a part of me that was uncomfortable carrying a weapon, but I knew they had a purpose. And my father wouldn't have me unarmed anyway. He was adamant that the monsters would wipe us out if they could. Hence the pistol at the small of my back.

"Shouldn't you be hunting the vampires during the day? When they're asleep or at least not fully awake?" I sat on the bed, my back to him, as I pulled the holster from my jeans and placed it in the top drawer of the bedside table. Right next to one of those hotel Bibles that, I shit you not, are real and not just in the movies.

"I'm glad you've been listening," he replied. "Yes, daytime is usually better for vampire hunting, but we're here now and we need to at least scope out where the nest is. Whether we go in tonight is another matter altogether."

I pulled off my flannel button-down, leaving me in a tank top and my jeans. I slipped off my shoes and socks and shoved them off to the side.

"Are you sure you don't need me right now?" I asked, the cynic in me wondering exactly what he was going to do while I slept. Of course, my body decided to take that moment to betray me with a jaw-cracking yawn.

"Get some rest, kiddo. You're going to learn to get it when you can."

Another yawn ripped through me as I lay down on the bed, my back to my father. Despite my excitement about being on a hunt with him, my eyelids drooped as soon as my head hit the pillow. He'd wake me up before long, and we'd get on with the hunt. He wouldn't leave without me.

❖

I awoke to absolute darkness and shot up with the disorientation that only comes with that brief moment of wakefulness before the memories of where you are come back to you. My heart pounded in my chest as I waited for my eyes to adjust to the dark in the unfamiliar surroundings. There wasn't a sound in the room save for my heavy breathing, and I knew something was wrong.

It took a moment for my eyes to adjust enough to the darkness to embark off the bed to find the light switch. I squinted at the sudden intrusion of brightness in my life and waited once more for my eyes to adjust.

The room was empty. Almost empty. Dad's bag was still on the other bed, zipped up as if ready for a quick getaway. My bag was on the floor beside my bed, and I grabbed it up and pulled out my phone. It was almost half past eleven at night. I swore.

He'd left me behind. That son of a bitch left me behind! I restrained myself from destroying the room with my fury and instead focused on the piece of hotel stationery that sat tented on the bedside table.

The words were written in my father's flowing handwriting. I read the note. Reread it. Read it a third time, then crumpled it in my fist and threw it in the trash. That asshole. That fucking asshole! Brought me all the way here only to tell me that he didn't think I was ready and that I couldn't come on the hunt with him. And he didn't even have the decency to say it to my face.

"Not mature enough," I spat his words out into the air around me, the anger boiling up inside. "Not ready! Need someone to stay back!" I slammed my fist against the bed. "What fucking bullshit!" I hit the bed again, but stopped myself before I did it a third time. I was acting like a child having a temper tantrum. I was better than that. It just…it wasn't *fair*. He'd brought me all the way here just to leave me behind? And to tell me in a note, of all things, that I wasn't ready for this? Why the hell had he brought me along in the first place?

"Because he needed someone to drive the car, idiot," I told myself. I wiped at my eyes, forcing back the annoying tears that threatened to fall. Yes, I was pissed. Yes, I was hurt, but crying wasn't going to make anything better.

Well, he'd better not have expected me to wait around for him like a dutiful little daughter. I grabbed my flannel and shoes and socks, then tucked my weapon back in my jeans, making sure the flannel covered the weapon well. I grabbed my key card and phone and left the room, storming my way toward the elevator. My first thought was to head for the parking garage to get the car, but I reasoned that Dad would have taken it—and the weapons—with him. With a frustrated sigh I hit the button for the lobby instead. I couldn't just sit there in the room alone. I couldn't do it. I needed something more. Wanted more than to wait around for him.

There was a restaurant off the lobby that looked like the bar was still open. I nodded to myself. A drink would be good. Two or three even better.

There was already a woman sitting at the bar, a tumbler in front of her and a bottle of what looked like something expensive beside it. The bartender was more focused on a television hanging over the far end of the bar top than on her, and I sidled up and plunked my ass down on a stool, leaving an empty one between us but making sure I got the bartender's attention.

"Kitchen's closed." He wasn't very happy that someone else had come to interrupt whatever he was watching—some recap of the news or something. I didn't care.

"Beer, Kokanee."

He eyed me up and down. "ID?"

I sighed and fished out my identification. Hey, I was of legal age, just let me drink. He gave the card a scrutinizing look, then nodded and handed it back.

"Bottle or tap?"

"Tap's fine."

He poured a glass and set it in front of me. I took a sip and choked back the slight burn of the alcohol hitting my throat. It was something I was still getting used to. I was a good girl. I didn't start drinking until I was old enough to buy it myself. Hadn't built up a tolerance to it yet, but I was working on it. The way my dad drank, it seemed to be a requisite for hunters like us. Probably to deal with the horrors of what we saw on the regular.

But all that was neither here nor there. I was pissed at him and I didn't want to think about him anymore.

"Stupid," I said to myself and took another sip. Movement to the side drew my attention to my drinking partner.

She very carefully poured more of an amber liquid from a bottle into her tumbler. Semi-melted ice cubes clinked around in the glass. She moved with deliberation, like she was already three sheets to the wind and knew it. I took a better look at her.

She had light brown hair in a pixie cut with sweeping bangs that kept threatening to cover her eye. She wore a nice dress, not evening-gown nice, but definitely something that made me think she'd been on a bad date or something. The dark dress fell to her calves, and a pair of simple flats completed the picture. She looked like she was maybe a couple years older than me.

Her eyes caught mine as I was looking, and I fell into the amazing color that looked almost violet in this light. I couldn't bring myself to look away even for a second as she took her time with her own examination of me. I smirked as her eyes returned to my face.

"Like what you see?" I asked, trying to put all the confidence that I could muster into the line.

"I've seen worse." Her voice was soft, but had a strength behind it that belied what I thought was her drunken status. Those eyes only told the story better, showing me she wasn't nearly as out of it as it had seemed. "And how do I measure up in your estimation?"

"As the most beautiful woman I've seen tonight."

She laughed and made a show of looking around the empty bar. "There doesn't seem to be a lot of competition around."

"I call them like I see them." At this point my mouth felt like it was moving on autopilot. I couldn't even blame the booze—I'd only had a couple sips. "I'm just commenting on the company here this evening. It's rare to see someone as beautiful as you, here alone this late at night."

Her look told me she was skeptical, but I tried to keep my look as open and honest as I could.

"And you often go trolling hotel bars around midnight?"

I laughed and pushed back some hair from my shoulder. Her eyes followed the movement, and I had to wonder exactly what I was doing—and why I was enjoying it so much. "Who doesn't?"

"Married couples?"

We laughed together at her joke and I took another sip of my beer. She took a swig of the amber liquid, savoring it before swallowing.

"Then I suppose I'm barking up the right tree." Though I had no idea what tree that necessarily was.

I'd never thought about my orientation before. I knew I liked women better than men, but outside of a few fumbling experiences late in high school had found little taste for the more carnal desires. There were more important things in the world—monsters and villains and things to hunt and fight.

But tonight? Tonight, I didn't care about all that. The culmination of my childhood training and the mission my father wanted to pass down to me didn't matter when I was staring into her eyes.

"I am barking up the right tree, aren't I?"

"You are," she replied quickly, a twinkle in her eye. "Now, whether or not I'm interested is another matter."

"Well, you haven't told me to get lost yet, so I'm hopeful."

"Hopeful that you have a chance?"

I said the first thing that came to mind. "Hopeful that a beauty like you would take a chance on me, even if only for a night."

Oh. My. Gosh. Who was I and what the hell was I doing? My surprise and lack of confidence seemed to be well hidden, though, when the woman patted the seat beside her.

"Very smooth. Let's talk, then we'll see if you have a chance."

I resisted the urge to let out a sigh of relief. Was I really doing this? Talking up some woman at a bar? And to what end? But there was a side of me that wanted this. Partly to get back at my dad for leaving me alone like this, and partly wanting this experience for myself. This was the first thing I'd done for myself in a long time. I wanted it to work out. I wanted to find something that I wanted, for a change.

"I'm Ashly," I said, holding out a hand to her.

She took my hand. "Rias."

"*Ree-as?*" I repeated softly, drawing her name out. Beautiful, striking, and somehow fitting of her. "I like it. It's unique in the best of ways."

She snorted. "That's not the response I usually get."

"No? Well, that's a pity. Because it's a beautiful name for a beautiful woman."

"You keep trying to compliment me." She took another sip of her drink. "You must really be desperate."

"If I was desperate, I would be in a dingy hole-in-the-wall bar or a dark club or something. Instead, I found this beautiful woman staying in the very same hotel I'm staying in. And I hope she is of the same—or at least similar—persuasion as myself."

"We've already established that I am."

"Exactly! So, it's a wonderful coincidence that we happened to be here together at the same time, and I think we should take advantage of it."

"Really? How so?"

I took a swig of beer and decided to go all in. "I really wasn't expecting to have to explain the birds and the bees to you tonight, but when two people really just want to have sex with each other…" I waggled my eyebrows at her, and she gave me a soft chuckle in return.

"But why me?" She made a show of looking around the empty bar again. I followed her gaze. Other than the annoyed-looking bartender shooting dirty glances at us, there was no one present. "I mean, there've got to be better options in your hole-in-the-wall bar or club."

I waved my hand, dismissing her words. "You sell yourself too short, my dearest Rias. There are no options at other places that could be better than yourself."

"You flatter me too much."

"And you deflect said flattery too quickly."

"I suppose that puts us at an impasse."

I leaned closer to her, staring right into those gorgeous violet eyes. "I *suppose* that's up to you."

Who was this person I was channeling right now? I wasn't this smooth. I wasn't this good at talking to people. Get to the point, be direct, get in and out without a scratch. That's the kind of stuff I was used to doing. This…tête-à-tête was something beyond me, most of the time.

Rias sighed and turned away from my gaze. She pressed her glass to her forehead like she was trying to cool herself down.

"You certainly are direct, aren't you?"

I grinned but moved back, giving her back her space. "In this, I guess I am. But it means I know what I want and am driven toward it. There're enough things in life that aren't that simple or direct. This I at least have control over."

She sighed. "I understand that more than you probably realize."

"Then the universe definitely brought us together for a reason."

She sputtered into her glass, choking back more of the amber liquid through her laughter. I resisted the urge to pat her on the back, aware that unwanted touching might ruin everything. Whatever the hell I was doing here tonight, I wanted this. I couldn't even say for certain why, but I wanted her more than I'd wanted anything for a long time.

"Kiss me," she said when she got herself under control again.

My bravado slipped. "Excuse me?"

"Kiss me. Show me what I'm missing."

I'm not proud of the fact that I hesitated, only for a second. I wiped my mouth with a napkin and turned fully toward her as she turned on her stool toward me. I placed a hand on her shoulder to steady us both, then moved in for a kiss. I halted a half inch away, my eyes open and searching her face, waiting for that final bit of permission before I did this.

She closed the distance between us. Our lips pressed together, hesitant and awkward at first as we tested the waters, then evolving into something more. It was soft and wonderful, her lips tasting sweet, almost like caramel from whatever it was she was drinking. I grazed my tongue against her lips and she opened slightly, allowing me a deeper taste for only a second before I leaned back, not wanting to push her too far.

We parted from what had actually been a pretty chaste kiss, all things considered. The bartender's eyes were now firmly on the television, like he was trying to give us privacy. But I wanted more. I retreated a little bit back from her, unsure of how she would react, when her hand shot out and grabbed mine.

"Let's go," she said breathlessly, and threw a couple of bills on the bar. "Before I change my mind."

I gave her a wide smile. "Yes ma'am." I let her pull me off the stool and toward the elevators.

All thoughts of my father and what he'd done were burned out of my head as she pressed me against the wall of the elevator as it moved upward. We kissed again, hot and passionate, her lips sweet and warm and the most amazing thing I'd felt in I didn't know how long.

Whatever I'd thought I was going to do tonight, that plan changed the moment we stepped off the elevator onto her floor. I let myself go with the flow, and forgot about my father, about hunting, about everything.

There was only Rias and me.

Perfect.

CHAPTER THREE

Rias

Six weeks later

"And then what happened?" Natalie asked, her face in her hands, elbows on the table. Clearly hanging on every word I said.

I laughed, popped a french fry in my mouth, and chewed slowly, all the while enjoying the wild anticipation on my friend's face. It'd been a month and a half since my night in Vancouver, and since then I'd been on my own most of the time, working through what I remembered from my childhood in a bid to control my magic. As much as I didn't want to admit it, Brigid was right. I hadn't had any more episodes since my return. Not since that night with…

"I don't kiss and tell," I told her finally. I gave her a wide smile as she leaned back and pouted. The newly minted werewolf in front of me had only decided to stay here a couple weeks ago, after that disastrous battle with a rival pack that saw her almost get killed. Wren had turned her into a werewolf to save her life. Now they were happy together, a pack of three wolves with Heather. And I didn't have to drive to another province to find a friend I could confide in.

It was really, really nice, actually.

Sure, there was Wren, or Dr. Maru, both of whom would listen and probably try to tackle whatever problem I had head-on. And sometimes that was warranted. But Natalie *listened*, and that was what I needed more.

"You're not even going to tell me her name?" Natalie said. She was still pouting as she snatched up a fry from the big plate between us. "You can at least tell me that much."

I stretched my arms over my head, leaning back and grinning at her, enjoying the moment wielding knowledge over her. We sat in the rear-most corner booth of Wren's diner, the Tooth and Claw, where Natalie was often near her mate.

"Her name is Ashly," I said, remembering the strawberry-blond hair that cascaded down her back as she enthusiastically worked herself between my thighs. I had to rub my legs together for a second and realized just how noticeable the movement was when Natalie's face lit up and she giggled. Heat rushed to my cheeks and I glanced away. I grabbed a couple more fries and shoved them in my face, so I didn't have to say anything.

"So, are you going to see her again?"

Dear Goddess, how much I wanted to. I hadn't felt anything like it in years upon years. That's not to say I hadn't had fun in the past, but that was different. What happened that night was amazing. It was something I desperately wanted again.

"Probably not." I didn't like how wistful my tone became. "I mean, we were both staying in the same hotel. I don't know where she lives or if she's with someone else or what. I don't even know her last name."

"What do you know about her?"

I sighed and remembered Ashly as if she were standing at the end of the table. "She was a couple inches taller than me, closer to your height. Her hair was a few shades lighter than yours, more strawberry-blond than ginger. Her eyes were a gorgeous blue…" I wanted to continue gushing but stopped. This was getting a little too pathetic, even for me. "I mean, she was handsome, and amazing, and I'm never going to see her again, so there's no point in dwelling on it."

"I'm sorry." Natalie had the good grace to look slightly chagrined. "I'm just happy for you. I haven't seen you excited about anything like this before, and it's really a nice change."

"I'm not that grumpy, thank you."

"I didn't say you were grumpy. I just…I mean, it's nice to see you happy about something. You're usually really…reserved."

Reserved. Not a terrible word for it. And I couldn't argue with her. I'd been doing too much work by myself, and ignoring everything else. Reserved was putting it mildly.

"I know I've been kind of a hermit lately."

She shook her head. "I'm not judging, I promise. I notice these things because I know what it's like to shut yourself away from the world. It's how I spent a lot of my childhood."

"How did you change?"

She smiled. "Ran away from my parents, transitioned, started hormones as soon as I could. And I still needed a kick in the ass to get out of my hermit mode and meet people."

I laughed. "A kick in the ass called *getting turned into a werewolf*?"

"To put it mildly," she said. "Even when I was with my ex, I didn't really get out at all. Most of our friends were *her* friends, most of the things we did were things that *she* wanted to do. I thought I needed to be okay with that because she was the only one who would want me. The only one who would have me. Then…then I came here."

"And you found a family."

She nodded. "And you're part of that family."

I did my best not to shudder at the term but failed. "I never thought about it like that. I haven't thought I'd have a family in a very long time."

"Sometimes you need to find your family, especially if the one you started with wasn't so fantastic. Sometimes it takes time."

Time. Something I had in spades. A witch's magic could help them live for a few centuries, much like the shifters. Losing control of my power could have long-term consequences that could haunt me for years if I didn't fix it. So far things had been going well, but there was that gnarly feeling in the pit of my stomach that made me worry that it wouldn't be enough.

I was tempted for a moment to tell Natalie about my magic. I wanted to share the problem with a friend, come clean about what had happened, hell, even be honest about the reason for my trip to Vancouver. The excuse was for a vacation because I was burnt out—not far off from the truth in a way. What would Natalie say if I told her I couldn't control my magic? Would she be as frightened of it as I was?

"Natalie, I—" I began.

"Hey, Nat," a voice called from behind the counter. We both glanced over and saw Wren come out of the doors to the kitchen. "We should head out to Hikaru's."

"Oh right!" Natalie replied and eased her way off the booth cushion.

"You're going to Dr. Maru's?" I asked. "Are you okay?"

She waved a hand. "Oh yeah, it's fine. We're going to see her because…well…" She turned and looked at Wren. "Can I tell her?"

Wren hesitated for a moment, then nodded at her mate.

"We're going to talk to the doctor about looking into in vitro fertilization. See if sometime in the future we can have some puppies." Natalie let out a little laugh. "I mean, I don't know if it's going to happen, and it's just, you know, kind of just to see if it's doable and stuff…"

I stared at the two of them. The idea of it had never crossed my mind. I mean, Wren? With puppies? But I smiled instead and stood from the booth as well, then wrapped my arms around Natalie in a tight hug.

"That's amazing," I said as I backed off a step. "I really hope it works out for you."

"Thank you!" Natalie gushed as Wren stepped up beside her and put an arm around her shoulder. "I'll see you later, all right?"

I nodded and moved aside as they headed for the door of the diner. I sat back in the booth, staring at the fries in front of me. I felt the beginnings of tears start to collect around the inside corners of my eyes.

Okay, so I was a bit jealous of Wren and Natalie. They were like the perfect couple. But I guess that's kind of what you get when you're literally fated to be together. Natalie wasn't just Wren's mate, but her Fated Mate, a gift from the Mother of Wolves that the wolf shifters honored. Witches…witches didn't get fated mates. We usually kept ourselves within our covens, meaning whoever we decided to be with lived about as long as we did anyway. Those who left the covens for love usually didn't stay away for long, knowing that no one they found out in the human world could handle being with someone who looked twenty-five when they were north of sixty.

In a way, that was another thing my exile had cost me. The chance to be with someone who really understood who I was, what I was going through. I'd have to find another exile to be with, and the odd chance of that wasn't great. Especially when most covens were more likely to burn a witch than exile them. It was easier in the long run.

My mind turned back to Ashly without prompting. Images of her on top of me, her hand between my thighs, flashed through my head. I hid my blush in another mouthful of lukewarm fries. I wondered where she was, what she was doing. I wondered if I would see her again. I closed my eyes, reaching deep within and idly touching that pool of power that dwelled inside me. It leapt at my call, but I only grasped the smallest bit of it that I could. I wrapped the magic against one of the smallest, simplest spells I could remember as a child. Putting a wish out into the universe. It was an effort in futility, I knew, but it didn't matter to me.

"I want to see her again," I whispered to myself. "I wish to see her again." I let the magic go with the intent behind my words, and the power evaporated into the air with the tiniest pop of sound.

Suddenly I felt a pulling inside me and there was another popping noise, and everything on the table in front of me, the table behind me, and the end of the bar near me suddenly was hovering at a spot three feet in the air as if pulled there by a localized black hole. The plate, fries, napkin dispensers, salt and pepper shakers, and even a stool all hung in the air for all of five seconds before there was a third popping sound and everything came crashing to the ground.

I stared at the mess as footsteps pounded nearby. I looked behind me and saw the other patrons staring at the mess, then shooting me disgruntled looks. I ignored them, clutching a hand to my chest as I pressed down on my magic once again, trying to quell it. It went easily, as if happy to return back to its pool now that it had accomplished something large.

"Rias!" Heather's voice was shrill and panicked. "What happened? Are you okay?"

I numbly nodded, watching as Heather stood over the pile, confusion plain on her face. She stepped around the mess and stopped beside the booth, leaning down.

"Is something wrong? Did something happen?"

I felt nothing but numbness as my nod turned into a shake. I stared at the discarded fries and felt the tears starting to fall. I pushed myself up and out of the booth, and almost bowled Heather over.

"I'm sorry! I—I have to go."

I didn't give her a chance to speak as I rushed out the door. I leapt into my car and peeled out of the parking lot before I absolutely devolved into my panic attack.

"Oh Goddess! What the hell? What the hell was that?" I tried to focus on breathing and driving at the same time and barely managed to make my turn that would take me off the highway and toward my house. "Stupid, just fucking stupid! Using magic in public like that? What were you thinking? You're not some empty-headed schoolgirl fawning over some fucking crush. Putting your magic out into the world like that? You deserve what fucking happened!"

The tears wouldn't stop falling as I berated myself and tried to drive at the same time. I knew I was going under the speed limit, I knew I was swerving a little, but I made it home safely—thank the Goddess. I shut myself up in my house with a final, echoing slam and collapsed on the floor, gasping and crying.

Eventually I managed to calm myself enough to climb into my bed and cling to my pillow. As I fell asleep I could only hope my magic was sated.

Chapter Four

Ashly

"Ashly, are you listening to me?"

I rolled my neck a few times to try and work a kink out of it before I even considered trying to respond to the old man. He paced in front of my desk like an irate teacher who, if he could just thrust enough knowledge at me, could make me an apt pupil. It didn't matter that we'd been over most of this before until it was drilled into my brain and I wanted to spew it all out verbatim before I died of boredom.

Was it like this for all hunter families, I wondered, or was my father just that special?

When I finished with my neck I shrugged my shoulders and rolled them back too, the stiffness from sitting in this chair for the past three hours absolutely killing my body. And Goddess forbid I should slouch at all, or he'd yell at me for not listening.

"Ashly!"

Ah, yes, exhibit A.

"Yes, Father?" I replied delicately.

"You haven't paid attention to a thing that I've been saying for the past twenty minutes." My father was not a tall man, but he knew how to make himself seem bigger when he needed to intimidate someone. When I was a teenager it used to work wonders on me, but since my brother…let's just say it didn't have the same effect it used to.

"Not entirely true," I told him. "I pay attention when you have new things to say."

He stared down at me and I resisted the urge to bop him in the nose. Either that or tap him on the top of his bald head and watch his mouth pop open like some weird children's toy from the '70s. His green eyes bulged a little like he couldn't believe I'd have the audacity to not wholly agree with him and bow my head in shame.

"I go over the same things to make sure you learn before I send you out on a hunt and you get yourself killed! What we go over here could save your life. You would do well to listen better."

"*Dad,*" I said, "I get it, I do. But since you rarely let me go on hunts and definitely won't let me have one of my own, it's a little hard to pay attention to your doom-mongering about the state of the supernatural world."

He shook his head. "This is why we do what we do, Ashly. We are hunters for a reason. Because the supernatural world is a world where humans are prey, not predator. It's up to families like ours to—"

"To balance the scales, to make sure they don't wipe us out. To destroy the evil creatures wherever they may be found," I finished for him. I'd heard the speech before. Constantly.

"I am trying to prepare you for our family's duty," he said, "and you respond with nothing but derision and jokes. And you wonder why I haven't let you out on a hunt yet."

"I'm ready, Dad. You know I am. I can do just as much as any of the other hunters around here. Hell, probably better since we started training so young. You know I'm ready for this."

"You'll be ready when I can trust that you will not get yourself or someone else killed!"

"How am I supposed to prove myself to you if you don't let me go on a hunt?"

"By paying attention and doing what I say," he replied.

"I always do what you say."

He snorted. "Like you did in Vancouver?"

Just the name of the city brought back memories of my night with Rias. I did my best to keep from smiling widely as I remembered her silky thighs and amazing taste. I straightened in my seat and pinned my dad with a glare.

"Vancouver was bullshit and you know it. You dragged me all the way there then left me in the hotel room with nothing but a note? A *note?*"

"You weren't ready for the hunt," he growled. "You still aren't ready to go on a hunt. You aren't physically or emotionally prepared for it!"

We'd had this argument more than once in the few weeks since that night. It always ended the same way, with him refusing to apologize and me being too angry to properly express how I felt—not that he would care anyway. It wasn't like I could just tell him what I did that night anyway. He didn't know my preference for women, and I knew he would never accept it.

I couldn't argue with the part of me that swore he kept me away from hunts so he could make sure that I survived long enough to bear him grandchildren that he could train to hunt the monsters too. If ever that happened—which was highly doubtful—I really didn't want him anywhere near them. Not after what he did to my brother.

I shook my head before my mind went down that dark alley. Instead I focused on dear old Dad. "You could have told me to my face that you didn't need me. Instead of leaving a damned note."

"I did need you. I needed you to stay on standby and near the phone in case I had to call. And instead you went and did…whatever it is that you did. You didn't even stay in the hotel room!"

I had to fight back the smile again as I remembered waking up next to Rias that morning. We'd gone another round before I got dressed and returned to my own room, and Dad still hadn't come back yet anyway. The way that woman worked her way around me—and I around her—was indelibly imprinted upon my brain. If it was possible to fall in love at first fuck, then I would risk saying that was exactly what happened.

But it wasn't like I was ever going to see her again. I only knew her name.

"I still don't know what you did or where you went that night," he continued, folding his arms across his chest. I mirrored him, comfortable knowing that he never needed to know what I did that night.

"And you never will."

"Damn it, Ashly!" he roared, and took a menacing step forward. I slipped out of my chair and stood, waiting for him to make his move. If he thought I would take his shit lying down, he had another think coming.

Whatever he was going to do or say after that was cut off by a commotion coming from the other room. A moment later the door slammed open and my mother was there, blood on her hands.

"Meredith, what—"

"Allan, we need you," she said, cutting Dad off with a look. "It's Marcus. He was hurt."

Dear old Dad turned to me with a snarl. "We aren't done with this." He was out the door, my mom following quickly behind him.

I grabbed my flannel and pulled it on, knowing the house was about to get loud and bloody. They tended to drag injured hunters here, where my parents could assist. My mom, Meredith, had gone through several years of medical school and was dangerous enough to know her way around a scalpel, and Dad was a capable nurse of sorts, I supposed. I knew to stay out of the way when this kind of thing went down. I slipped into the front room where a pack of hunters were surrounding someone lying on the wide coffee table, my parents leaning in close. I moved past them all and headed for the front door. No one seemed to notice as I slipped outside and into the evening air.

The sky was darkening quickly now that it was fall. It wasn't that late into the evening, and the sun was already almost all the way down, barely a sliver of light brightening the cloudy sky. I took a deep breath and shivered at the slight chill in the air. I hated when our home became a sick house. I'd never tell my parents, but I hated the scent of blood, even the sight of it. The less I had to deal with it, the better, I figured. I wouldn't let that stop me from doing my job, of course.

"Needed a little fresh air?" a voice said.

I leapt back, reaching for my weapon, as I spun to look for the source of the voice. On the sidewalk stood a tall man wearing a heavy black leather overcoat, like he'd just walked out of an old-fashioned western movie or something. It even had the mantle, that extra piece that sat over the shoulders and fell to about his chest on both sides. His hair was long and dark and messy, pushed back behind his ears. His pale skin almost glowed in the dying light, and he smiled in a way that was more off-putting than friendly.

I kept my hand by my gun as I eyed him up and down and searched the darkness around him. Was this the man who had attacked the hunter inside? Who was he? *What* was he?

"Who are you?"

"You must be the daughter." He took a step forward and I drew my pistol, taking it in a two-handed grip, my feet settling into the almost habitual stance.

"I asked who you are," I said.

He raised his hands and backed up a step. "Easy there, kid. I'm a friend of your father's."

I didn't let my aim waver. "That doesn't tell me who you are."

He bowed, bending at the waist and throwing one arm wide as the other was tucked under his stomach. "I am Eric Ritten."

I shook my head. "That still doesn't tell me why I shouldn't shoot you."

"Because then you'd have a crime on your doorstep, and I'm sure your parents and the others in your house right now would prefer that what's going on in said house remain unreported to the local constabulary."

I wanted to wipe the smug smile off his face. I couldn't argue with him. If an ambulance or the police were called because I shot him here and now…

"Now be a dear and introduce yourself, since you know my name."

I growled. "You said you know my father, but you don't know me?"

"It's only polite to offer introductions, especially when one is pointing a weapon at the other."

"I'm Ashly Mercer."

"Ah, Ashly. The younger child."

"The *only* child."

"Really? But I could've sworn…" He shrugged, that stupid smile still plastered on his face. "Well, no matter. It's a pleasure to meet you, Ashly."

"Trust me, the pleasure is all yours."

My arms were starting to get a little tired being tensed up in this position, but something about him made me want to keep the weapon drawn. I didn't trust him. I had no reason to trust him. He was clearly used to being a smooth talker and getting what he wanted, which made me feel even more contrary, and so I refused to give it to him.

"You wound me, my dear. Here I am, trying to be pleasantly formal and—"

"What are you?" I demanded. I was tired of hearing him talk but needed the information.

"What do you mean?"

"No one without an agenda enjoys bantering this much," I told him, "so what are you? If you're trying to gain an invitation into my house, you're going to be out of luck." That was a thing, wasn't it? Fuck, I might have to start listening to my dad again.

"Once again you wound me, dearest. I need no such thing as an invitation to enter your family home. Least of all because I have been in there before. As I said earlier, I am a friend to your father. If you'd like, I can be a friend to you too."

The gun wavered a little. "Answer the question, then we'll talk about being friends."

"Ashly, Ashly, Ashly, there's no need for that weapon to be between us. I've worked with your father for a long time. I'd like to work with you too."

I snorted. "You're barking up the wrong tree. My parents won't let me hunt, never mind work with someone like you."

"And what's wrong with me?"

I started to answer but light suddenly illuminated me from the house.

"Ashly, put it away!" came the sharp voice of my father. I swiftly holstered the pistol and let the flannel cover my backside as if the weapon had never existed. "Ritten, what the hell are you doing here?"

Ritten laughed and took a step forward. I itched to draw on him again.

"Who do you think brought your hunter back in one piece? I was about to come in to tell you when I met your daughter here."

"Who is he, Dad?" I asked.

Dad shook his head. "Get inside."

"No."

"Do as I say."

"Fuck that."

Ritten laughed. "A chip off the old block, this one is. I wonder if she'd like to know about—"

"Shut up, Ritten." Dad's voice was almost loud enough to be heard by the neighbors. "Ashly, get inside now!"

I knew that tone too well to ignore it. I gave both men one more look, then went back inside. Marcus was still lying on the coffee table, swathed in bandages on his right side. Three other hunters I didn't know by name sat on the couch near him, nursing smaller wounds and talking amongst themselves. They ignored me and I ignored them and proceeded into the kitchen where my mother was washing up.

"You should have been in here. You need to learn some time."

"Learn what? How to sew up the menfolk?"

She threw a dirty look over her shoulder. "You know it's not like that."

"Sure seems like it to me."

"I'm not having this argument with you again. Next time you will stay and learn. Even basic first aid would be good for you to know, when you do get to go on a hunt."

I laughed. "Yeah, and when will that be?"

She shook her head. "You know you're not ready."

"That's what everyone seems to think."

She said nothing to that. She continued scrubbing her arms and I looked away. I considered heading up the steps to my room, but curiosity got the better of me.

"Mom, do you know who Eric Ritten is?"

She made a sharp movement and shut off the water, turning to face me fully for the first time since I came in the room. "Don't say that name."

"Why not? He's right outside."

"Damn it! Where's your father?"

"Outside with him. What's the big deal?"

She shook her head again. "He's a witch."

I blinked. "A witch? Seriously?"

She gave me a harsh look. "Yes, seriously. He's a powerful witch, and we are all very lucky that he's on our side. He comes to us when he knows something unsavory is in the area. And he helps us hunt other witches—something we need. Witches are not to be trifled with."

"He said he was friends with Dad. That he wanted to be my friend too."

"I don't want you to have anything to do with him. You stay away from him. Let your dad deal with it."

I let out a sigh. "Of course. Because heaven forbid I should get to do anything in this family."

"You are barely twenty. You have your whole life—God willing—to do things for this family."

"I know. Sorry."

She turned back to the sink and I headed for the stairs.

"Wait."

I turned back around. Mom leaned her arms on the counter and sighed, then walked over to me. Her hands went to the back of her neck, and a necklace that I'm pretty sure she always wore came off in her hands. It was a simple pendant bearing a small green stone, something like an emerald.

"Here. Take this."

"What is it?"

She shook her head. "I don't like Ritten. I don't trust him. I don't know why your father does. But either way, this will help you keep a clear head if you ever have to deal with him."

"I don't understand."

"It's called leechstone. It protects people from the magic of witches. You can't be put under a spell while wearing it, and other magics won't work, or won't work as well on you. If you've attracted Ritten's attention, you might need it more than me."

I put it on and fingered the small pendant, surprised that something so small could be so useful. I nodded to her. "I'll be careful. I promise."

She gave me a look that said she only partially believed me, then returned to the sink.

It felt like a good time to go and lock myself in my room. I turned on my stereo and got ready for bed, but the sound of people downstairs was still too loud. I switched to a pair of headphones and lay down, letting the sounds drown out the ruckus. My mind raced with new information. Witches, Ritten, something that he knew that my father didn't want me to know. It made it difficult to relax, until my mind returned, as it always seemed to, to Rias.

As I thought about the other woman, I finally succumbed to a sweet, dreamless sleep.

CHAPTER FIVE

Rias

Seven months later

Oh, this was a bad idea.

"Get out for a change. Meet some people. Indulge in a hobby," I muttered, staring at the sea of people before me. "Damn it, Natalie."

It had seemed like such a good idea at first.

Even now, months later, I couldn't stop thinking about Ashly and the night we'd spent together. I had been certain that the memory would fade with time, but it only got stronger to the point where I was pining for the woman. I needed that connection again, desperately, but I had no idea where I'd even start trying to find her. And I did not dare use my magic to try and find her for fear that it would all go so very wrong. I needed something new, some kind of connection with people outside of the tiny sanctuary of Terabend. My weekly lunches with Natalie were the one thing I looked forward to most—the rest of my downtime was spent trying to regain control of my magic. Imagine my surprise the day I accidently let slip to Natalie that I was into anime and always wanted to go to a convention. That conversation eventually led to me booking a hotel and buying tickets for the both of us to Otafest in Calgary. She'd been just as into it as I'd been, but with the arrival of the new wolves last month, the Lupa had more responsibilities now and didn't feel like she could get away. For some reason she'd insisted I go anyway. Of course, it could've been worse. Nat had wanted me to dress up for it.

The most annoying part was that she wasn't wrong. If I had the social skills of someone who grew up outside of the witch covens and knew how to mingle, this might be a great opportunity to make a friend or get to know someone. You know, standard human things.

The problem was I didn't have those social skills. I was taught to keep humans at arm's reach, to never get too close lest they happen to notice that I was something…not human.

My magic had been behaving for a while now, but I still wasn't confident that it would continue to do so. Especially when I was anxious like this. It was like a living thing inside me, reacting with every wave of panic and anxiety that crashed over me. But this was a good test for my control too. Because I needed to get back to a life where I wasn't afraid to do things because of my magic. I wanted to be able to live my life, not hide at home scared that someone might come after me.

"Let's stop thinking about that," I said aloud. Instead of obsessing about my past, I pushed away from the wall and joined the crowd.

Okay, so it wasn't as bad as I thought it would be. People were surprisingly polite, if a little single-minded in what they were focused on, and clumps of stragglers tended to stay to the sides instead of taking up space in the middle of everything. I let myself move with the crowd, enjoying the sights of the costumes and the people whose conversations went entirely over my head but seemed to make sense to them. I clearly had a lot of anime to catch up on, though I did recognize a character or two in passing, and that made me feel like less of an interloper.

By the time I finished my second panel—about voice acting on English dubs—I was getting a little tired, but was proud of myself for having managed to make it this far. I was doing well, and my magic was cooperating, which gave me a chance to live my life. It was something I never thought I'd have.

With that happy thought, I headed for the marketplace and artist's alley. It was the area I was looking forward to the most. I wandered up and down the aisles, enjoying the artwork and the things on sale. I picked up a few prints I thought would look nice, and a necklace from one of my favorite games. It was like I was in a different world, one where my past wasn't a factor anymore, one where I could do or be whatever I wanted. Whoever I wanted.

And it all came crashing to a halt when I heard a single word shouted near me.

"Rias!"

I turned around, looking for someone who might know me, someone familiar, but there was only a crowd of unknown faces.

"Rias!"

I focused on the person calling my name, a young man with a woman on his arm. But neither of them were looking at me. Instead they were looking at a cosplayer only a few feet from me, standing in front of another table.

"Rias! Can we get a picture?"

The cosplayer turned to them and gave a bright smile. "Of course! But let's move to the side."

I watched her walk away with them and felt like I could barely breathe. She was wearing what amounted to a school uniform in a lot of anime, with long red hair that nearly swept the floor and breasts that looked too large and perky to be natural. Black wings jutted out about a foot from each shoulder blade, and it took a keen eye like mine to realize they were ingeniously sewn into the back of the shirt. The outfit looked amazing, and she smiled wide for the picture and waved as the two fans walked away.

I felt the magic inside me stirring. It wanted to break free, but I kept a firm grip on it. Not today. I wasn't about to let it slip away. Interested, however, I did move toward the cosplayer.

"Excuse me?" I said as I joined her beside a table in the artist's alley.

"Oh, hi! I didn't see you there!" she said, her voice bubbly and welcoming. She gave me a sweet smile. "Did you want a picture?"

I shook my head. "Oh, no, no, I was just going to mention that I love your cosplay. It looks really amazing."

"Thank you! I worked really hard on it."

"I was wondering, can you tell me who the character is? You look familiar, but I don't remember if it's something I've seen or only heard of."

"I'm Rias Gremory, from High School DxD. She's kind of a badass devil-witch person and I absolutely love her!"

I did my best not to flinch at the word *witch*, and nodded. "I haven't seen that one, but it's definitely something to put on my watch list. Thank you."

"Of course!" She smiled and moved on as I headed in the opposite direction. What the hell were the odds that there was a damned anime character—a *witch-like* character—with my very name? My family name, really. Was it a stupid coincidence or did someone know something? Was this all an elaborate ruse by the covens to draw me out of hiding?

I shook my head. No. No this was not a rabbit hole I was going to fall down. Not today. Not here. There was no way someone from the covens would know this was where I would be and that they could find me here. There was no way they would know about what happened in Terabend last summer. It wasn't happening.

I took a deep breath in, held it for a few seconds, then out again. I repeated the process, trying to find some inner peace. But it didn't come. The panic was too far along for that, and the magic inside me was making its displeasure known. I forced it down, pushed it back, but a sliver of it managed to break through my grasp.

There was a sudden cacophony of sound as a group of tables that sat empty in the far corner of the room flipped into the air, crashing around on the floor. No one was nearby, but the noise was enough to draw frantic shouts and stares from everyone close enough to witness the strangeness. I blanched at the sight, knowing it was my power that had flipped over three tables without a single person being nearby.

As quickly as I could without appearing suspicious, I headed straight for the exit of the marketplace and back toward the lobby. I had to get out of here, back up to my hotel room. That would be the safest place for me right now.

"Rias?"

I stopped. The voice sounded familiar this time, and sent a slight shiver down my spine. I glanced around, expecting to see the cosplayer or a similar one nearby, but there was no one.

"Rias, is that you?"

I looked forward again and saw a woman striding toward me. Tall, strawberry-blond, with beautiful blue eyes that I remembered seeing so full of pleasure and satiation. I stared at her for a long moment, barely able to believe who I was looking at.

"Ashly?"

She grinned, wide and cocky, her hands on her hips. She looked far too good, like she was walking out of the beginnings of a wet dream or something. Tight black jeans looked like they were almost painted onto her thighs, and a tight tank top spread over her chest. Her purple flannel flared a little as she walked, and I desperately stopped myself from grabbing it and pulling her to me. "Well, I guess today's my lucky day, isn't it?"

"W-what are you doing here?" My eyes were drawn to a shininess at her throat, a small green stone set in gold that hung around her neck. Something absolutely pretty that suited her so much. Something new that I didn't remember from Vancouver.

She looked around as if trying to see someone, then took my arm and led me away from the crowd and toward an empty corner with fewer people. I let her lead the way, part of me still certain that I needed to head back to the safety of my hotel room where I could deal with my magic appropriately. But it was in the presence of this woman that my magic settled down, almost came to a complete stillness like I had rarely felt recently.

That was interesting.

"I live here."

I glanced around. "You live in a hotel?"

She laughed. "No, I live here, in Calgary. This is my city. What are you doing here?" Her gaze darted over my head, scanning the crowd as if looking for someone.

I lifted my purchased swag in a half-hearted shrug, unsure where this unexpected meeting might lead—and knowing exactly where I wanted it to lead.

"I'm here for the conve—" My words were cut off as she held my face and pressed her lips hard to mine. I melted into the sudden kiss and she dipped her head further down into me, as if she were trying to devour me whole. My magic awoke with the sensuality of the touch and coiled up inside me, but not in the way that it had been. No, now it was more like it wanted to see her, to meet this woman who was making me feel all these things that I hadn't felt in…well…ever.

When she pulled away it was far too soon, and I surged after her like water rolling down the beach after the tide. I noticed her eyes widen in surprise but didn't care as I kissed her again, pulling her down into me. My body caught fire with the intensity of the kiss, the sweet, terrifying warmth that was quickly putting all thought of hiding safely in my hotel room out of my head. An obscene sound slipped out of me that gave me the briefest pause, but I didn't care if we were going to draw an audience.

But Ashly seemed to. She pulled back slowly, a wild smirk on her lips, and her hands firmly on my shoulders.

"Well, that was certainly something."

Heat crept into my face and I found myself unable to look her in the eye. "S-sorry."

"Oh, don't be sorry, I'm certainly not."

"W-what was I saying?"

"I think you were mentioning that you were here for the convention," she said, much more smoothly than she should have been able to after kissing me like that. Maybe I was a little jealous. Maybe.

"Right…right. The convention." I shook my head, trying hard to put my thoughts back into something resembling order. "W-what about you?"

"I was in the area and decided to pop in, see what all the fuss was about." She looked over me again, her eyes searching for something I couldn't see. "Imagine running into you of all people. It must be the universe's way of bringing us together again."

She smiled like she was joking, but I knew too much to dare argue against the idea that the Goddess might have made this little meeting happen. And while there was clearly something she wasn't telling me, I didn't want to have her disappear on me. Not only did she have an amazingly calming effect on my magic, but I wanted her close to me all the time.

"Well," I said, trying to sound as smooth as she was and probably failing, "then, for the sake of the universe and everything, maybe, perhaps, you might like to maybe go out for dinner…with me?"

She reached for my hand and brought it up to her lips, planting a kiss on my knuckles in such a weirdly gallant gesture that I had no idea what to do but swoon a little. "I would be delighted to accompany you."

The words brought the image of Ashly in shining armor riding a massive horse, her smile warm and infectious and her arms waiting to swing me up behind her into the saddle and whisk me off into another life. A new life.

Wasn't that what I wanted? Did she?

"L-let me just drop off my stuff, and we'll go," I stammered like I was a lovesick puppy.

"Might I escort you?" Ashly asked, giving me an honest-to-Goddess bow as she asked, and I had to force myself not to drool. Chivalry was clearly only dead to straight men.

"Um, sure," I managed to squeak out.

Ashly was patient and gallant enough to wait outside the room as I dropped my things off and made a quick dash to the bathroom to primp myself up a little for my sudden date. I had not been expecting anything of the sort and now had nothing to wear and didn't bring the right kind of makeup and I wasn't sure what I should even be wearing or if I—

"Stop it," I hissed at myself. This was just dinner with Ashly. The woman who I'd been clearly obsessed with since we slept together once. This wasn't anything more than that. But oh, Goddess, how I wanted it to be more than that. How I needed it to be.

I touched up the minimal makeup I was already wearing and

switched from a T-shirt from one of the bands that I liked to a nicer black blouse with semi-transparent sleeves. I kept my jeans and shoes on. I knew that comfort would be good for this, and it would maybe remind me to keep my senses around me while I was trying not to swoon over the handsome woman standing in jeans and a flannel who happened to be right outside my door.

"Dear Goddess," I swore under my breath, "please, please don't let me be completely hopeless."

Night fell as we left the hotel and went to a nearby restaurant. I let Ashly take the lead; after all, this was her city and she was certain she knew where best to go. I wasn't sure I liked following her around like a lovesick puppy, but it was taking me too much time to try and put myself back together after the two kisses we'd shared—and then a third one outside my hotel room that almost made me want to pull her into the room with me, dinner be damned.

The restaurant was not one that had loud music or lots of television screens with various sporting events, for which I was grateful. Those places often made me feel less comfortable, with so many different things vying for my attention. No, this place had dim lighting, with soft music and a more intimate atmosphere. Ashly had picked well.

We were shown to a dark booth along one wall across from the bar and Ashly popped quickly into the side of the booth that faced the front. I normally would have taken that seat, wanting to keep an eye on whoever was coming in, especially after my magic slip-up earlier, but right now I couldn't care. But there was still something odd about her behavior, something that didn't quite fit with how chivalrous and courteous she'd been.

I ordered water and a Diet Coke, wanting to stay away from the alcohol tonight. Oddly enough, Ashly did the same, and ordered a water and regular Coke. She didn't say anything about my choice, so I decided not to question hers.

"So, you're into anime?" Ashly asked after we had settled in with our drinks and I was glancing over the menu. She was holding her menu in one hand and playing with her necklace with the other, flipping it around and over her fingers in a way that was almost hypnotic to me.

I flushed a little but there was no sense of accusation in her tone.

"Yeah, I mean, sort of. I used to watch a lot of it when I was—I mean, years ago. I kind of stopped for a while, though."

"Can I ask why?"

I shrugged. "Had a hard time finding shows I wanted to watch for a while, then kind of forgot about it. Life got in the way, I suppose."

She nodded sagely. "I understand what that can be like."

"What about you? You a fan?"

She laughed. "No, no, I've never actually watched any. I know of it through…like…word of mouth, basically. I wasn't even sure that's what the convention was for. I thought it was either anime or video games, from the colorful costumes I saw."

"So why were you there?"

She gave me an odd smile, one that didn't reach her eyes, and opened her mouth to speak when the server reappeared and took our orders. She was quick to order prime rib with baked potato and asparagus, while I hemmed and hawed over the maple glazed salmon and got the dirtiest look from the server when I asked for a side of steak fries. What? I'm a simple gal. Fish and chips is more my speed.

With the orders taken, I turned back to Ashly to find her giving me a look that I couldn't quite describe.

"I, uh, guess we didn't really talk about ourselves much last time we were together."

"No, no there wasn't a lot of talking involved, outside of some—well…you know."

She gave me a soft smile. "I never thought I'd get to see you again."

"Me either."

She shook her head. "This has to mean something, right? Like, I can't stop thinking of Vancouver. Of you. Even now."

I hesitated. I wasn't about to start invoking the Goddess right now, especially because people tended to look at me weird when I did, but she wasn't wrong that this felt like something was bringing us together.

"I…I think this is what we make of it. What we want to make of it." I reached out, took one of her hands across the table, and rubbed my thumb over her knuckles. "For what it's worth, I couldn't stop thinking about it either."

"I've never felt this way about someone before. Like it's more than a crush, but I don't know how to…to quantify it." She shook her head. "I just mean that I want to tell you things that I'm not supposed to. To be honest with you, like I haven't been honest with anyone in my life."

I kept her hand tight in mine. "I want you to be able to be honest with me. I'd love to know more about you. I'd love to tell you about me. I want this to be more than just…what it was in Vancouver."

She let out a soft sigh, as if she was relieved. "Me too."

"Well, in that case, for the sake of honesty, I should tell you I'm older than I look."

She smiled. "Oh, yeah?"

"Yup. I'm twenty-six." I gave her the age on my license. It was as honest as I could be. How could I possibly explain that I'm a witch and I'm actually about sixty-seven, and that witches age so much slower than other humans.

"I just turned twenty-one, so we're not far off." She glanced down at our hands, still clutching each other on the table. "I guess, I guess I should be honest too."

"Please do."

"I wasn't at the convention because of anime or video games or whatever. I was…I was looking for…"

I nodded as if I understood. "You were looking for someone to spend the night with," I suggested helpfully.

"What? No!" she was quick to sputter. "No, no, that's definitely not why I was there. Running into you was just…a very, very happy coincidence." She pulled her hand back out of my reach, hunching her shoulders as if trying to make herself seem smaller. "Truth is, I was being chased."

"Wait, chased? By who? Do we need to go to the police? Are you okay?" I was half out of my seat, ready to reach for her when she shook her head, but the pain on her face was too real.

"No, no it's not like that." She took a deep breath. "My father is a private investigator. I work for him, and he's training me to help him, to be his partner someday."

"And this involves people chasing you and you—I'm assuming—using the crowd at the convention to lose them?"

"Got it in one. It's a game to him. He won't let me out on a hu—case on my own yet. He decided to send a couple of his friends after me today, saying if I could stay away from them for the rest of the day, then he'd consider giving me a case to work on by myself. I jumped at the chance."

I remembered how her eyes kept looking over me and around and even the intensity of the first kiss. Was that just an act? I pulled my own hand back, suddenly feeling less comfortable.

"That first kiss you gave me," I said quietly.

She nodded. "Public displays of affection make people uncomfortable sometimes. Some people like it, others will turn away. I took a chance." She caught my eye and held my gaze. "But I promise you, I did it because I really wanted to do it. Please believe me on that."

I tried, but it was like trying to keep water in a leaky bucket. Even my magic was starting to react to the change in mood, roiling ever so slightly inside me as if ready to lash out.

"Then I kissed you."

Even though I wasn't completely sold, the smile that bloomed across her face told me everything. "Yeah. Yeah you did. And it was amazing."

My face had to be turning red permanently at this point, the way she was making me feel. "So, when does this little game of yours end?"

She glanced at her phone for a moment, then tucked it away. "About twenty minutes ago."

"You know, you don't have to—"

She held up a hand to cut me off. "Don't go there, Rias. I'm here because I want to be here. Seeing you today was a massive bonus that I hadn't anticipated. One that I wouldn't give up for anything."

I was quiet for a long moment, trying to sort through my own emotions. I wanted her. I wanted to be with her. But I didn't want to be an excuse, or just a rebellion against her father. I wanted something more than that.

But those thoughts were the farthest from my mind when I opened my mouth and shyly said, "Danaan."

"I'm sorry?"

"My name, it's Danaan. Danaan Rias."

Her grin almost stretched from ear to ear. "Ashly Mercer. A pleasure to meet you, Danaan Rias."

I shivered as she said my name and was thankful for the brief respite given by the arrival of our food. I used the time to steadily regain whatever composure I could muster. The way she spoke my name, my full name. It wasn't something I heard often. A lot of people didn't even know my first name. But to hear her say it…

She tore into her steak with a single-minded intensity as I watched, wondering how often she did something like this. With the way it sounded like her parents controlled her, probably not a lot. She didn't exactly have the decorum that they were probably used to in a nicer restaurant like this, but then neither did I. But neither of us cared. She looked up over her dish and gave me a toothy smile that I couldn't help but return. Just a couple of cavewomen enjoying a nice meal.

"Does your…" I began, but drifted off when I realized the question might be too personal.

"Does my what?"

I bit my lip. "Does your father often do things like this game of yours?"

She took a moment to chew on that. "Too often. He thinks that because I'm his daughter, he controls my life. Like I have no autonomy of my own. But at the same time, I let him, because it's all I know. He's always been there, poking us, pushing us in the direction that he wanted us to grow up in."

"Us?"

She just shook her head. "I mean me. He was always rough, but when I was a teenager it got worse. He was dead set on me following in his footsteps, to the point where it was always constant training, fighting, survival skills, the like."

I raised an eyebrow. "All that just to be a private investigator? Sounds more like doomsday prepping."

She barked out a laugh. "Right? I wish I had the courage to say that to his face, I'd love to see his reaction. Doomsday prepper. I love it."

I idled for a moment before deciding to ask my next question. "Is that why you have a gun at the small of your back?"

She looked up sharply. "You noticed it?"

"Yeah, I felt it during our second kiss."

"You didn't say anything."

I shrugged. "I figured there was a reason for it. You know it's illegal to carry concealed, right?"

"I know. Dear old Dad insists that I go everywhere armed. As long as I don't go flashing it around, I should be okay." She smiled and started to laugh. "Unless you're a cop or something."

I only gave her a look, and whatever laughter had been building up died in her throat.

"You're, uh, a cop, aren't you?"

"Sheriff's deputy, actually. Back home."

She was quiet for a long moment. I could have put her out of her misery, but honestly this was much more fun.

"Well," she said slowly, "you haven't arrested me, so that has to mean something, right?"

I folded my arms across my chest in mock sternness. "It means I figured there was a good reason for you to go armed and I wasn't going to bring it up until I felt it was appropriate."

"So, are you going to haul me in, copper? Arrest me? Handcuff me?"

"There might be some handcuffs involved." I gave her a sly smile.

"Really?" She raised an eyebrow and we shared a laugh. "So, where's home, if I can ask."

"A small town a few hours west of Edmonton. Called Terabend. It's a tiny place, nothing really going on."

"It's got something going on if you live there."

I blushed again and waved a hand but secretly loved the compliment. We shared a few more personal facts about ourselves as we finished eating. The check came and Ashly snatched it away. She claimed her father could at least pay for the meal, since it was his fault we were together. I didn't argue. She needed to be able to have some sort of rebellion against him.

As we left hand in hand and headed back to the hotel, I realized that I could be that bit of rebellion for her after all. As long as I was more than just that in the long run.

Chapter Six

Ashly

We were on each other the minute the hotel room door closed. I pressed Rias up against the wall, and my lips met hers as her arms wrapped around me and pulled me in close. I pressed my tongue against her lips and she opened for me, letting me in. I put my knee between her legs and she ground down on it as she gave a loud moan that didn't get much farther than my mouth. I deepened the kiss and held the back of her head, and combed my fingers through her short hair.

I pulled her shirt over her head and started to work on her jeans as she gripped my shirt and tried to pull me into her. I had her almost naked before she seemed to realize it, when she backed off for a second to look me up and down.

"You are overdressed," she breathed as she kicked off the rest of her clothes.

"Maybe you should help with that," I said with a wink. It was all the permission she needed.

My shirt disappeared almost immediately, pulled up and over my head and tossed away to land somewhere as she attacked my jeans. I helped her, wary of the weight at the small of my back that was attached to the pants. If she noticed she didn't say anything as I kicked my jeans off, making sure the weapon wasn't in plain sight. A second later, I'd removed my shoes and socks and turned on her. I grabbed her hands and pulled her to the one king-sized bed in the room.

We fell onto the bed together and Rias wrapped an arm around my head to pull me close. I pressed my face against the delicate swell of her breasts and darted my tongue across her nipples. I sucked and tugged, which made her moan in my ear as her back arched and I caressed the silky skin on her back. I pressed my thigh between her legs and she let out a long moan that made me wetter than I ever had been before.

Rias rolled us so she was on top, straddling my thigh. She grabbed my wrists and held them above my head, almost hitting the headboard. She leaned over and put those wonderous lips of hers to my ear.

"Keep these here for a minute," she whispered and I could only whimper in response. In a flash she was gone, searching for something in her luggage, as I lamented the loss of her body heat. Then she returned and climbed on top of me. She leaned over and wrapped something leather and sturdy around my wrists. I glanced up at the belt she was tightening and flinched. This wasn't something I'd done before.

"Is this okay?" she asked, breathless and needy. I could only nod. It was more than okay. There was a weird kind of freedom in having my hands bound. I was certain I could slip out of the belt if I really tried, but I didn't want to. I tested the bonds and shivered a little, knowing that I could trust my partner.

How the hell did I know that? I barely knew her. And yet it didn't seem to matter.

I gasped as Rias trailed kisses from my lips down my throat and across my chest until she reached my breasts and started nibbling. Her hand reached further down and I could feel her fingers questing between my thighs as if she were exploring uncharted waters. She slowly entered me with her fingers, first one, then a second, and I shifted slightly, trying to push them deeper without the use of my hands. Rias gave me a soft chuckle before her mouth found one of my nipples.

"R-Rias," I moaned as I used my legs to thrust myself onto her fingers. She pulled her head back until I could see her feral smile, her eyes sparking with desire.

"That's it, kitten," she said, "keep fucking yourself on my fingers."

I couldn't stop the little whimper that came out of my mouth at her words. I'd never been with someone who took control like this before. It was…intoxicating. Wonderfully so. I never thought I'd be the kind of person to enjoy this. Clearly Rias was proving me wrong. She curled her fingers deeper into me as she pressed her lips to my cheek, and leaned forward to whisper softly into my ear.

"Next time I'll bring my handcuffs. Maybe tie you down properly and have my way with you. Would you like that, kitten?"

I nodded wordlessly as her fingertips reached inside and found a deliciously sensitive area inside me that made me arch my back. She pressed her thumb to my clit and rubbed it gently as I felt myself getting closer and closer to release. At that point I think I'd have agreed to just about anything to keep her touching me like she was. But there was also something else there. I should have noticed it the first time we slept together, but she hadn't been quite this domineering then. Tonight… well, I couldn't deny I was enjoying myself.

"Please," I found myself whispering against her soft skin, "more. Please more."

She laughed in that delicious way that sent shivers down my spine. I hungered for more, desperate for it. Whatever it was about being vulnerable to Rias was making me feel amazing, and I didn't want it to stop. My orgasm almost snuck up on me, coming quick and hard, and I screamed my pleasure out into the room as the woman atop me kept going, kept pushing me to the brink until I fell over that waterfall again. My hands, still bound, reached for her, desperate to touch, but the moment my wrists came off the bed, she stopped moving entirely and gazed at me with patient eyes.

"What did I say, kitten?"

I groaned and moved my hands back above my head, but the slight reprieve was welcome as it allowed my body to come down from the massive highs of the multiple orgasms. Rias seemed to notice this and she slowly removed her fingers from me, holding them up between us and casually licking them clean. I felt like I could die and go to heaven right there, watching her do that. I wriggled against the belt, and her eyes darted to my restraints.

"Want some help there?" she asked, her voice back to something like the shy, less domineering Rias I remembered from last time we were together. Not that I was complaining.

"Please," I said softly, and she unwound the belt and tossed it to the side of the bed. She rubbed her hands over my wrists as if checking for any lasting effects, then curled herself up around me and held on tight. I wasn't prepared for the sudden cuddle session, instead hoping to give as good as I got, but when she let out a long, soft breath of relief, I figured I'd let her continue to take the lead in what we were doing.

I just didn't want to get a rep for being a pillow princess, honestly.

"Thank you," she said, after a few minutes of soft breathing as we both took the time to recover.

"For what?"

"Letting me do that to you."

"It's not like it was one-sided," I murmured. I nuzzled into her and took comfort in the warmness of her body.

"You didn't exactly sign up for it going in."

"I loved every minute of it, thank you."

She paused for a long second. "Really?"

I turned so I could look at her face. She had her eyes screwed shut as if she were afraid of what I was going to say. I drew my thumbs across her face, over her eyes, and caressed her cheeks and her lips. She was beautiful to me. She was amazing to me. I didn't want this to be the last time we saw each other.

"Really," I whispered to her, "it was amazing. I didn't know I'd enjoy it that much, but you were just…amazing."

"I tried to make sure I didn't go too far."

"I think you went just far enough. Maybe…"

"Maybe?"

"Maybe I enjoyed it just as much as you did."

She opened her eyes and stared into my face. "Really?"

I nodded. "How could I not? You were with me the whole time, you checked in, made sure I consented." I let a smile bloom as I leaned in and kissed her on the forehead. "And maybe I enjoyed being called your kitten."

Rias giggled and wrapped herself tighter around me. "Thank you."

"What for?"

"For talking me through it. For letting me do what I did." She took a deep breath, as if preparing herself for a long speech. "I know what I like. I've known for a while. And it's been too much in the past."

"Until me?"

"Until you." She shook her head. "What is it about you that makes me want to tell you everything, show you who I am?"

"You make it sound like no one knows you."

Rias didn't reply to that. Instead after a long moment she let out a strangled little laugh.

"Isn't this sexy?" she asked. "Having a philosophical conversation about the whys of the sex we just had?"

"I've had worse pillow talk." As minimal as my experience of pillow talk had been, this really wasn't the worst.

She laughed again, but this time it sounded more genuine.

"How do you always know the right thing to say?"

"Just lucky I guess."

She snorted and it made me smile. Her words seemed to have run out as she snuggled in closer to me. Her eyes closed and her breath eventually evened out until I was certain she was asleep. It wasn't long before the softness of her breathing lulled me into my own slumber.

I had no idea how long we were asleep before a faint buzzing sound woke me. Rias had moved in her sleep, pulling away from me slightly as she snored. The buzzing continued and I propped myself up on an elbow as I searched for the source. It was coming from my jeans, and my heart sank. I knew exactly what that was.

I crawled from the bed without waking the beautiful woman beside me and reached for my pants, to grab the phone that was still going off. I hesitated. If I let it go to voicemail, he'd only call again and again until I answered. If I didn't answer at all, it was only a matter of time before he tracked me down. If nothing else, he was good at that.

I fiddled with my necklace for a second before I answered the phone.

"What?" I kept my voice low.

"Where are you?" my father asked.

"Does it matter?"

"No, no I suppose it doesn't."

He was speaking like it didn't matter, like I didn't matter. If that was the case why was he phoning me at all? He had all the help he normally needed, why bother calling his wayward child?

"What do you want, Dad?"

"You need to come home. We have a hunt to prepare for."

"You don't need me for that. You've made that pretty damned clear."

I expected him to get mad again, maybe yell and tell me what an unappreciative brat I am. But he surprised me. I heard him take a deep breath over the phone, and shock the hell out of me.

"I'm sorry."

"What?"

"I said I'm sorry." There was a moment of silence in which I tried to decide if he was being honest or if this was a case of invasion of the body snatchers. "I spoke to your mother." Ah, that explained it. She was good at making people feel guilty about things they wouldn't normally feel guilty about. "She said I've been too hard on you. That I need to give you a chance."

As much as I wanted to call him on his bullshit, I also wanted him to believe in me. To trust me. I was his kid. He was my dad. I just wanted to make him proud of me. I didn't want to always feel like a disappointment.

"What are you saying?" I realized my voice was getting a little loud and I pulled myself to the edge of the bed, trying not to awaken Rias.

"I'm saying that I want you on this hunt with me. You've shown your knowledge and your readiness. I want you to work with me on this one."

I didn't know what to say. Suddenly he thought I was good enough to join him? What the hell had Mom said to him?

"Are you only telling me this to make me come home?"

"It's the middle of the night. You should be here so we don't have to worry. Too many things might try to go after you in retaliation for us hunting them. You never know—"

"Dad!" I all but shouted. I glanced over at the woman in the bed with me and held my breath. She didn't stir, and I let it out slowly. I continued at a lower volume. "I'm fine. I won the bet, I deserve a night to myself. I'll be back tomorrow and we'll talk about this, okay?"

"Tell me where you are."

"No, Dad. I'll see you tomorrow." I hung up before he could say anything else and let out a long sigh. He wouldn't be happy about it, but I didn't want to ruin this wonderful night with his bullshit. I was my own person and I deserved to have a life outside of him, even if he didn't like it. I turned off the phone and tossed it on the bedside table, hoping there was no way he'd be able to track it or something.

Knowing him, he'd try.

There was a gentle stirring beside me and I leapt to my feet, ready for anything. Rias was watching me with wide eyes, surprise written on her face.

"Are you okay?"

"I'm fine," I snapped, too harshly.

She looked away and I felt immediate regret.

"I'm sorry, I'm sorry," I said quickly. "I don't…I mean…I just don't know how to talk about it."

"Your father?"

I nodded and settled back on the bed. Rias moved and wrapped an arm around me, and I had never felt more comforted than I did in that moment. I brushed away some wetness from my eyes as I sank into her embrace.

"He thinks he controls me. That he owns me. That I should be grateful to him for everything simply because I'm his daughter and he's raised me like he has."

"Has he always been this way?"

I nodded slowly. "Always, but it got worse after…"

"After what?"

I hung my head and felt Rias shift on the bed behind me. She wrapped me in both arms this time. I coughed, and tried to find my voice.

"You don't have to talk about it," Rias said softly.

I shook my head. "No, I want to. It helps." I took a deep breath and let it out, trying to find something to center my thoughts, but my head was a whirlwind of good and bad and terrible memories that had haunted me my entire short life.

"I…I had a brother. Older than me," I told her, and even I could hear the shame in my tone. "I don't know what happened, but when we were younger he said something to my father. Something bad. And he got hurt. Badly."

"I'm so sorry. Is he…did he…?"

"No. He ended up in the hospital, though. Dad wouldn't let anyone in to see him, or let him talk to anyone. Just an accident when we were out hiking. Fell down an embankment. Normal kid stuff." I faltered and her arms tightened around me, skin on skin, in a warmth I didn't deserve. "I don't even know why I'm telling you this. I haven't told anyone this. Ever."

Her hand found mine and squeezed tight. "You can tell me anything. I want to know everything about you, Ashly. What happened to your brother?"

"He ran away. Got past one of our uncles and snuck out of the hospital with a broken leg. He got away from the pain, from the abuse, the fighting and training and survival." I turned in her arms so I could face her, but couldn't bring myself to meet her eye. "I wished for months afterward that I'd been able to go with him. To get out from under my parents. I blamed him for leaving me behind."

"That doesn't make you a horrible person."

"I am a horrible person," I whispered, so soft I wasn't even sure she heard me. "I have been for a long time. I forgot about him. I let myself forget about him because it's what my father said to do. Said I was his only child now."

"You didn't forget him. You remember him even if everyone else tells you to forget him. That's not on you. That's on your father, on your family for doing what they did in the first place." She took my face in her hands and forced me to meet her eyes. "You are not to blame."

I sniffled and let out a wet chuckle.

"Isn't this sexy? Blubbering in front of you? I bet you didn't sign up for this when you offered dinner."

"I don't know what I signed up for, but I'm in for all of it."

"Wait…what do you mean?"

"I mean I want more than just this. I want more than just tonight, and last time. I want you, Ashly."

"But, I mean, I don't know if I can, and there's my dad, and I don't really even control my own life. And you have your life in Terabend, I can't just up and leave everything I know just to…"

She shook her head. "I'm not asking you to. I get it. I can't just leave my life, you can't just leave yours. We've only just gotten to know one another. So we'll take it slowly."

"A-are you suggesting a long-distance relationship?"

She shrugged. "It's better than nothing, isn't it? Better than hoping and praying that the universe brings us together a third time? Maybe make it a bit easier to plan things and get together and have more amazing nights like this."

I brushed the wetness from my face and took my time trying to find the right words. What she was suggesting was amazing, on paper. A relationship with this wonderful woman. Taking the time to get to see her, be with her, but not too much too soon. It sounded like a dream come true. But immediately, the pessimistic part of my brain started to wonder how long it might be until one of us slipped or messed up in a million little ways.

Damn it. I wanted to be the strong one, the confident one, but this idea was making me feel like the scared, naïve woman I was underneath. This was my chance to have something outside of my family, outside of my parents. It wasn't hunting, it wasn't fighting, or survival. It was something new and exciting and wholly my own.

I wondered how my father would take the news, then realized I didn't have to tell him. I was an adult. I didn't need to ask his permission for this. I could make this work and it would be awesome. And if it wasn't, well, then that would be a life lesson learned.

"Okay," I said finally and felt a surge of joy burst in my heart at the smile that spread across her face. "Let's do it."

Chapter Seven

Rias

I picked up the discarded belt from the floor and stared at it for a long moment, relishing the memory of the night before. It had been amazing. Satisfying. Wonderful. And a memory I would cherish for a very, very long time. Ashly was perfection, and I'd been sad to see her leave in the morning, but we promised to keep in touch and had already sent a couple of texts to each other with all the information we could think of to stay connected.

I wasn't going to let her get away again. Not like last time.

Now I was packing my suitcase, getting ready to check out. It was the last day of the con and I was headed home after one last trip through the dealer's room. I missed my house, the diner, Terabend, and the lack of people in general. But now I knew I'd miss something here too. I'd miss Ashly.

It was strange to me, to have something to leave behind. I hadn't felt that way since the coven. Everywhere I went after that, there were no bridges left unburned that would make me miss anything. It made me think of Terabend and how hard it would be if I ever had to leave that little town.

But that was a problem for future Rias. Present Rias was too busy trying not to touch herself because her mind was on the beautiful blonde that left the room about an hour ago. I shook my head and threw the belt into the suitcase and zipped up the whole damned thing.

It didn't take long to get downstairs and check out, then head for the elevator. I stepped inside and hit the button for the parking garage. Right before the doors closed an arm blocked them, forcing them to reopen as a tall man in a dark trench coat slipped into the elevator with me. I moved to the side a little to give him room, and he gave me a little smile. I couldn't help but notice what looked like a shiny bit of gold on one of his teeth.

I focused my thoughts away from him and toward Ashly, wondering if she had made it home safely, or what she was doing.

"Enjoying the convention?" The man's voice broke me from my thoughts. I fought not to do something awkward as I gave a slight nod.

"Oh, um, yeah. It was, um, fun." I watched the man's fuzzy reflection in the burnished metal of the elevator walls, wondering why he was even talking to me. There was something about him, something that felt familiar, though I was certain I'd never seen him or his gold tooth before.

The elevator came to a stop before he could talk again, and I slipped out the doors as they were still opening, and pulled my suitcase along behind me. I focused on making it to my car as quickly as I could manage, even as I swore I heard him leave the elevator a few seconds behind me.

I popped the trunk of my car, a four-door Toyota Yaris, with the key fob and tossed my suitcase inside. I'd just closed the trunk when a pair of arms appeared around me and I let out a sudden screech before a hand covered my mouth.

"Now, now, there's no need to be doing that here," the man from the elevator said. I struggled against his grasp as we backed away from my car. "I've been looking for you since I met your wolf friends in Edmonton last month. Imagine my surprise when I sensed your little display of magic yesterday. So, what did you do, hmm? Put a mind whammy on someone to get a better deal from one of the vendors?"

I kicked out behind me as hard as I could, but I swore the man had tree stumps for legs for all my battering accomplished. Instead I let go of my keys, drew on some of my magic, and held the keyring aloft with my power. Then I brought them up and flung them as hard as I could toward his face.

He shouted and dropped me. He used his arms and hands to protect his face from the sudden onslaught of keys and fobs, and I twisted and reached for my sidearm. When my hand slapped pants, I remembered I wasn't exactly on the clock here and swore as I threw myself back and away from him. I ran for the next row of cars before I held up my hands and brought the keys back to me.

"I don't know what you're talking about!" I shouted as I looked for a way out or a way to get around him or something. I didn't know what, but there had to be a way out of this.

"Oh, I'm sure you do, *Rias.*"

I swore under my breath.

"Who are you? How do you know my name?"

"You don't recognize me?" He grinned and threw his hand forward as if to toss something toward me. A blast of pure force slammed into the car beside me and I had to toss myself forward to avoid being crushed between two vehicles. The wash of power over me felt familiar, like something I'd tasted before. "You undid my ever so careful work before, I figured you'd smell it the moment I was within ten feet of you."

I shook my head. "I don't know who you are and I don't care. Leave me alone!"

"Now, now, I can't do that." He tossed another bolt of force at me and I moved again, sprinting between cars, trying to find a way out of here. This was oddly public for anyone to be showing off their magic like this, but he acted like he didn't even care. Whoever he was, he wasn't with a coven. "My name, little witchling, is Eric Ritten."

He said it like it should invoke fear in me, but I only shook my head.

"No? Doesn't ring a bell? Your little wolf pals didn't tell you what happened?" He lobbed another bolt of force toward me, but this one I caught on my own web of magic, spinning it quickly into a sticky magnet for magic that I used to catch the energy. I felt it tumble through me, making me shake in my sneakers as I instinctually grounded the transferred energy into the pavement below me. Holy shit, this guy was strong if he was throwing around that kind of power just to come after me. Stronger than most witches I'd encountered. Almost as strong as me.

"What the hell does that have to do with me?" I demanded. I wove my magic together and made something of a cat's cradle with the power around my fingers as he launched another blast at me. I swung my hands sideways, so the woven magic sliced through the air and deflected the bolt into a nearby car. It shattered the windows and crumpled the trunk.

"You're my ticket to the big times, dearest Rias."

I swear he had the most boisterously annoying voice I'd ever heard, and he took great joy, clearly, in using it like a Saturday morning cartoon villain. "I take your magic from you, that sweet, sweet power that you have, and I can finally move on from this stupid exile in this backwoods territory and take my revenge on the covens."

Yup, definitely a Saturday morning cartoon villain.

I released a blast of my own power, pure magic shaped into a thin arrowhead that I launched toward him. It wasn't meant to do physical damage, but instead to disrupt his magic should he choose to defend himself. Which he did.

"Damn it!" he roared, loud enough that it echoed through the parking garage. I glanced back at him and watched as he doubled over for a second before picking himself up again, his eyes full of rage.

Well. Looks like that just pissed him off.

Still, my attack gave me the opportunity to book it back toward my own vehicle, still grasping my keys in my off hand. I slammed the door closed behind me and started the engine, not even waiting for a second before I threw the small car in reverse and pulled out of my spot. Something slammed against the back of the car and spun me a little, but I managed to course correct and speed toward the parking garage exit. I slammed on the brakes before I hit the slowly opening exit door and closed my eyes to weave a new spell right on the bumper of my car.

I was glad I did.

A moment later something exploded right at the back of my car. Fire spread like a living thing around the shimmering, nigh-invisible barrier that I'd just put up as I waited impatiently for the exit door to go up. I caught sight of the nearest video camera near the exit and whispered a quick hex, sending a sliver of power into it. Hopefully that would destroy any footage the camera and any others like it had gotten for the past ten minutes at least. I didn't need my image to get involved in something like this.

I sped out of the parking garage with fire behind me and slipped onto the surface streets. Once I was away from the hotel, I slowed down and kept my focus on the road. I had to navigate the one-way streets in the downtown core of Calgary before I was able to head north, cross the river, and open up when I hit Deerfoot Trail.

I was almost to the city limits before letting out a breath of relief. There was no way Ritten could be on my tail. Who the hell was this guy, and why did his power feel so damned familiar? There was no way he was part of the covens. They'd never accept someone who so flagrantly displayed their power in the middle of a busy city like that. If there had been witnesses, I worried what might happen to them to keep his power a secret.

A man like that was dangerous, for humans and witches alike. And he wanted me, my power. I knew there were spells that could drain a witch of their powers, give them to another, but that kind of magic was forbidden. It just wasn't used. That an exile could have gotten himself that kind of power made me wonder just where the hell he'd come from.

And what the hell was his deal with the wolves?

By the time I got back to Terabend, my brain hurt with trying to suppose and conjecture and decide what would be the right thing to do. I needed more information on this man, and I thought I finally figured out where I knew his magic from. But I needed to talk to some of my favorite wolves first.

I pulled into the parking lot at the Tooth and Claw diner and parked at the far end of the lot where the new bar was still being built. The Wolf Den was almost ready to open, with only some inside stuff to finish up and a new picture window to replace the damaged one that an irate werewolf had tossed a cinder block through a week ago. I headed for the bar, certain at least one of the wolves I was looking for would be there.

I entered the bar and heard more than saw the flurry of work going on to make the place ready to open soon. But all sound and movement came to a halt the moment the door shut behind me.

"Deputy." A tall, fit-looking wolf addressed me cautiously, like they thought I might be there to cause trouble. V was Heather's mate. The nonbinary wolf was taller than their mate, their dark, almost black hair long, save where it was undercut on the right side. A stern demeanor belied a soft heart and a solid mind for change. They had tried to get their father, the Alpha of their old pack, to bring their pack into the twenty-first century, to do away with centuries-old traditions and aspects of pack life. It didn't happen, and our little town with its small handful of wolf-shifters suddenly found itself with a good dozen refugees from the other pack.

"V," I nodded as I looked around the room, "I need to speak with you and Wren—and your mates."

"I'm pretty sure Wren is at the diner," they replied.

"This is a…private matter."

They stood with their hands on their hips and watched me for a long moment. I still wasn't completely sure what I felt about V and the other new wolves that had come to town. Don't get me wrong, none of them had been anything but cordial, especially to me, but it was a lot of new people at once and they came from a place that wasn't so great. That had to leave some scars, I'd think.

The moment passed and V turned to the workers in the bar. "Take a break, everyone, go get some lunch or something. Take an hour."

There was no arguing with the pack's Beta, only a mass exodus as most of the wolves headed for the door. Only one lingered, his eyes on me as if he wasn't sure if he should trust me.

"Cale, can you go to the diner and ask Wren and Natalie to come here, please?" V asked without taking their eyes off me.

"Yeah, I can do that," he said before leaving.

Once everyone was gone, V waved me farther into the bar and toward a door near the back of the main room. I could see where the booths were going in—tables were pushed against one wall to keep them out of the way as the rest of the construction finished—and at least one billiard table had already been set up for the wolves to play on in the rear area. Apparently I'd interrupted a game, judging by the balls on the table. V led me through the rear door into a room that looked pristine and new, a private room that had a large booth taking up most of the far wall with room for other tables or for standing room loiterers. I supposed, anyway. I'd never been in a private room of a bar before. I didn't know what kinds of things got underway there.

"We got our first shipment of drinks in yesterday," V said, their tone still not friendly per se. "Do you want anything?"

"Just a water, thank you," I said as I sat down in the booth, almost letting out a groan at the plushness of the cushion. They nodded and exited the room.

I let out a long sigh. Now that the danger was over, the drive was done, and I was able to sit and rest for a second, the fatigue set in. I'd used more magic today than I had since I was a child. More even than I had freeing Heather from her curse. And Ritten had thrown just as much back at me or more. It was hard to conjure up pure force. A lot of power had to be used to focus that much energy into a blast like that, and he had been flinging them around like he didn't care. Was he just stupid? Not caring about how drained he made himself? Or was he truly that strong?

And I was exhausted. I felt drained from trying to keep his magic away from me. There had to be a better way for him to try and take me, instead of just throwing force around like that.

And yet…there was a part of me that was ecstatic over what I had accomplished today. Without warning, without training, I had managed to turn a witch's attacks away and against him. I'd never had to defend myself like that—hell, I never knew I really had it in me. I sobered quickly, however, realizing that if the fight had gone on much longer, I might not have walked away from it. At least not whole.

The door opened and I had the briefest moment of panic before V stepped inside, Heather at their side. V carried a tall glass of ice water and put it on the table in front of me, but I was focused on Heather.

"Rias!" Heather said, opening her arms and moving in for a hug. I got up and gave it to her, holding tight for a moment before letting go. She was doing better since she'd gotten back to town with V and the other new members of the pack a month ago. Having a mate suited her, though I think it was more the fact that she wasn't blaming herself for every small thing anymore that was having the most positive change. "I didn't know you were back yet!"

"I just got back a couple minutes ago," I said, taking a sip of water to try and quench my parched throat. A moment later the door opened again and Wren appeared, followed quickly by Natalie, who was carrying several drinks from the diner.

"Rias!" Nat said. "How was the convention? Did you have fun? Did you make any friends?"

At the mention of friends, I felt my face heat with embarrassment. But now was not the time to talk about that.

"I might've," I said softly, as the four wolves took seats around the table. I moved to the door, ensured the thing was closed tight, and then pressed some of my magic against it with a whispered word to lock it. When I turned back, all four sets of eyes were focused on me, three looking puzzled, and only Natalie looking on with a kindness and understanding that made me want to weep. "But there's a bigger problem than my social life."

"What happened?" Nat asked.

"I was attacked this morning. By a witch who called himself Ritten."

At the name I saw Heather go pale and clutch onto V, who held their mate close to their chest. Natalie and Wren only looked at each other, then back at me. I sat back down, nursing that glass of water, as Natalie pulled out her phone.

"Is this about what happened in the parking garage?" she asked.

"How did you know about that?"

"It was in the news this afternoon, something about a fire in the parking garage of the hotel. Apparently, the police think it was an arsonist."

I shook my head. "No, it was much more than that. And he happened to blame it all on a group of wolves." I eyed them, but kept a smile on my face to let them know I wasn't overly angry. "So, my group of wolves, is there something you didn't tell me about your trip to Edmonton a little bit ago?"

Wren and Natalie's eyes turned to Heather, who was still cuddling in close with V. V's eyes never left their mate, but they spoke. "Ritten was the witch my old pack hired to break our mate bond."

Heather's voice was small and muted by V's chest. "And he was the one my mother paid to curse me in the first place."

I clenched my fists under the table but did my best not to show the anger I was feeling to my friends. I knew it wasn't easy to talk about all that had happened in Edmonton, for Heather and V especially, but if there was something that involved a witch, I should've been told about it.

"That's why his magic was familiar," I said softly, "I'd seen it before, when I broke your curse."

Heather nodded. "He said he had an affinity for working with wolves."

"I guess that's a way to put it," I said, "I wouldn't even know where to begin to try separating your very essence from that of your wolf, like he did with that curse. That's some shifter-specific stuff."

I told them what happened in the parking garage, ending with getting the hell out of there in a burst of fire.

Heather sniffled. "Someone needs to stop him."

I shook my head. "That someone isn't me, so don't even ask."

She pulled away from V a little and stared at me as if she couldn't believe what I'd just said. "What do you mean? The dude attacked you! He cursed me and tried to kill me and V! Someone needs to step up and stop him."

"And someone else can," I said harshly, then bit back whatever else I was going to say before I got too worked up. "Listen, I get it, I do. He fucked with you too much and I get wanting him gotten, but I'm not the one to do it. I barely got away from him in the first place, and if he was willing to set the damned hotel on fire to get me, he's not someone I want to go after. At all. Period."

She opened her mouth but Natalie reached over and put a hand on her arm. "Easy, wolf. It's not her responsibility."

"B-but she's a witch!"

"A witch with her own life, who isn't someone who goes hunting after other witches. At least as far as I know." Natalie shot a small smile at me with that comment.

I didn't allow myself to react, but I was happy that someone at least seemed to understand where I was coming from. I wasn't a hunter. I wasn't someone to go toe to toe with another supernatural individual and expect to beat them in…what? A duel or something? Because yeah, that sounds like a fantastic idea.

"But he can't be allowed to keep doing what he's doing!" Heather insisted.

"No, he can't," Wren agreed softly, "but what would you have us do, Heather? Hunt him down and attempt to take a pound of flesh for what he did in the past? How many wolves would you be willing to sacrifice to go up against him?"

Heather gritted her teeth. "Someone needs to do something."

"And if he comes here and causes trouble, then I promise you he won't walk out alive." Wren spoke as if she were talking about some casual topic, like the weather or a local sports team. The fact that she was talking about killing a person sent a slight shiver down my spine—and not one of the good ones like I got from being around Ashly.

Oh, Ashly. The thought of her shunted me out of the moment and back into my memories of the night before. A much more pleasant place to be.

I shook my head. There would be time to think of that later. Right now, we had to figure out what we were going to do about Ritten.

"Look," I said, knowing Heather needed more than what her Alpha was saying. "I get it, I do. He's an asshole who doesn't deserve the power that he has, but I'm not the one to go after him. If he makes the mistake of coming here, there's half a town gunning for him, and that's going to have to be enough." My phone vibrated in my pocket and I pulled it out. My heart beat faster when I saw Ashly's name on the message, but I managed to put it aside for the moment.

"I just…" Heather began, looking in my direction but refusing to meet my eyes. "It's just that he found out about you because of me. It's my fault that you had to deal with him today, that you almost died."

I shook my head. "It's okay, Heather. It happened and we're here now. I'm just not going to go looking for trouble." I knew it wasn't what she wanted to hear. I knew she wanted me to put on my cape and spandex and ride to the rescue like I did when I broke her curse. But this wasn't the same thing. I was lucky today. Half of what I did was done out of instinct, the other half out of survival. If I went looking for trouble, I wasn't confident that my magic would come at my call like it did this morning. He was just too strong, and I wasn't in the mood to have my magic drained. "If he comes here, just be careful. Whatever abilities he has over wolves may make him a deadly adversary."

"Well, hopefully we'd have a witch on our side to help," Wren said. I gave her a smile that probably looked more like a grimace as I got out of my seat and pulled out my phone.

"I have to go," I told them without looking away from the notifications. "I just…I wanted to let you all know about Ritten," I ended awkwardly. "If he shows up here, give me a call or something. I'll do what I can."

I headed for the door.

"Rias—" Natalie started, but I didn't wait for her to finish. I was out the door and stormed through the bar, more upset than I really should have been. I wasn't some sort of avenging witch. I wasn't going to get into a fight with another witch that I couldn't guarantee I'd win.

I was back in my car before I stopped long enough to take a deep breath and try to push the conversation out of my head. I stared down at my phone, thumb hovering over the notification from Ashly.

Why was I hesitating? I tapped on the message. Read it, read it again, then let out a little sigh. There were a couple messages there, the first few just wondering how I was doing, telling me that her dad was a little pissed, but things were okay. The last one drew my attention most, a panicked text sent almost an hour ago. She'd clearly heard about what happened at the hotel and needed to know that I was okay. I sent her a quick text, telling her that I had been driving and I'd just arrived home. Which wasn't far from the truth.

I wasn't home quite yet, but it was close enough that I could assuage her fears. I told her I'd left before whatever happened. She didn't need to know the truth, no matter how much I wanted to tell her. I swore under my breath and tossed my phone on the passenger seat, then started the car. It was time to go home and figure out what the hell to do about Ashly, about Ritten, the wolves, everything.

Fuck, I needed a vacation.

CHAPTER EIGHT

Ashly

I stared at my phone, waiting for a reply from Rias. I'd sent her so many messages. Like, too many, honestly. But I needed to make sure she was okay. At first it was just a couple, you know, just to say hi and tell her to message me when she could. I knew she had a bit of a drive back to Terabend, so it might be a bit. But then I heard about what happened at the hotel. About a fire in the parking garage, and vehicles being damaged. The police weren't even sure exactly what had happened, but I could feel in my gut that it was something from my father's line of work. My line of work.

I paced back and forth in my tiny bedroom at home, wearing a damned trail in the carpet. I thought about this morning, waking up next to Rias, curled up together as we lay basking in the afterglow of a beautiful night together. I'd told her things I'd never told anyone before. I'd been vulnerable with her. And she accepted me for it.

It was something I never thought I'd get to have. I thought I'd always have to be *on*, to be the monster hunter, the tough, smart one who was ready to help at a moment's notice, like I saw my mother often being. Or even my father, the man with the plan, the one the other hunters looked up to. Even if I desired a relationship of some sort with one of them, could I ever be as vulnerable with them as I was with Rias? Would they accept me for who I was at face value, like she did?

Would they accept that sweet submissive streak that Rias brought out of me last night? I shook my head. The answer was painfully obvious. The moment I showed weakness of any kind they would look at me differently, treat me differently. It was already rough sometimes, being my father's daughter. They expected more from me, and I wasn't always sure I could deliver. But if they knew what I'd done in bed last night, they'd never come to respect me. And if I ended up in a relationship with another hunter, I could be damned sure that whatever happened in the bedroom would spread through our community like wildfire. Locker room talk, indeed. I knew more about Marcus and the other hunter's sexcapades than I ever wanted to.

I rubbed at my wrists, remembering the tightness of Rias's belt binding them together. The thought made me close my eyes and rub my thighs together for a moment, the pleasure of the memory rolling through me. Such sweet surrender to her. Something I desperately wanted, needed. But I couldn't trust anyone else with this side of myself.

My phone buzzed and I launched myself at it, but it was only an email notification. Stupid emails. Stupid phone. *Tell me that Rias is okay*. I knew it was irrational. Even the story from the police, what little they managed to say, claimed there were no injuries, no victims, but how could they be sure when they didn't know what I knew? If someone on my side of the tracks, my family's side of the tracks, pulled something in daylight, the police would have no idea what was going on anyway, and victims can always be found after the fact.

I forced myself to stop and breathe for a moment. I was getting a little too intense about this. I just…I didn't want to lose her the moment I found her. And I couldn't help but feel like whatever happened at the hotel was something to do with the supernatural. It was an instinct, something my father had helped hone, and now was apparently wrong, according to him.

He wasn't very happy with me when I got home. As much as his words on the phone the night before were mildly apologetic in the overall tone, he was still pissed that I took the night to myself. I was a hunter. I didn't have a life except for what I did for the common good. The needs of the many, blah, blah, blah. And the worst part of it was that he was right, to an extent. I didn't regret a single second of my time with Rias, but how was I supposed to prove myself as a hunter if I let dalliances like that get in the way of my work?

I wanted both. I wanted both lives. To be a hunter, help people, rescue them from the things they barely knew existed, but I also wanted a life outside of that. To be one with another person. To have a life that had meaning outside of the fighting and tracking and blood that came part and parcel with it all. But those lives seemed like they were mutually exclusive. Only one could win out. And despite wanting it for so long, the hunter life was looking less and less appealing the longer my father kept me from the true work.

"I'm just trying to keep you safe," he had said when I got back today. I hadn't left Rias until around ten in the morning, so it was almost noon by the time I decided to get home. I'd texted her a couple of times already before then, knowing she'd get the messages in a couple hours when she got back to her small town. "I know how hard it's been for you lately, and I'm willing to work with you to find a good place to fit in the hunter hierarchy."

I shook my head at him. "I want to be taken seriously. I want people to look at me the way they do you and Mom. They know who's in charge. They know who to come to if there's trouble. If they need a plan. If there's a tough hunt that's going on. You're the one they come to. I want to be that person too. And there's no way that anyone will accept me as a hunter if you never let me actually do anything!"

He had crossed his arms and looked at me steadily, but I swear there was something like a bit of pride in Allan Mercer's eyes. "You're not wrong. I've kept you from the brunt of everything, and in doing so, have done you something of a disservice. I wanted to keep you safe, to make sure that you came back home every night. But I guess, especially after last night, I have to accept the thought that you might not come home every night. You are your own person, and you are old enough to make your own choices. In life, and in hunting."

"I'm not asking to go off guns blazing on difficult hunts by myself. I know I'm not quite ready for that. It's about things like Vancouver, or even these little tests you have for me like yesterday, that make everyone still think of me as nothing but a child! I'm not a child anymore, and as much as you want to protect me, I want more out of life than a bubble."

I fiddled with the necklace my mother had given me, twirling it in my fingers. More and more often I found myself doing that, playing with the little pendant and watching it catch the light when I was trying to figure out exactly what it was I wanted from life.

If my father ever noticed that Mom had given me her necklace, he didn't say anything. Instead he carried on as usual, acting like everything he did was for the best and that I needed to suck it up and follow his lead. I was getting tired of being treated that way, but knew it was the only way he knew to keep from losing me. Or so it seemed.

It was hard to argue with someone when you could see their point of view. But I wasn't a child anymore, and he couldn't keep treating me like one.

"I will take your wishes into account," he had said at the end of our conversation, after we had both been about as honest as we could be about what we wanted from each other. I left out Rias entirely. I wasn't going to tell him that I was having a relationship with a woman. Not right now, not when I was so close to getting what I wanted. "And I will work with you on finding hunts that you can *actively* assist on. Sometimes that will mean assisting from home or a place of safety, but other times that means in the field. You will work with the other hunters and get to know them, and they you, so that one day when I retire you will be ready to step into the same role that your mother and I share."

I stared at him for a long moment. "You think they'll look up to me like they do you?"

He shrugged. "I can only try to prepare you for it. It would probably be easier should you choose another hunter to court or allow to court you."

I froze, shaking my head as if to clear it. Court? He wanted me to *court* another hunter? "Wow, Dad, what an archaic way of trying to set up an arranged marriage."

"It isn't like that and you know it," he growled. "But you are getting toward a…an age where you may want to consider a…a partner of your own." He faltered, looking as if he was saying something that would give him apoplexy.

"Is this *the talk*?" I asked sweetly, giving him absolutely no wriggle room or grace for what he was trying to say. "You know, the one that most kids get as a teenager. The birds and the bees? Who wants to date a werewolf hunter? A vampire slayer?"

Okay, to be fair, if someone asked me if I wanted to date Buffy the Vampire Slayer, I always would say yes. Both movie and television versions.

"You understand what I am trying to say. It is safer to date and… have a relationship within our own community than to try to bring outsiders in. Most of them have troubles believing in what we do. They need to see it firsthand before they can be an up front and honest partner for us. Like your mother and me. We both knew what was out there when we first started our relationship. We knew that our lives weren't necessarily our own, but we could make something work between us and still protect the lives of so many others." He shook his head. "To try and court someone outside of all this, I worry it will never end well."

Ouch. If that hadn't been a punch to the gut, I don't know what was. I'd managed to keep it together, though. Maybe he suspected that

I was seeing someone, considering I was gone all night. Maybe he was just implying that he wasn't keen on a series of one-night stands, which was inaccurate because last night had been the second night, after all. But either way, what he was saying wasn't wrong. I couldn't be honest with Rias and tell her that I had to go away to hunt a werewolf or a ghoul or a shifter or something else and have her wave me out the door and wish me luck on the hunt. Would she ever be able to believe me that the supernatural was very real and very, very dangerous?

With a sigh of frustration, I pulled myself out of my stupor and grabbed my phone. I stormed out of my room and past the group of hunters that seemed to almost live in our house with us before heading into the kitchen and beyond, onto the back porch. I leapt the railing instead of walking around to the stairs and stalked across the well-manicured grass of our lawn toward the back gate.

Our house backed onto a greenbelt that dipped into a heavily wooded ravine. It was a place I liked to go to think, to consider things, like the life I wanted, the life I could have. It was my time to be alone with myself in a way I couldn't be, cooped up in my house. At least it used to be.

There was a walking path paved through the ravine, an easy sloping path that most people took to get from one end of it to the other. It stretched for several kilometers and was a quick and easy run when I needed to get the blood pressure up and going. But there was another path, a trail worn purely by feet and wheels that meandered through the trees and all around, going for the harder inclines and climbing up and down. It was that second trail that I stared at now. A trail I hadn't touched in years.

The trail we took the day my brother got hurt.

I shouldn't even have been thinking about it. The fact that I let out the whole sob story to Rias the night before was completely irrelevant. I hadn't thought about the pathway, about him, in so long. I hadn't thought about that morning when Dad tossed him down the embankment, such a look of pure anger on his face, in too long. I hadn't thought about my brother at all, until last night.

But that wasn't entirely accurate, was it? The thought of my brother was always at the edge of my mind. I was always comparing myself to him, to what he could do or what we used to do together. Was I good enough for him? Would he come back and find me? Would I ever see him again? I wondered what kind of person he'd become. Three years older than me and probably living a wonderful life with nary a care in the world. Not knowing what was really out there. Not knowing that somewhere, someday, he could turn the wrong corner at night and get his face eaten off by a starving vampire.

I stared at the path and wondered what kind of bliss it must be to live like that.

I turned around and headed back toward the house. I leaned against the back fence, not wanting to go back inside yet. The fresh air was good for me, soothing, comforting, in a way I hadn't felt since I left Rias's embrace that morning. I turned around and slid down the fence until I was sitting in the grass, idly playing with my necklace.

A soft, crunching sound came from my left and I glanced up in panic, already reaching for my pistol, until I saw the ratty trench coat and flashing tooth and realized it was just Ritten. I'd seen him a few times since that first night and decided he was *mostly* harmless. He seemed to take what we did seriously, and was there more often than not to assist and aid us in the more dire circumstances. Turned out it was handy to have a witch on your side sometimes, at least from what I heard. So his sudden appearances didn't do much to faze me anymore.

"Ritten," I said, settling back down on the grass.

He stopped a few feet from me, giving me space. I'd threatened him before about personal space and it seemed that he took the hint, which was surprising because other people often did not. He slipped down onto the ground, his back to the fence, and started picking at the blades of grass around him.

"Ashly," he said, mimicking my neutral tone.

"What brings you out here? The hunters are inside."

"I bet I know what they're talking about," he admitted. I turned to him and raised an eyebrow. "The hotel."

I blinked at him. "You know about that?"

He nodded. "I was there."

"The fire in the parking garage, that was you?"

He shook his head this time. "No, not entirely. I was trying to stop the witch."

I let out a long, thin whistle as I considered his words. He was never big on details, so you had to read between the lines with him. That he'd gone off to fight a witch on his own seemed like a poor idea though. "You know you could have asked for help."

He shook his head. "I thought I had this one in the bag. A quick and easy job to stop a witch from hurting people at the convention this weekend." He frowned. "I was too late. They'd taken what they wanted, hurt people, and then got away."

I clenched my fist. The supernatural world strikes again. "The police didn't report on any casualties."

He laughed. "You won't hear about them. Witches are good at what they do. They can make people disappear like *that.*" He snapped his fingers. "And this one was strong. Powerful. Stronger than me. It scared me a little, I'm not going to lie."

Well damn. I'd never seen the man look so dejected. But I guess that's what failure did sometimes. Sure, it was a learning tool, but the fact was that it stung too. It always stung.

"Well, next time you'll call for help. You know we'll come running."

He chuckled. "I might just do that." He turned to look at me and there was something in his eyes, something a little wild and ferocious, like he was putting himself back together after a good, long bout of self-flagellation. "You're awfully candid today. Did something happen?"

I sighed. I wanted to talk about it. I wanted to talk about everything. Everything I wanted to say to Rias, to my dad. To explain to them both that I wanted two lives, to have the best of everything. And I realized there was no better person than this witch who might understand where I was coming from. How did a witch function in a world where they couldn't tell people who they were, what they could do?

"I feel like I'm being torn in two different directions," I told him, then told him about how my father was going to give me more responsibility, but at the same time how I wasn't sure I wanted it because I wanted a life outside of my hunter priorities. "And I don't know what I should choose to follow. I could try and live a life pretending I don't know what's really out there and just ignoring the world, but I don't know if I'd ever be satisfied."

He nodded, humming a little as he listened to my diatribe. It was the first time anyone outside of Rias actually made me feel listened to. It was an odd sensation. I certainly didn't feel anything for the man like I felt for the woman who'd rocked my world last night, but maybe this was what it was like to be able to talk to, dare I say, a friend?

"Is there a particular reason you're feeling this way right now, as opposed to earlier?" he asked. "I mean, last time we spoke you were pretty hung up on the whole hunting thing. Now it sounds like you've had a taste of a life outside of it and aren't so sure what you want anymore."

It took me a long moment before I replied.

"I know what I want to do with my life. But I know what I want outside of that too. I don't want things to have to be all or nothing, one way or the other. I don't understand why I can't find a balance to things that makes both sides happy."

"The problem is, it's not always possible to have your cake and eat it too."

"I know, I know." I sighed and pulled out my pendant again, fiddling with it. It was warm from sitting against my chest, the stone glowing slightly in the slowly setting sunlight. My phone buzzed and I jumped, scrambling to get the damned thing from my pocket.

It was a message from Rias. I read it. Then read it again. And I laughed with relief. She was all right. She'd just been driving and couldn't text back. I knew it had been something simple like that. I'd told myself time and again that that's all it was. But there was that part of me that didn't want to listen to rational explanations and was so sure she was in trouble. And that part of me was quick to describe in great detail exactly how I would drop everything and go to her rescue. Because who wouldn't?

I gripped my phone tight and held it to my chest before typing out a response. I barely remembered that Ritten was there beside me before he cleared his throat and I put down the phone.

"Sorry. I was waiting for a message and got really excited."

He waved a hand. "Far be it for me to come between you and your young paramour." The way he said *paramour* made the word sound overly dirty, and I could feel a flush heat up my cheeks a little. "Congratulations, by the way. Who happens to be the lucky lady?"

I stiffened. "Who says she's a lady?"

He laughed. "You did, just now. But honestly, I'm a witch, remember? I know these things."

I was pretty sure there was no spell or anything that gave him an intimate knowledge about the inner workings of my brain and sexual preference, or if there was that he'd bother using something like that on me of all people, but it was something of a word of warning that I had to be a little more careful.

"Don't tell my parents," I said quickly. "They...wouldn't understand."

He mimed locking his lips with a key. "Not a soul, I swear."

I looked down at my phone and gave a small smile. "She's amazing. And she's mine. I never thought I'd have someone like her."

There was a long, long silence before I glanced up to find him looking at me funny. I couldn't read whatever he was thinking, but he didn't look as jovial as he had a few minutes before.

"Well," he said finally, "I hope for your sake it goes well. And congratulations. Again."

He got up and walked into the backyard, as if heading for the house. I let him go. Instead, I stared down at the picture on my phone I'd just saved to my lock screen this morning, a selfie with Rias, smiling warmly at me as I made a goofy face.

Maybe I did want my cake, and to eat it too. Would that be so bad?

Chapter Nine

Rias

Four months later

I could barely wait until we got into the hotel room before my hands were all over Ashly. I couldn't help myself. It had been one month, ten days, seven hours, and forty-seven minutes since the last time we were together. It was the longest we'd gone without seeing each other since we started the whole long-distance thing. When we met up this evening for dinner and a date, I was about ready to say screw it all and drag her to my hotel room without preamble, but I was a good witch and ate food and had good conversation before suggesting we skip some boring movie and take it back to my bed. Ashly had been quick to agree.

She made the sweetest noise as I shoved her against the wall, my mouth on hers, my hand flitting over her body. I didn't know where I wanted to touch her first. I didn't know where I wanted to taste her first.

"Rias!" she breathed, and it pulled me back to the moment. I pressed my lips to her cheek, then trailed kisses down until I pulled aside her shirt to reach her collarbone.

"I'm going to kiss you for every hour we were apart," I murmured into her skin. She nodded against me, moaning as I pushed her jacket from her shoulders and let it fall to the ground. Her shirt was next, then I trailed my kisses down her chest and onto her beautiful breasts. I moved to one of her nipples and wrapped my lips around it, sucking on it until it hardened in my mouth. I moved my hands down her body to work on her jeans, then pulled them loose and let them fall down her legs.

Not to be outdone, Ashly pulled my blouse from my skirt and

undid the buttons faster than I noticed. I was thankful she didn't just rip the damned shirt off me. I kept my attention on her breasts as she pushed the shirt off my shoulders and I shucked it off, then she attacked the zipper on my skirt. I shimmied out of it, leaving both of us in nothing but our underwear.

I gave her nipple a gentle nibble. I loved the way she gasped and writhed against me as I held her firmly against the wall. She could probably overpower me easily, but instead she was putty in my hands—just the way I wanted her.

"Are you going to be a good girl for me?" I whispered in her ear, pushing myself onto my toes to sink my teeth into her earlobe and pull slightly.

"Y-yes, yes please! Rias!"

I wrapped my hand in her hair—her strawberry-blond now streaked with a purple that I absolutely loved on her—and pressed her toward my chest. My bra went the same way as my shirt, and she eagerly attached herself to my nipple as I threw my head back with a loud groan. Goddess, this woman was going to be the death of me.

"B-bed?" I stuttered, dragging her from my chest with an audible pop when she refused to let go of my nipple.

"Please," was the only word that made it out of her mouth before she went back to her mission of pleasuring me. I let her go with wild abandon, dragging us both toward the bed and pushing her down onto it. I didn't leave her alone for long, climbing on top of her and pressing my chest back to her mouth.

"More," I whispered and she went to it with a will. As I wrapped my arms around her head and held her close, she moved her hand down my body to the spot between my thighs. She edged my already soaked underwear out of her way and started massaging my outer lips as her teeth grazed my nipples and I gasped her name into the air. "A-Ashly!"

She twisted her fingers and entered me easily with how wet I was. I moaned into her as her fingers curled and found that perfect spot inside me. I pressed kisses against her head as her mouth continued to play with my nipples, giving each of them equal time, and I swore I was hers.

"I-I want to taste you," she gasped from my arms and I nodded quickly, desperate to have her mouth on me. I pulled her hand from between my legs and held it up to her lips. She took them into her mouth, closing her eyes and moaning with pleasure as she did. I pulled her fingers back to me, sharing with her the taste of myself, and we pressed our foreheads together in a soft moment. "O-on me, please, Rias."

Anticipation built inside me as I moved up to straddle her head. She gasped as I pressed myself against her quickly, soaking her mouth in my juices. I settled myself over her and she went to work, grasping my thighs as she used tongue and teeth and drove me wild. I tangled my hand in her hair, pulling her further into me as I ground down on her mouth and chin. Whatever she was doing down there, she was hitting all the right spots. Her tongue and lips were amazing against my clit, sending shock waves of euphoria roaring through me.

I glanced down at her, catching her eyes from between my thighs. I fell into that blue gaze, so obedient and ready and willing to pleasure me. She looked at me like I was something divine and it ached through every single part of me. Pleasure throbbed through me, stretching from my head to my toes and settling in my core as she worked me hard enough that I almost couldn't stop myself from coming right on that pretty little mouth of hers. I tried to take more control, slowing down and speeding up to control my own orgasm, but like a crashing wave it crested over me when I wasn't prepared and I slipped under the water, unable to keep my voice down as I screamed her name out into the world around me.

I collapsed into her, my hand still tangled in her hair, as I came hard on that beautiful face.

"Holy shit," I gasped, rolling off her as I allowed my orgasm to fade. Still, the aching need to have her more was there, only spurred on by whatever else I felt inside me. My magic was desperate for more, reaching out for the woman beside me, wanting to help me to pleasure her. The idea of so many different spells ripped through my head, different ways to bring this woman to pleasure and give me another mind-blowing orgasm.

One day, maybe, I'd be able to show her what I could really do. I allowed myself only a moment of that daydream, knowing that in truth it would never, ever happen.

Before I could turn melancholy, I looked at Ashly, happily licking her lips as she cleaned her face from what I had gifted her. She looked overly satisfied with herself, and I couldn't stop the smile that spread across my face.

"I think that's the hottest thing we've done yet," she murmured breathlessly.

"I concur." I pressed a kiss against her lips, tasting myself on her and feeling another blast of pleasure deep in my belly. I slipped a hand down between her thighs and she gasped, grinding in toward my fingers as I massaged her labia. After all that, I was not about to leave my lover unsatisfied. I kissed her again and again, feeling her squirm underneath me as I worked my fingers closer and closer to her center. I pressed my thumb against her clit, and two fingers slipped through her folds as she bucked up into my hand and I kissed her hard again.

"Rias, please—" She gasped and I pressed my lips to hers once more, biting at her bottom lip and pulling softly. Her cry was muffled by my mouth as I felt her muscles clenching my fingers. I hesitated, then added a third finger, filling her tight and curling to reach that most sensitive spot inside her. I left a trail of kisses down her neck and throat, using my teeth to nibble at the skin as I went, desperately wanting to mark her more heavily but knowing that it might cause awkward questions. I reached her breasts and latched onto one of her nipples, sucking hard enough I knew she would have a mark around her areola.

Dear Goddess, this woman was perfect. I loved how she felt under me, inside me, touching me, and me touching her. I couldn't get enough. My body was caught up in the melting-hot pleasure of just being with her, and as I brought her closer and closer to completion, she began to cry my name as if it was a mantra she was trying to memorize.

"Come for me, kitten," I whispered in her ear as I felt her on the cusp. "Come for me and scream my name."

"R-Rias!" she cried and bucked against me again. "Rias! Rias! Danaan!"

I froze only for a second, hearing my first name come from her lips. It had been a while since anyone called me Danaan, but to hear it from her…it made me feel more than just pleasure inside. It brought out more in me than just that, but I was scared to even think the words, never mind say them.

I patted her head, running my hand over her hair softly as she came down from her orgasm. My other hand found a place in my mouth and I sucked her arousal off my fingers as she stared at me with a look of…I wasn't sure. I wanted to call it devotion, but that couldn't be it. Could it? I kissed her cheek once, twice, thrice, trying to fulfill my promise of kissing her for every hour we'd spent apart. When she was able to move again she turned her head toward me, taking my kiss on her lips and groaning into me as our tongues danced together.

"Fuck, Rias," she breathed, and I gave her a moment to finish catching her breath.

"You all right, kitten?"

"Never better." That look flashed in her eyes again, and it sent a feeling through me that was so much more than mere arousal. But there was that too and I grinned at her.

"Ready for round two?"

Her smile matched my own as she pushed me over onto my back and climbed on top of me. "I thought you'd never ask."

❖

I had a smile plastered on my face for the next week. Even when I had to say goodbye and head back to Terabend and Ashly had to return to her parents' house, the kiss we shared as we parted promised so much more—when we could find time to be together again.

That was always the hardest part. We'd only actually seen each other in person a couple of times over the last year, and each time was an amazing day and night and maybe the next day before we had to return to our regularly scheduled lives. It was bittersweet, every time.

Goddess, I missed her. Even a week later after coming home, I couldn't keep her off my mind. That look I saw on her face that night, the feelings I was having for her not just during our amazing sex—there was something there that I think both of us were afraid to talk about. Instead we talked about everything but what we were doing. We texted every day, called once in a while too. We sent each other long messages about our day or what we planned to do the next time we saw each other. We talked about what we hoped for in the future or bitched about what we were being forced to do by other people in order to make a living.

But through all our talk there was never anything about where we were headed. What we were going to do. It'd been four months so far, and as much as we were making this work, I still yearned to hold her in my arms every night. To come home to her every day. I watched the happy couples around Terabend, not just the old, established relationships but even the new ones that seemed to be blossoming under Wren's roof at the diner. I watched Natalie and Wren, and yearned to have a relationship like theirs. I watched Heather and V and saw the softness between the two of them, the care that they had for each other, and the closeness that I was entirely jealous of.

But I couldn't have that.

That kind of relationship was reserved for the people who could be completely open with their partners. And that wasn't something I could do. What would happen if I told Ashly I was a witch? At best she would accept it as a quirk but wouldn't truly believe in my powers. At worst… well, my mind could go a lot of different ways when it came to deciding what the worst outcome would be. *Laughs in my face. Never wants to see me again. Starts a whole new inquisition.* Just normal things that one does when they find out their lover is a magical being that can affect the laws of physics with a wave of the hand and a thought.

And then there was the idea that I would outlive her several times over…

"Fuck," I muttered under my breath. These were not things I wanted to think about right now.

Natalie slipped into the booth across from me, breaking me from the thoughts that had clouded my mind for the past hour or so that I'd been sitting in the diner. My breakfast was long gone and I was nursing my third or fourth cup of coffee, but Natalie brought with her a plate of fresh fries and her own drink. She placed the plate on the table between us, almost like a peace offering, and I couldn't stop myself from reaching out and taking a bite of salty goodness.

"Damn it, you always salt these so damned well. Not too much, not too little." I wasn't even looking at her as I spoke because I knew she would see my desperation to do something I couldn't do.

"I know how to make a good french fry," she replied. "It's about the only thing I know how to cook, really, though Wren's been trying to remedy that."

"And how's that going?"

"I haven't burned down the house yet, so, well, I think."

"That's not much of a barometer for whether you can cook or not."

"It works for me."

When I was confident I could school my face into a look that didn't betray my deepest desires, I looked up at the open and honest face of my friend and immediately felt the tears start to fall. I couldn't even say why, but there was something about Natalie that reminded me so much of Ashly, and I missed her so damned much.

"Oh, oh, honey." I heard Natalie say, then felt her slide into the booth next to me. A pair of arms wrapped around me and I found myself leaning into the safe warmth of the other woman as the tears continued to fall and I tried to keep my sobbing to a quiet roar. "What happened, honey? What did she do?"

I shook my head against her, sniffling as I tried to find my voice. "Nothing. She didn't do anything. She's perfect, you know? She's great and perfect and she's not here!"

She held me tighter until I felt I could sit up and be an ordinary human-like being whose eyes weren't leaking saline for a bit. I felt Nat pull back a little, but she kept one arm wrapped around my shoulders as if in reminder that she was here. As much as I wanted to pull away, it was nice to have someone, to need someone like this. It had been a long time since I felt I could rely on anyone quite like this.

"I'm okay," I mumbled, but Natalie stayed beside me. "I promise, I'm okay. It was just…it was just a moment. I'm okay."

"So, I don't need to hunt this woman down and kick her ass?" Natalie asked. I glanced up at her, noting the soft smile on her lips. If I said the word, it wouldn't surprise me if she found a way to get it done, either. But only if I said so, and I made sure I shook my head in the right direction to tell her no.

"I'm okay, and she's perfect. No need to send out a wolf hit squad on her."

"I'm just saying, the option is there."

"Appreciated, but unnecessary." I let out a long breath and tried to rein in the waterworks a little bit more so I could focus on my friend—and the plate of fries in front of me. Nothing like french fries to console a heartbroken woman. "I just really miss her. I mean, I saw her last week and I can't stop thinking about her."

"Sounds like you've got it bad."

"I have since that night in Vancouver. I never thought I'd see her again, but then we met at the convention, and now that we're seeing each other…I don't know. It's like she's burrowed her way into my heart and mind and lives there now, and each time I have to come home alone I feel so…"

"Alone?"

"Yeah, alone. Like, I logically know that we have this relationship, and there's nothing wrong with it. We even made tentative plans to see each other again next month, as long as we can both make it work. But I think I want more than that. I want her here, with me. Or even me there with her. I would be okay with that. I would be willing to get back to living in the big, wild city if it meant being with her, and that's something I never thought I would do again." I wiped away the last remnants of tears and sniffled a little. "That's unreal for me. I swore off cities a long time ago. But being with her makes everything…better. Quiet. Being with her brings me a peace I haven't known in a long time, more even than I had before I broke Heather's curse."

"You mean with your magic." She kept her voice low and I smiled, loving that she was aware of talking about that kind of thing in public and acted accordingly.

I nodded. "It's…it's been problematic for me, since I broke the curse." This was the first time I'd said anything about it to anyone but Brigid, back in Vancouver. It felt good to talk about it, to tell someone who might just understand. Maybe she didn't have magic that threatened to break free and cause havoc, but Natalie had been through her share of shit in life. And she was nothing if not empathetic. Wren was as lucky to have her as a mate as Natalie was to have Wren.

"You haven't seemed like anything was wrong," she said quietly, her arm tightening in a sort of half hug for a moment. "Did I miss something or were you hiding it?"

"I hid it. When it comes to my magic, I hide pretty much everything." And I told her about how I was having trouble controlling my magic. That for the past year I'd been going back to basics, trying to learn how to get it back to a point where I didn't have to worry about it slipping out of my grasp. I told her about my slip-up at the convention. I told her in detail about the fight with Ritten. And I told her how much my magic quieted when I was with Ashly—like it never did around anyone else.

"It sounds like she's good for you, this…what was her name again?"

"Ashly," I said wistfully, snagging a fry from the plate. "Ashly Mercer." I was lucky I'd turned to look her in the face when I said Ashly's name, because something flickered across Nat's visage. Something I couldn't put into words. Recognition, maybe?

"What was that?"

She shook her head. "I…the name sounds familiar, is all. Growing up in Calgary, I knew an Ashly Mercer, but I'm sure it's probably a different person."

"I didn't know you grew up in Calgary."

She shrugged. "I don't talk about my childhood a lot. Honestly, it feels like it happened to a different person, sometimes. Like I didn't really even start my life until…until I was able to be myself."

That made a whole lot of sense. As much as I did know about Nat's past, which wasn't a whole heck of a lot, it was something she didn't talk about much. And I didn't blame her. It's not like I talked about my past in the coven either. Some things are just hard to talk about, especially if others can't really relate.

"But honestly, Rias, if you want something more with Ashly, you need to talk to her about it. I know you've got your life here, but that might need to change if you want something this badly."

I shook my head. "I can't just make that kind of decision for her. That wouldn't be fair to either of us."

"I'm not saying make the decision for her, but you need to talk to her. Communication is key."

"But what's the point when it will never work? I'm a witch. I have my magic. I'll outlive her possibly several times over. And I can't even be honest with her about who I am. And she has a life of her own, a world of her own that I don't know if I'll fit into. I highly doubt her parents would appreciate a woman taking her away from them from what little I've heard her talk about them."

I had to admit, I hated how self-pitying I sounded. I honestly couldn't remember the last time I'd felt so damned insecure, and I wasn't exactly relishing the feeling. What if Ashly wasn't as into all this as I was? What if she didn't want anything more than the odd night together and just talking at each other? Did that even make any sense? That look in her eyes that night…it had me thinking of things I shouldn't be thinking of. I groaned and covered my face with my hands.

"Hey," Nat said softly, "hey, don't do that to yourself. Don't beat yourself up."

"How do you know that's what I'm doing?"

"Because I know too well what that looks like. I lived through it often enough. Still do, sometimes, when my brain runs away on me."

"Then please, oh wise one, tell me what to do." The words came out far snarkier than I meant them to and I looked up, ready to quickly apologize. Nat just gave me a look like she knew exactly what was happening in my head and wasn't taking offense. This time.

"Don't borrow trouble," she said simply. "Don't let your brain tell you that there's all these problems that aren't actually there. They might be in the future, true, but right now you and Ashly are together in a way that makes sense for both of you. It may not be perfect. You might be pining for more. But until you can make that work, then this is what you have. Enjoy it."

That…was a hell of a lot easier said than done, but she wasn't wrong. Building up trouble in my head was just a recipe for disaster.

Never mind spelling disaster for my magic. It wasn't exactly being silent during this tumultuous emotional barrage I was having. It was a testament to my practice and learning that I was able to keep it in check without overtly thinking about it, but even that bit of control was starting to fail.

I glanced at the ketchup bottle on the other side of the table and, after a quick glance to make sure no one was looking, swiped my hand through the air. The bottle leapt into my hand with a little too much force, but I managed to catch it and put it down softly on the table, taking a moment to breathe and let my magic relax again before opening the bottle and putting ketchup on the plate of fries. I glanced toward Natalie, who was looking at me oddly.

"I thought you were having troubles with it."

I nodded. "It helps to do small things if it's already worked up. Kind of like taking the edge off." I sighed, dipping a fry into the tomato and sugary goodness, and munching on it happily. "I never would have even considered doing something small like that in public before all this happened. I've had to relearn and change my view of what my magic is and how I can use it. It's been a lot of work, but worth it, so far."

"Do you have better control over your magic now?"

"I wouldn't necessarily say it's better, but it's different. And it fits how my life is different now, thanks to you wolves."

She grinned. "What can I say? We live to change lives."

I laughed with her. "I was so scared of the covens coming after me for so long, it's like I forgot that there was this entire other part of me. I can't even say what prompted me to tell you that I was a witch in the first place, never mind offer to help with the curse. I hadn't used my magic in years before that, and honestly, I didn't even know if I *could* help with anything. But I did it, and it's like my magic woke up with a vengeance."

"Well, you know that all of us are grateful for what you did for Heather."

"I know, but it's nice to hear. I'm just glad I was able to help."

"Even with the trouble it's brought you?"

"Even with. It's no way to go through life, feeling only half of yourself. Something I've learned too."

"Sometimes we learn that as kids, sometimes as teens, sometimes as adults. And some people don't learn that lesson at all. We deserve to live life fully as who we are, supernatural or not, transgender or not, straight or not. It's not fair to force us to live a life hiding who we are just so others are more comfortable."

"Too true," I said, snatching another fry. Natalie took one of her own and we ate in comfortable silence for a few minutes before she spoke again.

"So…I really wanted to see you here because I wanted to tell you something, as my best friend."

I looked up at her, a little shocked. "I'm your best friend?"

"Yeah, one of a few. Is…is that okay?"

I don't think I could properly express what it felt like to have someone call me their best friend, so instead of answering I merely gave her a tight hug.

"I'll take that as a yes."

"Of course it's a yes, silly," I said after releasing her. "I just…it's a little…" I shook my head. "What's the news you had?"

"Oh right, that." I watched a blush creep up her cheeks and became even more intrigued, putting aside the whole friend thing. "Well, I know I told you last year that Wren and I were talking to Dr. Maru about IVF. Well, we started the process more recently and…"

She trailed off and my mind started following the logical route. She didn't seem upset, but instead excited, maybe a little embarrassed, but happy. That really led to a single conclusion.

"Wren is pregnant?" I did not remember to keep my voice down.

She shushed me, slapping my shoulder lightly, but clearly couldn't keep the wide grin off her face as she nodded happily.

"Yeah! We just found out. It's only like a month in or so, and I know you're technically not supposed to tell anyone for the first while in case something happens, and we've been keeping it from the rest of the pack, but I *needed* to tell someone!"

"Oh. My. Goddess, you're going to have a puppy!" I hissed, wrapping her into another hug. "That's amazing!"

"I know, right? I'm so excited. I mean, I never thought anything like this would happen!"

"Why not?"

"Well, I mean look at me." I did and still didn't see anything wrong. I eyed her severely, though, and she seemed to get it. "I know, I know. I just…I spent so much of my life not thinking that I'd have the things I wanted in the future. Thinking I wasn't good enough to have them." She shook her head. "When I started my hormone therapy, my doctor was insistent that I freeze some sperm. I refused at first, sure I'd never have an opportunity to need it. Now, though…I'm so glad I did it. Wren is carrying my baby!"

"That's amazing Nat, it really is. I'm so happy for you."

And I was. But there was a bit of jealousy too. Not necessarily that Wren was pregnant, but because of the relationship they had. It was just another sign of what was wrong with what Ashly and I were doing. Yes, it was easy to say that I just wanted whatever I could have, but the truth was I wanted more. I wanted that kind of togetherness I saw the others have. I wanted to be with her.

I shook my head, not willing to go down that road again.

"Thanks Rias, I really appreciate it. Thanks for letting me tell you."

I sighed, grabbing another fry. I was her best friend. She could tell me anything. Or that's how it was supposed to work, wasn't it? Then why didn't I want to tell her more about Ashly, about what I was pining for? Maybe for now I'd keep that to myself. Just until I could talk to Ashly again. Maybe next time we saw each other, we could figure something out. That idea brought a smile to my face. Maybe something could change.

I could always hope.

Chapter Ten

Ashly

Seven months later

When one is hunting vampires, it's best to be quiet, stealthy, and as unseen as it's possible for a human to be. So when I slipped into the abandoned house, I attempted to be all of these things. The man who walked in behind me was none of them.

"This is pointless," Marcus said, and I fought the urge to unload my hand crossbow into his chest. "You've been hunting this thing for weeks. You really think it's in this shithole?"

His sentiments weren't entirely baseless. Most vampires, I'd been told, preferred much more posh surroundings. But sometimes beggars couldn't be choosers, and I'd run this bloodsucker down for weeks. I knew where she was, and I was going to show my parents I could take care of a hunt by myself. Then the asshole behind me scuffed his boots on the ground.

Right. Not entirely by myself, I amended.

We were in the woods outside Rocky Mountain House, a little more than an hour from Calgary. We'd parked down the road leading up to the house, using the trees as cover until the house came into view. The place was decrepit with age and all but falling apart. A dangerous place that only brave teens and other students used as a dare to prove how unafraid of death they were. The perfect place for a young vampire to lie low, especially one that couldn't yet stand to be in daylight.

Depending on the age, it was easiest to hunt for vampires while the light of the sun was overhead. The younger of the species couldn't handle it, and even the older ones were weakened enough to make them viable targets for the hunt. Dusk was coming on strong now, and I knew in the back of my mind I should be doing this tomorrow, but something inside me said it couldn't wait.

Ever since my father had his epiphany—his word for it, not mine—I'd been on several hunts now. Never by myself, and usually only as backup or support, as they called it. But I'd faced down a couple other vampires now, and another werewolf. The latest had been a young woman who turned into a panther on me. My father had been knocked away by the beast, but I was quick to put a silver bullet in its eye.

I might have thrown up afterward, but that didn't matter. I was doing my job. My job was to hunt monsters and that's what I was doing. Despite how wrong it felt sometimes.

This was my first chance to hunt without my parents present. I wanted it to go well, to be able to tell them that I took care of it mostly on my own. Maybe then they'd let me go on one on my own.

So I ignored Marcus's words and continued my silent recon of the dilapidated house. Half the thing had already collapsed in on itself, but most of the main room was intact. The stairs to the second level were collapsed about halfway up, but I wasn't worried about that. I wanted an entrance to the basement. It wasn't far, through another room, around the corner from the collapsed stairs, and through a broken doorway.

It was like walking into a different world. From the ruined and broken wood walls of the old house to a solid foundation of mortar and rock like root cellars of old. I crept down the steps with Marcus hot on my heels until the stone floor spread out before us. I stopped a few steps in and waited for Marcus to plant his feet before I tried to peer through the darkness. No windows, no source of light at all. The basement was pitch-black.

"This is pointless," Marcus said. "Let's get out of here and get back on the trail."

"Shut up."

"I'm serious, Ash, we're wasting our time here."

"Don't call me Ash," I snapped. "And I didn't ask you to come with me."

"No, your father did."

I snorted. "Yeah, that's what I want to hear right now."

"You know you're not ready to go on a hunt by yourself."

"Says you."

"Says everyone."

"Well *everyone* can go fuck themselves." I threw an elbow back and connected with his gut. "Now shut the fuck up and let's get moving. I want that vampire dead tonight."

A throaty laugh rolled through the darkness.

"I believe you will be sadly disappointed, little blood-sacks."

I turned toward the voice, leveling the crossbow into the blackness. I felt Marcus at my back, muscles tense, sure his own weapon was ready to go.

"Turn on some lights and we can have a nice conversation," I bantered.

That laugh echoed around the cellar once more. "Yet is it not more humane to leave the cattle blinded before slaughtering them?"

I couldn't help but smile a little. Some monsters were not fans of some light banter before we killed them.

"Is this a philosophical question?" I asked the darkness.

"Alas, if you'd not come to kill me, then perhaps we could have such a discussion."

"Why don't we have it now?"

"Certainly not, because you are attempting to aim crossbows at my heart." Her tone was dripping with sarcasm. I couldn't resist playing with her, but with each back-and-forth I could feel Marcus's tension growing.

"And if we put them away?"

"Well, then surely I would come out of hiding."

I waited for her to laugh again before I whispered to Marcus. "Flare."

"What"

"Flare!"

I shut my eyes as I heard the distinct scratch and hiss of the road flare and the red light shone even through my eyelids. "Past me!" I told him and the light moved, flying over my shoulder to illuminate the cellar.

At least most of it, I realized when I opened my eyes. Either the vampire had done some remodeling, or it was someone else who'd owned the place, but most of the far wall had been knocked out into some natural cavern or something. The flare's light faded into the darkness beyond the cellar, and nowhere did I see the source of the laughter that had cut off the moment the light had flared.

"Well, so much for humane." The vampire's voice drifted on the air, and I turned, spying her standing at the top of the stairs. She was tall, lithe, pale in all the best ways, and had long hair that fell in unearthly waves of golden blond. The air was filled with the pure sensuality that most vamps in my brief experience had. I could feel the pull toward her and cursed that it actually worked on me.

Still, Marcus had to be getting hit harder than me. He sure didn't seem like it, though. He was quick to snap to the top of the steps, crossbow at the ready. He let the bolt fly, and she disappeared a second before it smashed into the stone wall.

"Reload!" I yelled at him as I swiveled, trying to find her again.

"Urg! Grk!" was the reply.

I leapt away quickly, rolling across the floor to come back up with crossbow ready. The vampire had Marcus in the air, one hand wrapped around his throat. I leveled the crossbow at her.

"Put him down!"

"Are you sure? Would you not rather I put him out of your misery?"

As tempting as it was to let her do it, I instead leapt sideways to get a better angle and fired the crossbow. It took the vampire in the leg, making her shriek and drop the idiot. She disappeared again, and I dropped the crossbow to swing the shotgun on my back around into my arms.

The vampire appeared like a ghost from the darkness, and I fired point-blank into her chest. She fell back and I pumped another shell into the shotgun and put another round of buckshot into her leg. She screamed as I pumped it one more time.

"Any more shit you want to say?" I quipped. She opened her mouth, her body already healing the damage. I fired before a word was spoken, taking out her entire head. A few seconds passed before the body stopped twitching.

"Fuck!" Marcus coughed, over and over again.

"Spit it out, fuckwad," I snarled. I leaned over the vampire and rummaged through whatever was left of her bloody clothes. Damned gorgeous dress—but it didn't have pockets.

"You almost got me killed."

I turned on him, pumping another shell into the shotgun as the flare stuttered a little. "I told you I could handle this alone. You decided to be a dick and come with, only to question me the whole fucking time. You almost got yourself killed, asshole."

"Fuck you," he said, coughing all the while.

I rubbed my forehead, trying to ease some of the tension that had taken root. "You sound like you're choking on a dick, fucknut. Cough it up already and let's get out of here."

He coughed one more time, then seemed to get enough air to stop. "This is going in my report," he wheezed.

I sighed. "Like I give a shit anymore," I said, "let's go report back to my parents. They'll desperately want to know how *you* saved the day and I became the damsel in distress."

Marcus was already halfway up the stairs as I finished speaking. In the slowly dimming light of the flare I looked to the vampire one more time. Her skin had gone ashen and gray, and I gave a slight nod. That's how you knew they were dead. I nudged her with my foot and bits of skin flaked off like they were dust. A part of me was almost sad to see her like this. A beautiful creature like her deserved better.

I swallowed hard and tried to keep my rebellious stomach from heaving. I moved away from the body but something lingered. A smell, maybe, or maybe it was just me, but I lost the war and found myself doubled-over in the corner of the basement, losing my supper. I wiped my arm across my mouth when I was done, glad Marcus wasn't around to see that.

Not for the first time, I was definitely reconsidering whether I was cut out for this life. When I felt sorry for a damned vampire and couldn't stand to look at the corpse, there had to be something wrong with me, right?

I sighed and followed Marcus up the stairs and back to the car. He had it already started by the time I got there, and I was a little thankful he didn't just up and leave me in the middle of nowhere. I tossed the shotgun and crossbow into the trunk under a false lid where we hid most of the weapons, then settled into the passenger seat for the long ride home.

As they always did when I had a moment where I didn't have to worry about impressing my parents or fending for my life, my thoughts turned to Rias. I let out a long breath, closing my eyes and remembering the last time I'd seen her, about a month ago now.

That night had been amazing. That morning had been torture. Leaving her at the hotel was the hardest thing I'd had to do in a very long time. There was something about her, about us, that made me never want to leave her. Even when I knew I'd have to.

Fuck. I wanted to be honest with her. I wanted to tell her everything. What I did, why I did it. I wanted to tell her about what was really out there. I wanted her to believe me and stay with me and need me just as much as I felt like I needed her.

I let out a long sigh, earning a glance from Marcus, but he didn't say anything. Probably didn't want to, with his throat half-crushed. Already a massive bruise was showing in the shape of a hand on his throat, and I fought the urge not to snicker. It looked like he'd had some bedroom play gone wrong—not that I'd entertain the thought of being in a bedroom with him. Not a damned chance. Those fantasies were reserved for Rias. I rubbed my face to try to clear those particular thoughts out of my head. Now was not the time for that.

I knew what my parents would say if they knew I was pining over a woman. I knew what they thought my duty was. I was a hunter, after all. And I was a woman, as much as the two didn't seem to mesh all that well in my father's head. I knew he wanted me to be with a man, to start popping out little hunters for him to train into adulthood and keep his legacy going. It was going to be a rude awakening for him when he found out I had no desire to be a parent anytime soon, never mind be with a man. I wanted Rias. I wanted to be with her until the world ended and we were the only ones left. I would protect her, keep her safe from the monsters that were out there in the world. I wanted to tell her exactly what was out there and have her look at me like the champion I was, not an unbalanced person who believed a little too much in ghost stories.

But was I a champion? Did that even matter to me anymore? Maybe I just wanted to be a standard, minty-fresh person. Someone with a day job, a rent or mortgage, maybe a dog. Someone who could be with Rias and not be considered anything but ordinary. Maybe I just wasn't meant to be a hunter.

A year ago, that thought would have been anathema to me. Now, it only made me wonder what else I could have.

My father's words rang in my head, and I fought not to grimace.

Remember, Ashly, no matter what they look like, a monster is always a monster.

Maybe I was naïve, but after seeing the beautiful creature I had just slain, I wanted to believe that it wasn't true. I wanted to believe that some of the so-called monsters just wanted to live their lives, not hurting anyone. But so far, what I'd seen, what I'd been told—none of it added up to monsters just wanting a peaceful life.

As lovely as she had appeared, that vampire certainly hadn't wanted peace. She'd left a trail of victims while I tracked her down and I only wished we'd gotten to her sooner, before so many people had died of unexplained blood loss. But we'd stopped her. *I'd* stopped her. She wouldn't hurt anyone anymore, and it was another notch on my belt. I didn't know if I wanted any more notches, honestly.

My thoughts drifted all over the place as we drove back into Calgary, spending most of the drive with my eyes closed and wandering the halls of what I knew and what I wanted. By the time we got back to my parents' place, I was in a worse frame of mind than when we left the dilapidated house. My mind juggled the idea of telling Rias about who I was, and having her fall into my arms all over again as she thanked me for keeping her safe from the monsters, but I knew that this idea was the least likely outcome. She would probably be more likely to stare at me like I'd lost my mind, then politely suggest we go our separate ways.

And I didn't want that. I wanted to be around her more, not less. I wanted that kind of life where I got to see her every day, I got to wake up in the morning and kiss her on the cheek and make her coffee before we both went to work for the day and then we couldn't wait to see each other that night so we could tell each other about our days and how the world was so unfair but at least we had each other and holy shit did I clearly have it bad for her. Like so fucking bad.

I was so lost in my thoughts that I didn't even notice that Marcus had left the car until the door slammed shut, knocking me from my reverie. He entered the house first and I lingered outside, knowing my presence wouldn't be demanded until after Marcus had given his report. And honestly, I didn't want to hear what the asshole had to say about me. I knew what went down. I knew that he'd almost gotten us both killed because he couldn't keep his mouth shut. But the bullshit artist would spin a tale that put me in the asshole seat and ensure I didn't have another chance at a hunt until my father felt kind enough to throw something at me out of pity.

The front door opened again a second later, and Ritten, in all his glory, stepped outside. He saw me and smiled that stupid, apparently disarming smile of his, then stepped to the side as if to let me in. He pulled out a pack of cigarettes and offered one to me, but I shook my head. He shrugged, drew a cig, then fumbled around in his pocket for a light.

"You're a witch," I said blandly, "just use your magic."

He laughed, the unlit cigarette dangling from his bottom lip as only the seasoned pros seemed to be able to do. "Sometimes I do, but I find that sometimes it's better to do things the mundane way. Elsewise, one might forget how to do things without magic."

He finally found a match in that overdone coat of his and struck true, then lit the cigarette. I took a step back as he belched out a cloud of smoke from his first drag, and I eyed him with suspicion.

"What are you doing here?"

"Nothing nefarious, I promise you," he said smoothly. "Your father is simply helping me with…well, I suppose you could call it a mission, of sorts."

I crossed my arms over my chest, shivering slightly in the spring breeze this late at night. "What mission? Is it something I should know about?"

"My dear, sweet Ashly, you have enough to worry your pretty little head about. A few witches on the docket for you hunters is beneath you."

"Witches? You're hunting witches with my dad? Is this about the one that got away from you at the convention?"

He frowned for the first time and took a long drag from the cigarette. "*That* one…has proven elusive. I tried following them home once, but they have a formidable Genius Loci protecting the area."

I blinked. "A Genius Loci?" I'd never heard of such a creature.

Ritten waved a hand. "Ask your father about it," he said, stepping away from the house, "for me, the night is young. I have business with some witches."

I watched him go with a bit of longing, actually. As much as it felt like I could come and go as I pleased, sometimes the reality of my cage really hit me. As long as I lived under my father's thumb, I would always be in it—and always be jealous of that man's ability to be able to do what he wished.

I closed my eyes for a moment to keep my emotions from slipping onto my face, and when I opened them again the man was gone, leaving only the lingering, burning scent of the cigarette. I glared at the front door with distaste, debating whether or not to go in.

"Damn it," I whispered, sitting on the stoop and pulling out my phone instead. My finger hesitated over my messaging app, noting a couple of missed notifications from Rias. The urge to read them was intense, but I didn't want to feel like I was obsessing over the woman any more than I already did. I just…I'd never felt like this about someone else before, and I wanted her so damned badly.

I opened the app, ignoring messages from others, and focused on Rias. I'd warned her that I wouldn't be communicative today, so nothing was too important, but she did say that she was thinking of me, which left a really warm feeling in my gut. Her final text had me biting my lip, a promise for the next time we saw each other. I couldn't wait. I wanted to be with her now, screw everything else.

But I had a job to do. I had a family to be a part of. Could I really just up and leave it all behind for her? Before I met her I'd never have thought of such a thing. Now, it was constantly on my mind. *She* was constantly on my mind.

The door behind me opened suddenly and Marcus came storming out. He didn't even bother looking at me before he marched down the walk and got in his car. I shook my head, flipped him the bird for good measure, then headed inside for the inevitable confrontation.

I barely got two feet in the door before my father cleared his throat, watching me from the living room couch. I turned toward him and knew this wasn't going to be a fun conversation, but I had to be careful. As much as he'd been better this past while, he could take it all away too. I didn't want to anger him to that degree.

"You're late."

"I figured I'd give Marcus a chance to give you his report first," I told him.

"You were supposed to be back from the hunt yesterday. You also refused to listen when a more experienced hunter told you what to do, which is what we had agreed upon, if you remember."

I snorted. "If I'd listened to Marcus, we'd still be hunting the vampire—or we'd be dead."

"I don't care. It was your job to see it done, and it took you weeks. The delays cost more human lives."

I started to argue with him but gave up before the words could come out. He wouldn't listen anyway. Everything was a teaching moment, and I never impressed.

"This is how dire our work is, Ashly," he began, clearly gearing up for one of his grandiose speeches about the fate of humanity being in our hands. "As long as these creatures stick to the shadows and prey on humanity, it will be our job to hunt them down and destroy them. There truly are monsters in the world, and we are the only line of defense mere humans have against them. We have to remain strong, resolute, in the face of these creatures who defy logic, defy what we know as true. We must—"

"I get it," I snapped, tired of hearing the same rhetoric over and over again. "I get it, Dad. I know what our job is."

"It is not a *job*, it's a calling," he said. "There are only a handful of us to do this work, and I have done my best to train you to follow in my footsteps—"

"Maybe I don't want to follow exactly in your footsteps! Did you ever think of that?"

He stared at me with a shocked expression, like he couldn't comprehend what I was saying. Of course he couldn't. He couldn't fathom anyone reconsidering their role in this…this war.

"What are you saying?"

I shrugged, knowing I'd just put my foot in my mouth and said something I'd never even considered telling him. "I'm just…I'm having troubles wanting to be a part of this battle like you want me to be. You don't trust me when I tell you I'm ready. You don't listen to me when I tell you what happened; instead you believe what another hunter tells you. I might as well save my breath." I shook my head. "You want me to be a hunter but don't want me to go out and get hurt, or worse, and I get that. But I'll never be good enough for you if you don't give me the chance. It makes it hard to want to be a part of all this."

He was silent for a long moment. "I…I don't…is this about that boyfriend of yours?"

I stared at him. "What? B-boyfriend?"

"You must think your mother and I are blind or something." He shook his head. "Did you think we hadn't noticed your distance? That you've disappeared off and on over the last several months, and that you're on your phone far more than you ever have been?"

I mean, I hadn't really thought about it from their perspective, but I supposed I was a little more distant with them than I was before. I knew I had been preoccupied by this long-distance relationship. The fact that he assumed it was with a man irked me, but now wasn't the time to have that conversation with him, either.

"Um, yeah. I mean, kind of. It's hard because sh—uh, he's not… he doesn't know about the monsters and everything. So I have to keep all of that a secret and it's hard and it hurts. It hurts a lot because I really like—uh, him."

"That's the danger of dating outside of our calling. You will never find someone out there that understands what we have to do."

"Surely new people have been brought into this life. You can't tell me everyone involved has come from a hunting family."

He squirmed a little under the accusation. "There are some who are affected by the monsters and decide to start hunting. We often take them under our wing to make sure they survive. But I can promise you that your mother and I both came from very successful hunter families, thank you."

I rolled my eyes. "I know, Dad. I wasn't arguing your damned pedigrees."

He shook his head again. "I'm not saying that pedigree matters, though you might want to consider it when you start dating within our world instead of outside it."

"What are you talking about?"

"You'd be better off with someone like Marcus than with someone you feel you need to hide from your parents. Someone you can't be completely honest with."

I almost choked on the bile that tried to climb up my throat at the mere thought of being with Marcus for…anything really.

"That's never going to fucking happen!"

"Well, if not Marcus then another hunter. It would make much more sense in the long run."

I sneered. "And give you little hunter babies to raise and train like you did me? Like you did my *brother*!"

He stared at me with a look devoid of any sort of emotion, the same mask he always wore whenever anyone said a single word about my brother.

"You don't have a brother. You know that."

I shook my head. "Just because you refuse to acknowledge him doesn't mean he isn't out there somewhere."

He just kept that cold look plastered on his face. "This is not a conversation we're having."

"It's a conversation we need to have."

"It is no such thing. You don't have a brother and that's final."

I stopped myself from saying anything else. Whatever I had to say would just escalate things, and that wasn't what I wanted to do. Instead I just stared back at him, trying to put on my own cold, unfeeling mask, before I turned away and left the room. That was not an argument I was going to ever win.

I breezed past my mother, who didn't even try to stop me to talk. The look on her face told me that she'd heard everything, and she'd hardened herself too against the claims that I even had a sibling. Both of them were so into the lie that they couldn't even fathom me talking about it. But I couldn't forget. I wanted to know who he was now. Where he was. I dreamed of it sometimes—when I wasn't dreaming of Rias.

Thinking of Rias again—because she was never far from my mind—had me pulling out my phone as I climbed the stairs and headed for my bedroom. I'd gotten a new text from her, asking if I was available to spend time together in a couple of days. I enthusiastically agreed and lay down on the bed. My brain ran with the idea of telling her everything. Telling her exactly who I was and what I did for a living. What my family did. And I wondered what it would be like not to be beholden to them anymore. What kind of life could I have with basically a doomsday prepper's skills and little else. I shook my head. First, I had to get her to believe me, and if there wasn't a handy-dandy werewolf nearby to show her the truth of my words, she'd probably break up with me on the spot.

I sighed, uncertain what I should even do anymore.

Chapter Eleven

Rias

I poured myself a glass of whiskey on the rocks, the amber liquid filling half the glass. I liked mine chilled, personally, though I knew it wasn't always drunk that way. I pulled a bottle of water and a can of Coke from the fridge too and carried it all to my kitchen table, where my two friends were sitting and laughing together.

"Thank you," Wren said, accepting the water in one hand as her other went to support her distended abdomen. She groaned as she sat back in the chair, and I placed the Coke in front of her mate. "Remind me whose idea this was again?"

"Are you tired of it yet?" I asked.

She laughed. "Only every moment, but not really. It's worth it." She wrapped an arm around Natalie at her side and I felt a pang of jealousy for the closeness of their relationship. Damn it. That's what I wanted with Ashly. I wanted to introduce her to my friends, to be that cute a couple. I took a sip of my whiskey and checked my phone idly, but there were no new messages from her. She'd said she'd be busy for most of the day, so it wasn't surprising, but damn did I want to hear from her.

"It won't be that much longer, my love. That pup is about ready to come out," Natalie said.

I couldn't help but laugh at her use of the word *pup*. "That pup is about to knock you both on your asses. I'm so happy for you."

"Thank you, Rias." Natalie smiled. "I don't think we could've made it this far without your help."

I shook my head. "All I did was help with Wren's morning sickness, you know, herbal draughts and stuff. Nothing huge. No big deal."

"It was a pretty big deal when it felt like the baby was trying to come out my mouth instead of waiting in my stomach," Wren said, laughing.

I held up my hands. "It was honestly the least I could do for the two of you."

Natalie beamed. "Hey, we're always here for you too. How're things going with Ashly?"

Wren perked up at the conversation change. She always did when we started talking about the lover that no one had met. I did my best to keep my smile plastered on, but it was hard. And Natalie, being as damned intuitive as she always was, noticed it quickly.

"What's wrong, is everything okay?"

I shrugged. "It is and it isn't. It's the same as it was last month. As it was half a year ago. As it was a year ago. I miss her. I want her here. Or I want to be there with her. I want more than what we have, but I'm not sure if she wants the same." I let out a long sigh. "I saw her last month, and everything was pretty good. But it's almost like since then, things feel a little off. I mean, we still talk, but even that feels… stunted, lately. Like we've run out of things to talk about. Like there's a lot we're not saying to each other."

"What do you want to say to her?"

"Everything! I want to tell her about magic and that I'm a witch and that I want to be with her even though I know it might not be forever. And that I don't need to think about the future. I want her now. I want her in the present. And I'm willing to risk throwing it all away to do it."

Both wolves were silent after my outburst. I covered my impatience to hear what they had to say by taking another sip of my whiskey. The ice clinked against the glass as it shifted, and I stared at it as I set it back on the table, unwilling to look at my friends.

"It's not like this stuff is easy," I said. "You know, we don't have fated mates or whatever to help us find a person who fulfills us and makes us whole. Shifters are kind of lucky that way. I don't know how she's going to react if I tell her the truth. I don't know if she'll think I'm losing it or be cool about it all. I don't know if she'll try to kill me or end up telling the wrong person and suddenly I'm being burned at the stake by the covens." Natalie gasped, a hand over her mouth. "It's true. If the covens found out I'd revealed my existence to a human, neither one of us would be safe. And still I want to try because I want to be with her." I shook my head. "It's ridiculous how much I'm overthinking all of this, but it's all valid and all a real risk that I can't be sure if I should take or not."

I avoided their gaze and stared at my glass. I shouldn't have opened my mouth, but it was like once I'd started I couldn't stop. Everything that was built up inside just decided to come falling out, and my dignity and probably my friendship with both wolves was about to fall out with them.

"I mean, the whole *fated mate* thing isn't exactly perfect," Natalie said, and I glanced up to meet her eyes. Her gentle, almost knowing look made me want to run and hide and pretend that no one was actually home—which was far too late, but hey, it made sense in my mind for a second. "You know my and Wren's story—you lived it with us, especially near the end. You know how close it was that we didn't have each other, that Wren would miss out on having someone who loved her for exactly who she was and I'd…well, I'd be dead. Or worse." She shook her head like she was dispelling the negative thoughts that might come with remembering those harrowing hours after Wren had shared her power and turned Nat into a werewolf. "You're not wrong for feeling the way you do. There's nothing wrong with wanting more. But you need to decide if it's something you can live with if it goes wrong."

"I just…I just want to be with her."

"Then go be with her."

Wren looked sharply at her mate. "What are you saying?"

"I'm saying that she should go be with her." Natalie smiled at her before turning back to me. "You don't have to stay in Terabend. Sure, you're an exile from the covens, but it's not like you'd go out and settle in their territory, right? You can go to Calgary, be closer to her. Be with her. And you can choose to be honest with her. And maybe she'll be honest with you too."

I blinked. "What do you mean? You think she's not being truthful with me?"

"I think, as you said earlier, that it feels like there're things that neither of you are saying. We know what you're not talking about, but what about her? Maybe being honest with her will allow her to be honest with you."

The idea that Ashly might be hiding things from me made my chest ache, and the magic inside me reacted violently. I barely managed to wrestle it down, pushing myself away from the table and the wolves before I lost control and hurt someone. It was something I didn't want to think about, something I didn't want to consider. Had she found someone else? Someone closer to her? Someone she could see on a regular basis. Was I nothing more than a fling to her?

The magic slipped my grasp and lashed out. It slammed the chair I'd been sitting in sideways until it hit the wall with enough force to leave a dent in the drywall. Natalie was out of her chair in a flash and moved in front of Wren protectively. Wren levered herself to her feet, looking perturbed but not saying anything. I huddled on the other side of the kitchen, fighting to focus and quell the power inside.

"I'm sorry," I gasped, wrapping my arms around myself as I struggled to control the power. I shook my head. "I'm sorry."

"It's okay Rias." Natalie's voice was soft, wary, like she was talking to someone dangerous. I guess she kind of was. "Are you okay?"

I wanted to nod. Wanted to say yes, but I didn't want to lie to her. I wasn't okay. Even now, after so long working with my magic to keep it under control, I still had troubles. I still lost control and it tried to wreak havoc.

"It's like no matter what I do, I'll never be able to control it like before."

"Because you weren't controlling it before. You were ignoring it."

"How do you know that?"

"You told me yourself. Before you helped Heather, you pushed your magic aside, refused to use it. Now that's no longer an option. You need to stop acting like you can go back to that. You need to find your new normal."

There was something about the softness of her voice, the conversation, even just being able to talk about it at all that helped quell the magic inside. Enough that I could force it back down until I drew on a small amount and held my hand down in my sink and flipped the cold water on. I wove my magic around my hand, creating a barrier of heat that hit the cold water, and immediately steam began to rise from the sink.

"Rias!" Natalie said, but I shook my head.

"It's fine," I said, gritting my teeth. It hurt a little, but it was the only way I could think of to drain off the excess magic that had built up during my brief panic attack. If I was going to continue having those, I needed to find a better way of bleeding off that extraneous power. "I'm fine, I promise."

I ran the water until the steam stopped rising and I felt in control again. Natalie moved my chair back to its proper place, but I didn't sit. I kept my back to my friends, unwilling to let them see the start of the tears that welled up in my eyes. I tried to force them back but failed when a strong pair of arms wrapped around me in a soft embrace.

"It's okay," Natalie said.

I shook my head. "It's not, but I will be. I promise."

"You don't have to make any rushed decisions, you know," she said. "Take your time. Consider your options. Do what your heart tells you."

"And if it's dangerous to listen to my heart?"

Another pair of arms wrapped around both me and Natalie.

"Then you can listen to your brain," Wren said, and I felt her stomach press into my side as she tried to get as close as she could. I swore, for a brief moment, I felt the little pup moving around in there.

I took what comfort I could from the two of them and let the tears fall silently. It was a few moments of no one speaking, just being held, before I wriggled enough to extract myself from the wolves.

"Okay, enough with the doggy pile." I sniffed, wiping my face before turning back to look at my friends. "I'm sorry. I hope I didn't hurt either of you."

"We're fine."

"It'd take a lot more than a chair to hurt either of us," Wren added.

"Well, maybe not you right now." Natalie laughed.

Wren grinned and pulled Natalie into a warm kiss that turned very heated very quickly. Heat crept up my face just watching the two of them, and I had to look away.

"Get a room, you two." I shook my head. "Or better yet, a whole house. Your house. I don't need a repeat of what you did in my kitchen."

It was Natalie's turn for her cheeks to turn red as she separated from Wren. "We should probably head out anyways." She took a deep breath and gave me a hard look. "Are you sure you're going to be okay?"

"I'm fine, *Mom*," I said, then dodged her playful smack. "Go on, you two. Get home and have your fun times."

"As much as I can, anyways," Wren groaned as she started shuffling toward the front door.

"I'll meet you at the car, my love," Natalie said, giving Wren a peck on the cheek. She waited until Wren was out of the kitchen and almost to the front door before turning back to me. "I get why you panicked, I really do," she said quietly, "but try your best not to assume the worst, okay? Ashly makes you happy, you should try to hold on to that."

"But it's so hard not being with her."

"So remedy that."

I nodded. "Right. Right, I need to do that." I stepped in for one last hug. "Thank you, Nat."

"Anytime."

I watched the wolves drive away, still jealous of their closeness but hiding it well now. Besides, I had my lover that I had to win over. If only I could find the right words. And the right time. And figure out what I was going to say. Was I really going to ask her to leave her family for me? Or was I willing to leave everything I knew for her?

The more I thought about it, the more the answer to the second question was becoming a firm yes.

I chugged back what was left of my whiskey, letting the ice hit me in the face like a wakeup call. I coughed at the burn in my throat. That was not the way you were supposed to drink whiskey. But the shock to my system was almost everything I needed. Almost.

"Damn it," I muttered. I sat back in my chair, let out a long breath, then reached inside me for that well of magic that was still worked up enough that it wasn't letting me ignore it. I pulled a string of magic from the pool and wove it around my index finger, raising said finger into the air as I called the power to create a ball of witchlight. A blink of the eye later, a ball of light floated above my fingertip, casting new shadows around the room as it brightened and dimmed as I breathed in and out. I flared my other fingers out, holding them all up, and called up a little more magic. Three more balls of light appeared in the air, the same size as the first, continuing to dim and brighten simultaneously. With a thought I wove all four balls of light into a single one. It grew larger and brighter, casting deeper shadows throughout the room. I stared into that bright light until it was all I could see, everything else blank around it.

"Give me the strength to do this," I whispered to the magic that was still weaving its way from deep inside me to my fingertips. "Give me the strength to fight for what I want. To have something, someone, of my own."

I laced my words, my intent, my will with my magic and sent it into the witchlight. It grew even larger, until it was the size of a softball, then blinked out as I cut off the power. The ceiling light was still on, but it took a few minutes before my vision returned to normal and I could see again. Staring into the witchlight like that wasn't a grand idea, but it was how I could focus. And the weaving had worked. I'd controlled the magic. I was in control of it better than ever, in some ways. If I could just manage the sudden panic attacks, I'd be golden.

My phone rang, breaking me from my thoughts and practice, and I reached for it immediately, not even looking at the caller ID before answering.

"Ashly?" I asked, the hope in my tone surprising even me.

"What? No. Danaan, it's Brigid."

My mind took a full second or two working out that the person on the other end of the call wasn't the woman I was pining for, then another second to figure out who it actually was.

"B-Brigid? You're calling me? That never happens."

"Well, there is a first time for everything, my dear. But that's a conversation for another time. I need your help."

"You're always there for me. It's about time I can return the favor."

"I need you to meet me in Calgary the day after tomorrow. There is something going on out here that I cannot put my finger upon."

"What do you mean?"

"My contacts," she said and the stress in her tone made the magic inside me begin to roil once more. "My…my friends. Other witches that I know. Most of them have gone silent. Some have disappeared. Others have been killed."

"Killed?"

"By hunters."

I shook my head. "Since when do hunters come after witches? Especially ones that aren't a threat?"

"I do not know. But I need your help. I think I am being followed."

"Come to Terabend," I said immediately. "We'll help you—I know Vadi and the others would agree."

"Perhaps, after we meet, I will accept that as a course of action. But I do not want to draw danger to your sanctuary. I would rather settle things before risking such a thing."

"This doesn't make any sense," I said. "What the hell is going on out there?"

"I do not know, but it worries me."

"It's not…it's not the covens, doing some sort of culling, is it?"

"No, not that I can tell, anyway. This is something else." I heard her take a sharp breath like she was surprised by something. "I must go. Day after tomorrow, tell me you'll meet me."

"Of course. I'm there."

"Thank you. I have to go."

She hung up before I could say more. I blinked at my phone for a second and tried to control the sinking feeling in my gut that this was something far larger than either me or Brigid could handle. I took a breath, focused on my magic and keeping it in control until the feeling passed, then started putting together a plan. The day after tomorrow. That gave me time. Time I could use outside of the small town of Terabend.

I wasn't sure exactly what was going on, but damned if I wasn't going to take advantage of it. I turned back to my phone and sent a quick message to Ashly, to let her know I'd be in town tomorrow and I wanted to see her. I hesitated for only a second before hitting the send button. Brigid's call was like a gift from the Goddess. It gave me a reason to leave my comfort zone, my safe little town in the middle of nowhere, and find out once and for all if I could have something more with the woman I was very much growing to love.

"Love?" I wondered if that was truly what I was feeling. It sounded right. It felt right. I was in love with Ashly. And with that came the reality of pain. Lots of pain, if things went wrong.

I shook my head. It wasn't long before I got an enthusiastic reply, and I smiled down at my phone.

Tomorrow. Tomorrow I would tell Ashly everything. Tomorrow we'd find out if I could have what I wanted.

Chapter Twelve

Ashly

Something is wrong.

That thought echoed in my head from the moment I met up with Rias until now, with her asleep on one side of the bed, me wide awake on the other. Normally we'd be all over each other, at the very least with her holding me. But tonight her back was to me, like a barrier that I couldn't figure out how to overcome.

I wanted to be honest with her and tell her everything, but the words had refused to come out each time I had the chance. And it was making things harder between us. But I got the feeling it wasn't just on my end either. There was something she wasn't saying too, and I couldn't help but overthink about what that might be.

There was so much about her I did know, like where she lived and what she did for work, that it was hard to think of what she might be hiding from me. It wasn't like me being a hunter. I was lying to her face when I told her my dad was just a PI. That I was training under him. I hated that I had to lie to her, but would she believe me if I told her the truth? Could I be open and honest with her and risk losing her? There were too many questions and not enough answers.

Now more than ever, the thought of leaving my parents niggled in the back of my thoughts. The more I thought about it, the more I found myself pulling away from them. They weren't what I aspired to be when I got older. And for good reason. I wanted more to life than just hunting monsters. Sure, I wanted to save people, and I had the skills to do it, but there had to be more to life than work. It was all-encompassing for them, and I didn't want that life. I was certain that if I kept going the way I was going, that was exactly the life I was going to end up having.

Of course, the moment I started reconsidering my life, a buzzing sound broke the silence of the hotel room. I got out of bed without disturbing Rias and went searching for my pants. I answered the phone with a soft "Hello?"

"Ashly." My father's voice came over the line. "Where are you?"

"I'm with a friend," I said. "What do you want?"

"I need you for a hunt."

I snorted, too loudly. I glanced back to Rias, but she seemed to still be sleeping soundly. "Bullshit. You never need me—you've made that pretty clear."

"I don't have time to argue with you. We have a lead on a powerful witch that needs to be taken out, and you're the only one I can call. I need you as backup, Ashly."

I didn't say what came to mind first. I wanted to think that he wouldn't screw with me again. Wanted to believe it. But he'd burned me before. Instead I took a deep breath and tried to be at least a little more considerate than he deserved.

"What about Marcus, or Jared, or any of the other hunters? Why are you calling me?"

"The others are busy, and your mother is taking care of something else. You're the only one I have left to call."

That, at least, made a little more sense. Of course I was a last choice.

"Where do you need me?"

He gave me an address. I closed my eyes and envisioned a map of the city, pinpointing where I was going. It wouldn't take long, especially this late at night.

"I can be there in fifteen, twenty minutes tops."

There was silence on the line for a long minute. "Be faster." He hung up before I could reply.

"Fuck," I muttered, staring at my clothes strewn across the floor. Of all nights for him to actually want me to help. I turned back to Rias, still snoring lightly, her back to me and the rest of the room.

I climbed slowly back onto the bed, putting a hand softly on her shoulder and leaning over. I pressed a soft kiss to her cheek, trying not to wake her, and whispered softly. "I've got to go, beautiful. But I'll be back soon." I caressed her shoulder softly, almost desperate not to leave her. "We'll talk when I get back, okay? I'll tell you everything. I promise."

I dressed and grabbed one of the two room keys we'd gotten when we checked in, slipping it into my pocket. I made sure my pistol was firmly holstered at my back and left the room.

❖

I was surprised when I reached the destination that my father had given me. He was actually there, and without other hunters. Maybe he actually did need me.

We were parked in an empty lot across the street from one of the cheaper motels in the city. It was a little run-down but still functional, apparently had a swimming pool, and clearly still was doing good enough business to keep up with the times. No longer did the sign boast about having cable TV or phones in every room. Instead it proclaimed cheap rates per night.

"Across the street," my father was saying. "There's a woman in one of the upstairs rooms. I have confirmation that she's a witch. We need to find her and take her down before she can hurt anyone."

I glanced at him. "How do you know she's a witch? Did she turn you into a newt?"

He glared at me in that way that he always did. "This is not a joking matter. You need to be serious when you're on a hunt. Making a joke or being blasé about this is going to get you or someone else killed."

"I just want to make sure that this is someone who is a danger to people."

"She's a witch. Therefore she's a danger."

"But what has she done?"

"It doesn't matter. The fact is that she can hurt people, and probably will. Magic is something that no one should be able to do. There is too much risk in the power that they wield."

"What about Ritten? He works with you."

His face clouded over. "That's a special case."

"Because he's useful to you. Am I close?"

"Because he understands the danger of the power his kind can wield. He has his own reasons for wanting to get rid of some of the witches. He uses his power to help us, and in return we aid him in culling the witches that are a danger to humankind."

This was sounding more and more terrible by the minute, but I couldn't argue against him. It's what hunters did. We hunted things that weren't human. We ensured that people could live free of knowing what lurked out there in the darkness.

Damn it, I was getting tired of the spiel.

"Okay. Okay," I said. "All serious. We'll get this done. Where do you want me?"

He gave me a skeptical look. "Are you in this? Are you here with me tonight? Because if you're not, I can send you home and do this myself."

"No, I'm here. I'm in this."

"You better be. We can't afford to screw this up. We can't let another witch prey on innocent people."

"Another—"

He shook his head. "Never mind. Just listen." He laid out his plan in short, choppy sentences. The tension in the air could be cut with a damned knife. I'd never seen him like this, not even that first hunt we went on, back when he showed me what was really out there.

I nodded when he finished. "Okay, where do you need me?"

"When I draw her out of her room, I need you to cut off any means of escape. She won't want to draw a crowd, so she'll probably run. I want you at the bottom of the steps that lead to the second floor, ready to shoot." He glared at me. "And that means shoot to kill, Ashly. Not wound. We need to take her out before she has a chance to cast a spell."

"Got it."

"No room for error."

"I got it, Dad."

Together we moved in silence across the street and toward the motel. I took my place in the shadows at the bottom of the far stairwell. The concrete walkway above shielded my view of my father, but I knew he was working his way toward whatever room the witch was in. I felt my gut stir uncomfortably but pushed the feeling away and put a hand on my weapon at the small of my back, aware that we were still out in public. This wasn't some abandoned house in the middle of nowhere with a vampire hiding inside. This was a hunt in the middle of a city where people could very well see weapons and call the police. That would end badly.

I took a deep breath and focused on the issue at hand. I listened in the quiet of the late night, waiting for the first hint of trouble.

It didn't take long.

There was a loud banging noise and then I saw something fall from the upper balcony. It looked like a body. It looked like my father. I itched to run forward and see if he was okay, but that was the last thing I was supposed to do. Especially when a moment later I heard footsteps storming down the steps beside me.

A shadowed figure hit the bottom of the stairs and I moved out of the shadows, gun drawn, ready to fire. Then I got a good look at the taller woman as she stared in shock at me, then the gun, and shook her head.

"Why?" she asked, her tone almost void of emotion.

It took me a second to realize what she meant.

"You hurt people."

"I've never hurt a soul."

"Tell that to my father."

She looked confused, then glanced over her shoulder and frowned. "Wouldn't you try to defend yourself if someone came to kill you?"

I opened my mouth, but words escaped me. I panicked, thinking she'd cast a spell on me, and pulled the trigger. The bullet went wide, hitting the concrete side of the building. She froze and stared at me, and for the first time I noticed a phone in her hand.

"Calling for help?" I snarled.

"A warning," she said. "To you, little hunter. You are in over your head. You should quit—"

A second gunshot rang out in the night and the witch crumpled, falling toward me, the phone spinning out of her hand. My father stood feet away, limping slowly toward us.

"I told you to kill her, not talk to her."

I shook my head. "She distracted me. It won't happen again."

He snorted but didn't say anything else. "Get out of here. Before the police arrive."

"What about her?"

"I'll deal with it."

I didn't bother to try and argue. I holstered my weapon and turned away from the witch and the pool of blood that was slowly growing beneath the body. I snatched up the fallen phone, curious as to who a witch would call for help, and jogged back to the car across the street.

The phone was still unlocked, and I gave a sigh of relief that I didn't have to try and hack it. There was little on it from what I could find. A couple of apps, some messages from phone numbers, no contact names or emails or anything. Very bare bones. It made me wonder if she purposefully kept it this way in case someone like me picked it up, or if she just never learned what a smartphone was actually capable of.

I flicked into the recent calls. There was a number there that looked very familiar, called not five minutes ago. I stared at the number for a long moment, trying to place it. Who did I know that would be in contact with a witch? The only one who came to mind was Ritten, but I didn't have his number. He came and went as he pleased.

I pulled out my own phone and started checking the numbers I had saved. It didn't take long to find the one I was looking for. I looked from my phone to the witch's, feeling bile start climbing up my throat and threatening to choke me.

Rias.

It was her number.

Why would a witch have Rias's number?

I slammed my hand on the steering wheel. Why did that witch have my girlfriend's number? And she'd called it before, not just tonight. What was she planning? What did she want? Was Rias in danger because of me? Did someone find out about us?

There were too many questions and no answers. I slammed my hand against the wheel again, the frustration and anger too much to let sit quietly. I needed to know. I had to go back to the hotel and see her. I started the engine and peeled out of the parking lot, hitting the street, and accelerating as hard as I could push the pedal down.

It was only the distant sound of police sirens that made me slow down and act like a normal driver before the blue and red flashes came after me.

"Fuck!" I shouted. I pulled a sharp right and headed back toward the downtown core. I had to make sure she was okay. I had to be sure that I didn't get her into trouble. If the witches knew that a hunter had an ordinary, unsuspecting human girlfriend, they might not hesitate to do some harm. It was what my parents had warned me about for so long, why they pushed me to have a relationship with another hunter.

If Rias was a target, I was going to be there to protect her. Come hell or high water, no one was going to hurt the woman I loved.

Chapter Thirteen

Rias

I almost leapt out of bed as the sound of a heavy door shutting echoed through the otherwise silent room. I reached out to the other side of the bed, feeling for another warm body, but there was nothing but lukewarm sheets and an empty mattress.

Ashly was gone.

And it was my fault.

Because I was too chicken-shit to tell her the truth, to tell her what I really was. I wanted to stay in this honeymoon phase that we had every time we were together. I didn't want to see the look on her face when she decided there was something malicious or evil about my magic. Or worse, the fear when I showed her what I could really do. I felt myself tense, my magic working itself up as I did.

I closed my eyes, focused on my breathing. In on the count of one, out on the count of two. Breathing from the diaphragm. Deep, calming breaths. A trick I'd learned from the covens, when it came to trying to stay mindful and in the moment. To let the negative thoughts pass by. It wasn't something I did often, and I needed to change that.

That's what the covens were all about. Control. Of ourselves, of our magic, of our world. We learned guided imagery, meditation, deep breathing, all sorts of ways to keep ourselves in check. I had always wondered why when I was young. It seemed like a lot of work for something that should come naturally to us. But now I understood better. If this past year had taught me anything, it was that some kind of control over my magic was imperative. I couldn't just ignore it.

I didn't know how I'd gotten away with ignoring it for so long.

My slow, calm moment was shattered by my phone blaring

loudly from the nightstand beside the bed. I grabbed it and answered, wondering who the hell was calling this late.

"Hello?"

"Danaan!" Brigid's normally placid voice sounded strange being so panicked. "They're here!"

"What? Who's here? What's going on?"

"The hunters. They've found me." There was a fleeting moment of silence before she spoke again. "I don't know how. I don't know what's going on, but they're here."

"Where are you? I can help."

"A motel on the southeast side of the city." She gave the address but said it dismissively. I got up and started fetching my clothes with one hand as the other held the phone to my ear. "But I don't think you'll get here in time."

"There has to be something I can do."

"Listen to me."

"What?"

"I said, listen to me. There's something afoot. All the other witches who lived outside the covens in this area have been hunted and killed, or just disappeared. It was only a matter of time before they came for me too."

"I don't understand. Why are they hunting witches? We haven't done anything."

"You know as well as I do that it does not matter to the hunters. But still, you are not wrong. There is something happening that I cannot put my finger on, and we are out of time."

It was awkward trying to pull my leggings on one-handed, but I managed. I sat on the bed, out of breath from the exertion.

"I can come get you. I'm on my way now."

"Be quick, my dear Danaan."

I pulled on my dress, pulling the phone away from my ear for only a second. When I put the phone back against my ear, I could hear what sounded like a loud thumping noise from the other end of the line.

"Just hang on, Brigid."

An even louder crash erupted over the line, and I had to pull the phone away.

"Brigid? Brigid!"

The call had been dropped. I felt a surge of panic roll through me like an ocean wave, dragging me under. I couldn't keep my head straight as I moved away from the bed and slammed my hands against the desk on the other side of the room. I clenched my fists, the panic being pushed aside to make way for a new emotion: rage. How dare they go after my friend. How dare they go after any of us. We didn't hurt anyone. We weren't monsters.

I swiped my arms across the desk, knocking over the standard lamp and other things the hotel provides its guests. Even the crash of the lamp wasn't enough to satiate my anger, though. Instead I reached for my magic, and it leapt at my call, already driven wild from the initial panic. It formed a ball, one that I could envision inside me. A moment later that little ball burst out of me in a concussive wave of force that shook the entire room. Cheap paintings fell off the walls. The television screen cracked and shattered. Anything that wasn't nailed down was shifted inches if not feet away from their usual position.

And in the middle of this storm, I stood, staring down at the now smoking wreckage of my phone in my hand, the screen a massive spiderweb of broken glass. It had taken the brunt of the magic, it seemed. I scoffed and threw it on the ground, though the carpet was a relatively soft landing for it.

Shaking my head, I grabbed the rest of my things and threw the door open. I didn't care that I was leaving the place a wreck. Someone was after my friend, and I needed to make sure it didn't happen. I hurried to the elevator and took it to the parking garage and found my car. I was on the road in another minute, speeding toward the motel.

I needed to be there for her. I needed to help her. I couldn't lose her. Wouldn't lose her. Not tonight.

The feeling of dread that had buried itself in my gut became worse the closer I got to Brigid's motel. I slowed right down when I noticed the flashing lights surrounding the area and pulled into a parking lot across the street from the motel.

A crowd of people gathered near the police tape that marked off what looked like a crime scene. Several police cars were within the tape, along with a single ambulance, and a van marked Medical Examiner that had its back door open. No one was rushing or in a hurry, and I knew that I'd gotten here too late.

Brigid wouldn't have killed anyone, not outright. She wasn't that kind of person. But she would've defended herself from attack—so what the hell had gone down here? I watched it all with a keen eye, uniformed officers speaking with a small handful of bleary-eyed people beyond the tape. Witnesses, I supposed.

I got out of the car quietly and joined the crowd on the outside of the cordoned-off area. One or two of them gave me a look but quickly went back to gawping at the officers behind the tape as two paramedics worked a body bag over something that didn't seem to want to cooperate. I couldn't tell if it was Brigid or not, but something inside me told me it was, and it was all I could do not to scream her name and run past the tape to see her one last time.

She was supposed to meet me later today. We were supposed to talk, like old friends did. She wanted to tell me something important, and now was never going to get that chance. All because of the hunters. What the hell did they want from us? We left them alone, left humans alone. Why would they come after us like this? If what Brigid had said was true, then it was safe to surmise that I might be one of the last witches in the province who didn't live within a coven.

I shivered at the mere thought, drawing the attention of one of the other onlookers.

"Cold?"

I shook my head. "No, just…sorry for whoever that was." I nodded at the paramedics, who'd finally managed to get the body in the bag. "Did you see what happened?"

"No, I was asleep in my room when it all went down." He pointed to a door on the far side of the motel. "The sirens and gunshots and everything woke me up. I figured I wasn't going to get back to sleep, so I'd find out what's going on."

I nodded and moved away, ending the conversation. I needed someone who had more information. I needed to know more. I was happy to switch into a more analytical frame of mind, or I might have had to worry about my magic in my anxious state, but for now it was behaving. Still, it swirled around inside me, making its presence known.

I glanced over to where a uniformed officer was talking to an older woman, who kept throwing her hands in the air and talking vehemently. They were just out of earshot, but from the pad of paper in the officer's hand, he must've been taking witness statements.

I was tempted to walk through the tape, flash my deputy badge and ID, and ask what was going on, but I knew that was a terrible idea. I didn't want anyone to know I was here, and if the hunters found out about some out-of-town deputy involving herself in a case like this, they might put two and two together and come to Terabend. I didn't want to risk everyone else back home.

Instead, I found a spot with a clear line of sight to the witnesses and drew on some of my magic. I'd never done something like this before, but I needed more information than I had. I wrapped my intent around an invisible mote of power and gently sent it out toward the witnesses. I could see it only in my mind's eye, watching it traverse the space between police cars until it neared the several people standing by, waiting their turn. The magic struck the ground in front of them with an almost inaudible popping sound. The officer glanced around suddenly, like he'd heard something, but then shook his head and returned to his work.

I focused on that mote of magic and placed another tiny mote on the entrance to my ear canal, then tuned into the magical frequency.

"Ma'am, I don't need the specifics about your motel room," the officer's voice echoed in my ear, and I flinched from the volume. I tweaked the magic a little until I could handle it. "Just tell me what happened after you woke up."

"Well, I woke up when someone walked past my room on the upper floor. I'm a very light sleeper, you know, and the upper hallway here is something terrible for making noise whenever anyone walks on it."

The officer jotted down things in his notebook as I bit back my impatience. This was working okay. It was the best I had.

"And then there was a loud banging noise, correct?" He asked.

"Like I said the first three times," she said. "It was like someone was pounding on the door. Then a crashing noise, and I was out of my bed and heading for the window. There was no one out on the walkway, but I could hear running footsteps."

"And did they get louder or softer as you heard them?"

"Softer. Definitely softer."

He looked up at the motel, then down at his notes again, nodding. "She was running away from your room."

The woman snorted. "It wasn't exactly my choice to be two doors down from whatever was going on in there. Probably a drug deal gone bad or something. I know places like this are known for that kind of thing."

"I'm just looking for the facts, ma'am. Now, you say that the footsteps got quieter. When did you hear the first gunshot?"

"Um, a minute or two after the crash. Maybe less. I swore I could hear voices too. I opened my door to see what was going on, you know, to know whether I should run away or something."

"And what did you see?"

She shook her head. "Nothing to see. But there was another crack, like a gunshot."

"You say another, so that's two gunshots?"

She nodded. "Definitely two, but they sounded different."

He made another note in his book. "And after that, you didn't see anything else?"

"Hell no! After the second shot I closed the door and hid in the bathtub until you lot got here."

"And you didn't see anyone at all?"

"No."

"Not even passing by the window before the noises? The person who might have woken you up?"

"No."

He let out a heavy sigh and said, "Thank you, ma'am. I'll take your name and number—in case we have any more questions for you."

I kept listening for a little longer as he questioned two more people, a young man in dirty clothes that looked like he hadn't washed in a week, and an older gentleman who kept staring around at everyone with wide, unblinking eyes. He looked so strange and nervous that it made me wonder exactly what he was hiding. But he claimed that he'd been alone the entire time and was at the motel just for a night away from the wife and kids.

I called bullshit, but now was not the time to point out an adulterer.

I cut off the flow of magic, took a deep breath, then turned toward the ambulance. The paramedics had loaded the body onto a gurney and gotten it in the back of the medical examiner's van, and the ME was now talking to the police. I did the trick with my magic again, hoping to overhear something new.

"She's young, and pretty. Definitely not one you normally see around these parts."

"Did you get a name from the motel registry?"

This officer shook her head. "She paid cash but gave a fake name."

"How do you know it's fake?"

"Because I know for damned sure that she isn't Dolly Parton."

I had to hold back my snort of laughter. For all that I loved

Brigid, she had this infatuation with classic country music that I never understood.

"So what's the cause of death?" the officer asked.

"Preliminary findings suggest a bullet wound. Shot in the back. Died almost instantly."

"That's it?"

"I'll know more when I get her back to the shop."

I pulled back and cut off my magic again, not wanting to hear anymore. I knew it was Brigid. My Brigid. And she was dead. I wandered slowly back to my car, got in the driver's seat, and just sat there for a long moment. She was gone. My only witch friend, the only one who truly understood who I was and what I was going through most of the time. She had the magic in her too, why didn't she use it? What had stopped her?

Why did this have to happen tonight?

I reached for my phone before realizing I'd left it smashed at the hotel. I shook my head. That had not been the best idea. I started the car and pulled out of the parking lot quietly and headed for the highway that would take me north. Back to Terabend. Back home. I kept Brigid in my thoughts for the drive, hoping she'd found her way to something better than this life. We'd see each other again someday, Goddess willing.

In the meantime, I was headed somewhere safe. I didn't want to be next on the hunter's hit list, and I knew they'd never come to Terabend. Why would they? There was nothing there for them, that they knew of. I would be safe there.

I thought of Ashly and swore, wishing I could call her and tell her that I wasn't going to be able to see her for a while. When all of this hunter business calmed down, maybe we could do something together. But right now I needed to stay safe and alive, and that meant staying where I was protected, not just by a small army of werewolves, but ghouls and other supernatural people who also weren't big fans of being hunted by humans.

"Sorry, Ashly," I said as I hit the highway and sped up, leaving the city—and the woman I loved—in the rearview mirror.

CHAPTER FOURTEEN

Ashly

I made it back to the hotel in record time and broke several traffic laws along the way. I didn't care. Someone was gunning for my girlfriend. I had to make sure she was okay. I strode confidently through the lobby, earning only a passing glance by the person behind the desk, and headed for the elevators. I swiped my card and pressed the button.

Even without any stops on the way up, the elevator moved with excruciating slowness. The moment the doors slid open I was out and heading down the hallway, watching the numbers fly by in a blur as I ran, not caring about waking anyone else up. I found the room, hit the door hard enough to make sure I woke Rias up, then swiped the key card and barged in.

The room was a mess. I stared at the broken television, the shattered lamp, and pieces of debris on the floor. Her clothes were gone, the only sign that maybe she had gotten out of there before someone tried to get at her. The worst part was not knowing what the hell was going on. All I knew was that witch had Rias's number, and I wasn't going to let anything happen to her.

I pulled out my phone and dialed Rias, but there was no answer. A second later, I realized why. Her cell phone lay cracked and broken on the floor and didn't ring even once as I let the line go to voicemail. She was gone, but her phone was here. Did the witches take her? Or did she get out before they could?

"No!" I shouted as I smashed a hand against the wall and left a slight dent in the drywall. I drew back, let the pain wash over me, and tried to shunt my brain into thinking clearly again. I couldn't contact her. All I had was a phone number and the town where she lived. Not a lot to go on, really. I could try calling her in a couple of days in case the phone being destroyed had nothing to do with what was going on. But that might be a couple of days too late to save her if something else had grabbed her.

I wanted to be there for her. I wanted to save her. I'd promised I'd tell her everything anyway, and what better way to have that conversation than to assure her that I wouldn't let any witch or other supernatural creature come anywhere near her. Damn it, I wanted to tell her that I loved her.

Because I did. I loved her. I loved being with her. I loved spending time with her. This last day with her, when everything felt off, was still better than any other moment of my life. I wanted to be with her, to learn more about her. Hell, I'd move to that tiny town of hers, get a mundane job, do it all just for her.

My parents wouldn't be happy about that, but at this point I was ready to tell them to fuck off. I didn't want their lives. I knew what was out there. I could protect myself and my girlfriend from them. That was enough. I was pretty sure that would be enough.

"What are you thinking?" I wondered as I crouched down and picked up the damaged phone. "She's in trouble. She needs you, and you're lamenting how much you miss her? Grow up and do the right thing!"

But what was the right thing? Did I go after her? Did I even know where to go?

"Terabend."

If they had her number, they knew where she lived, I reasoned. If she got away, which it looked like she had despite the broken phone on the ground, then that's where she would go. Right? I'd run home if someone was after me. She might not believe in witches and shifters and the like, but she was smart enough to run home if someone was coming after her, wasn't she? Or was there an army of witches there waiting for her?

I shook my head. I was overthinking this. They wanted her because she was my girlfriend. If she was out of their reach, they'd come after me directly. If I went to Terabend, I'd be leading them right to her. I couldn't go out there if I was only going to draw her into the crossfire. Maybe it was better if I stayed here and didn't see her again.

Maybe Mom and Dad were right. Maybe it was too much for someone who wasn't a hunter to be involved with me. I didn't want Rias to get hurt, especially because I liked her as much as I did. I loved her, for fuck's sake. Could I really put myself into a self-imposed exile away from the woman I loved just because some assholes might try and hurt her? I shook my head again. I needed to be honest with her and tell her everything. Make her understand what was out there and how dangerous it was. Then I could teach her to protect herself, make sure she wasn't the soft target these witches clearly thought she was.

I stopped myself before I could fall down that rabbit hole any further. My mind was so full of things, my thoughts were getting completely twisted around. First, I decided not to go to her, then I decided that I needed to. I couldn't keep going back and forth on this.

I needed to talk to someone. Lay it all out clearly and in the open so they could help me make a rational decision. I couldn't talk to my father. He'd never agree to me dating Rias, especially after finding out that she's a woman. He already knew I was seeing someone who wasn't a hunter. He'd be the first to tell me to cut my losses and stop contacting her. My mother would probably agree. She rarely contradicted my father and was just as adamant as he was that I date within the hunter community.

The stupid thing was that the person I wanted to talk to about it was Rias herself. She was the one I'd go to, talk things through with, if I was faced with most other things like this. But that wasn't an option tonight.

I tucked the broken phone in my pocket and left the room, letting the heavy door swing shut behind me. I didn't want to be caught in there with the mess and the destruction. I headed to the car and barely took the time to start the damned thing before I shifted it into gear and pulled out onto the road.

Dad was already home from the hunt by the time I got there. I was sure his contacts on the police force would keep us safe from whatever repercussions might come from tonight. He'd never been caught hunting before and never suffered any consequences that I knew of. The lights were on inside the house. It made me wonder if they were waiting up for me or if something else was going on. I sat in the car for a few long minutes, and listened to the engine die down as I turned it off.

The silence was sobering. I didn't want to go inside. I didn't want to face down my parents, especially my dad. He would have nothing good to say about my performance tonight. Letting the witch live long enough to talk to her. That was a mistake. She could have easily cast a spell on me. Hell, I'm surprised she didn't. This had been my chance to impress my father, and I'd kind of blown it. Oddly, that didn't make me feel as bad as I'd expected it to.

"Damn it. I'm so fucking lost right now." Because talking to myself was clearly going to make things better.

I got out of the car and started a slow trudge up toward the house. I was about halfway up the walk when the door opened, and surprisingly, it wasn't one of my parents impatiently ready to admonish me for my work tonight.

"Ritten?" I said, loudly enough to ensure that he could hear me. "What are you doing here?"

He pulled the door shut behind him and sauntered down the steps toward me. His visage cracked into a wide smile.

"Ashly, my dearest, how are you this fine evening?"

I did my best to hide the shudder his term of endearment caused. It felt icky, coming from him.

I shrugged. "I'm alive."

"So you are! And your father too. I was worried that the witch I sent the two of you after would be too much of a handful for you. Seems instead you were able to talk her to death."

I blushed. "I wasn't prepared. I didn't know…I mean…she just looked so normal."

"Yeah, yeah, witches are like that. Not so monster-looking like shifters and vampires and ghouls and stuff, huh?"

"You should know."

He laughed. "You got me there."

"So why is a witch sending hunters after other witches in the first place? Why the hell is my dad working with you?"

"It's a mutually beneficial arrangement, my dear. I tip off your father on witches that are in the area, doing bad things, and I get to not have to worry about some enterprising young magic-users trying to set up a coven in my backyard."

"So you don't want to be a part of a coven?"

"Hell no. I don't work that well with others. With no one watching over my shoulder, I get away with pretty much whatever I want." I opened my mouth to respond but he cut me off. "Of course, I do it without hurting anyone. I help them."

"So, what do you do for people?"

"I find things for people. I give them what they want. I make deals with those who are more in the know about all of us supernatural peeps. That kind of thing."

I started to move past him, already kind of feeling sick about this conversation. If there was any witch we should be after, he was probably one of them. Whatever that woman tonight did, it couldn't be as bad as what Ritten was admitting to right now. Then I stopped, realizing that he might be exactly what I needed.

"You give information to hunters."

"Yup. Usually for a favor or two."

"I want to ask a question."

He laughed and clapped his hands almost like a child in a candy store. "Now this is an occasion. And I'll tell you what, I'll give you this one for free. For your hard work tonight."

"I'm not a charity case."

"I wouldn't dream of calling you such. Consider it payment. After all, you took out one of the stronger witches in the area without so much as a scratch on you."

I gritted my teeth at his sarcasm and focused on what I wanted to know. "I think the witches are after my girlfriend, Rias," I said slowly. "I found her number on that witch's phone. No messages, just the number."

He froze for a long moment, and his face turned somber. "Rias, you say? That's an interesting name." He shook his head. "Either way, they have her on their radar, that's for certain."

"What does that mean?"

"It means that for whatever reason, they're interested in her. I couldn't tell you why without meeting the woman, but you say she's your girlfriend?" I nodded. "Then I would go to her and make sure she's okay. Is she in town?"

"I don't know," I said. "I think she went home, but that's a few hours away. And I can't call her." I pulled the broken phone out of my pocket, showing it to him. "But I need to know that she's okay. I need to know that it's not my fault that they're after her."

"Your fault?"

"Because I'm a hunter. My parents are always warning me about the things we hunt finding out about an outside relationship. It's the only reason I can think of that anyone would want to go after her."

"If you're that worried, then you should definitely go to her. And I mean right now. You have no idea if another witch might be on her tail or if the one you took out tonight had backup."

"You're the one who sent us after her. Was she alone or with more?"

He shook his head. "I have no idea. As far as I'm aware it was just her, but witches are crafty, cunning creatures. We specialize in hiding in plain sight. It's how we've survived for so long. The Inquisition was a very real thing that the covens still remember. It didn't end well for our kind, but we survived."

"Maybe we need a new inquisition."

"That would be a lot more dangerous in this day and age. Would all humans be willing to hunt us if they found out what we could do? And would things escalate so much that we start pulling out nuclear weapons? There're too many unknowns about the world right now, the witches are happy to continue flying under the radar. Mostly."

"That's what you're doing? Flying under the radar?"

"Me? I'm just doing my part to make the world a better place." He grinned at me, but it disappeared quickly. "Honestly, though, go to your lady. Go make sure she's okay, and if you think she'll believe you, tell her what's coming. If you can warn her, protect her, you can make sure things will be okay."

I looked at him, then at the house, then back at the car. I didn't have to go in there. I didn't need my parents yelling at me for something that turned out fine anyway. And Rias didn't have a lot of time. If it was as bad as Ritten was saying, she was in trouble. The witches would find her, whether it was my fault or not. I had to protect her. I couldn't let anything happen to her.

"Go to Rias," he said, and it was like he was reading my mind.

I nodded, turned on my heel, and headed back to the car. I started the engine without really realizing what I was doing. I paused a moment to clear my head a little. Was I really going to do this? Go after her? Would she appreciate it? It didn't matter, I told myself. I needed to make sure she was okay. That she was safe.

I put my foot on the pedal and began to pull away, then stopped suddenly. I didn't know exactly where to go. "Stupid, stupid Ashly." I pulled out my phone and quickly typed *Terabend* into the navigation. The GPS lady started barking directions and I pulled away from the curb, leaving my parents and Ritten in my dust.

I yawned but kept my focus on the road. I wouldn't sleep until I knew Rias was okay. I couldn't. I needed her to be safe. I needed her.

CHAPTER FIFTEEN

Rias

The drive from Calgary to Terabend was way too long for my liking. It would normally take around five hours or so, but I had to stop several times along the way to discharge more magic. The magic wouldn't calm down, wouldn't settle, after what had happened in the hotel room. I'd left the place a mess and honestly felt bad about it, but if I'd stayed it would have been a lot worse.

Now it was like the magic inside me was stuck on high tide, flowing in and out of me without considering what I was doing or where I was. I was barely able to hold it in while I drove until I could find another turn-off or rest stop or somewhere I could get out of the car and throw a random blast of force out into the fields of plant life that lined a good chunk of the highway throughout Alberta.

The last rest stop I parked at was surrounded by forest. The spring sun was rising but the tall trees blocked most of its light this early as I looked around to make sure there was no one who could see me. I wandered down the ditch on the side of the parking area and back up toward the trees, barely able to hold the magic within me. It ebbed and flowed and churned and desired a way to be free, to be used.

Hidden within the trees, I pressed both hands against a thick trunk, my back toward the rest area. With one massive shunt of my power, the tree started to careen away from me. There was a massive cracking sound that sent animals scurrying as I leapt back to watch the tall, old tree fall as if something had torn it off its trunk. The trunk crashed to the undergrowth and caught on another tree and pitched it a different direction. I scrambled back and away, only to find myself on my hands and knees in the ditch until the trees finally landed and I was able to control my magic again.

I knew it wouldn't be long before I needed to let loose again. Since Brigid, since that call, my restraint just hadn't been working. All of my tricks, little witchlights, and small bits and bobs of magic—nothing was working. It was like the magic itself wanted vengeance. Knew that my friend had been killed and wanted someone to pay for it.

Hell, *I* wanted someone to pay for it. But I didn't know who, and if they were hunting witches, there was a chance they were after me too.

For a second my mind went back to Ashly, but I shook my head to clear it. I didn't have the luxury of thinking of her right now. Later, maybe, if I managed to get my magic under control. And after I got a new phone and all. But after all this, maybe I could go to her, and we could talk about everything that we didn't get a chance to talk about last night.

As if the mere thought of last night was enough to send my magic coursing through me again, it spurred me back onto my feet and back to my car. I was only another hour away, two at most. I could hold on for that long.

I hoped.

❖

My magic was ready to burst again by the time I saw the sign welcoming me to Terabend. It proclaimed to be a haven for outsiders, and it honestly was. Not just because it had a rather large supernatural community that had come to live within its borders, but also because it took in outcasts of all stripes with nary a worry. People like Natalie, who needed a new life in more ways than one, or even like me, who desperately needed a sanctuary to land in.

My mind was not on the sanctuary aspect of coming home right now, however. No, it was more focused on keeping the magic from bursting out of me again and causing me to veer off the damned road. By the time the actual town came into view, the first thing I saw was the diner sitting on the right, with the new bar across the parking lot. It was early in the morning, the sun only barely risen, but the diner was open all day and night, and I hoped I'd find some help there.

I pulled into the parking lot and parked across several spaces. I lurched out of the car and toward the diner, just in time to see Natalie and Wren pull up in Wren's Jeep.

"Rias?" Nat was the first one to notice me. I stopped and noticed

Wren's heavily distended belly. I didn't want to lose control near her. There was no way I'd get over it if I ever hurt that little baby in there.

"Stay back, Wren!" I croaked.

"Rias?" Wren echoed her mate. "What's going on?"

Natalie pulled open the diner door and ushered Wren inside but didn't go in herself. Wren made to argue, but a look from Natalie had her closing the door behind her. I saw V and Heather in the diner as they took charge of the pregnant Alpha. They must have worked the night shift. Natalie ran toward me, and I shivered when her hands touched my shoulders.

"What do you need?"

No preamble, no demands about where I'd been or what was happening, just a simple question that told me everything I needed to know about Natalie. If this woman didn't already have a mate, in another life we might have had something together. As it was right now, I shook my head.

"The magic. It's out of control. I can't…can't handle it."

She turned toward the bar. "C'mon. I'll get you somewhere safe."

"I don't want to hurt you."

"You won't."

"Or Wren."

"You won't."

"I'm not going in the diner."

"I know. I'm taking you to the private room in the bar, okay?"

She helped me move faster as I focused solely on controlling the roiling magic within. It felt worse than it had in the hotel, than at the rest stop, than anywhere else in the past hours. I stumbled forward with her hands on me. She held me steady and supported me as we moved across the parking lot toward the bar.

The bar was not open all night, so the door was locked, but Nat was quick to whip out her keys and unlock the door. She didn't bother to relock it behind us as she ushered me in and led me to the private room in the back.

"I don't know if I can hold it back." I groaned as I settled into the booth at the far end of the room. Natalie moved a few feet away, as if afraid to be at ground zero but unwilling to leave me completely alone.

"You don't have to. Let it out. Find a way."

"I don't want to hurt you, destroy anything."

"You don't have to. It doesn't have to be destructive, does it?"

I took a moment to breathe before answering. "N-no. No it doesn't."

"So do something else with it. Weave it into something else."

I shot her a look. "Weave it? How did you—"

"You explained it to me, remember? That destruction was—"

"Easy. Pure force is…simple, but unrefined," I continued her words, remembering the day we'd sat in the diner, and I told her what troubles I was having with my magic, and how I needed to fix it. I should have remembered earlier. Hell, I'd taken down a fucking tree. Sure, it wasn't that huge or anything, but it was big enough to notice. And the whole time, I probably could have avoided any large incidents if I'd just thought to *weave* the magic into a new spell, instead of just pushing the power out of me.

"Weave the magic into something stable," Natalie said softly. "Or something you can control better. Focus on the magic, nothing else."

For someone who wasn't a witch, she sure listened and learned when I was teaching her things. It was almost like the words had come from Brigid herself, telling me how to calm myself, calm the magic. I took a deep breath in, held it for a count of three, then breathed out. It let me think a little clearer, and as I repeated the exercise I could feel the panic receding enough that I could think through it.

It was time to stop letting my magic run the damned show.

I closed my eyes and started to hum to focus my concentration. I looked inward, toward that well of magic inside me. I pushed against the power, forcing it back until it felt like I was about to burst, then drew forth a thin thread of that power. I wrapped and wove and tied it into the shape of something that resembled a wolf, then released the power into the air with a sigh of relief.

I opened my eyes in time to see my small, witchlight-infused wolf run across the room until it drew taut to the power that was still tethered to me. I saw Natalie's eyes go wide, a smile on her lips as she watched it go by.

"Close your eyes," I told her, "it's going to get bright in here."

I closed my eyes again and started humming, then refocused on the magic and drew it into my hands in threads at the speed of thought. I wove those threads into different shapes and sent them out all over the room, and the witchlight shone even through my eyelids. There was a gasp and a thud, and I faltered, my concentration going toward Natalie and whatever had happened.

"I'm okay."

I nodded in her general direction and continued. With each shape, with each witchlight-infused creature that I manifested, the well of magic grew calmer, easier to deal with. I could tell when the magic started to dwindle, as if I had pulled too much from it. It had been a long time since I'd felt this empty. A very long time. Maybe it wasn't a bad thing to do, once in a while.

I stopped humming and opened my eyes.

Natalie was sitting on the ground, looking like she had fallen. I supposed one of the shapes might have floated right toward her and might have scared her enough to knock her over. Either way, her eyes were open, if squinting, and she looked around in wonder. I took a moment before I checked over my masterpieces.

Shapes made of witchlight floated in the air throughout the entire room. They danced in the air, giving off their light, and all of them were tethered to me by an invisible thread of magic. There had to be at least a hundred of them, maybe more. I hadn't bothered to keep count.

"Holy shit," I breathed. I couldn't believe what I'd done. I'd never made something like this before, something so amazing. So beautiful.

"Creating things is more beautiful than destroying," Natalie said in almost the exact tone of voice I'd used the day I explained it to her.

"Creation is hard," I said, lowering my head to the table. "Destruction is easy. Pure force, breaking the laws of physics, calling fire or wind to lash out. It's all simple, requires little thought, and wastes a lot of magic."

"Good in an emergency, when called for, but not for something like this."

I shook my head. "This is different. Very different. To create something and put it out in the world takes a kind of willpower I…I didn't think I had. I had no idea I could make something like this. I'd never thought to even try. One witchlight, maybe two, sure. But to make them into something, to make a field of lights like this, wrapped and woven into what I could see in my mind, never mind something I could do with my fingers…" I trailed off, feeling exhausted now that the magic was out of me.

Natalie looked around at the lights, then back to me. "How long will they last?"

I grunted. "Until I dispel them, I think. Maybe longer."

She nodded. "Maybe we'll keep the VIP room locked tonight."

"That might be for the best."

She moved around the lights until she could sit in the booth beside me. She reached out her hand and I felt it on my head as she idly brushed her fingers through my hair. It was such a soft moment that I could feel it in my heart. What the hell had I done right in this life to deserve a friend like her? That thought brought with it memories of Brigid, and my heart broke as the tears started to fall freely. Natalie didn't say a word, just kept working her fingers through my hair with a calmness I couldn't emulate right now.

I sobbed into the table for my old friend, covering my face in my hands. The hunters had taken her away from me. My mentor, my oldest friend. I wanted to make them pay. I wanted to show them what it was like to lose someone they loved. I sobbed under the hand of my friend and vowed that somehow, I would find a way to make the hunters regret ever coming after us. I would find out who got Brigid killed and make them pay.

CHAPTER SIXTEEN

Ashly

I didn't speed the entire way to Terabend, but I pushed the limit a little bit. The last thing I needed was to be pulled over by the police. I didn't think they'd accept my excuse as a valid reason to be speeding, and I really didn't want them looking in the trunk for whatever reason. We weren't stupid—open the trunk and there was nothing to see, but open the divider where the spare tire was hidden and you'd find the tools of our trade as hunters, and most of that was illegal in one way or another.

I shook my head and focused back on the road. No need to bring bad luck down on me in the form of cops. I needed to get my head straight and focus on what I was out here to do. The sun was already up in the sky this early on a spring morning, and the scenery out my window was absolutely lovely to look at. Not that I paid it much attention. I only stopped once, and that was to fill up with gas in Edmonton before heading west.

My phone buzzed again in the cupholder, but it wasn't the GPS with new directions. It buzzed a few times, then went silent, and I cursed. My father, probably. And it wasn't the first time he'd called from the missed call notifications. I'm sure he wanted to know where I was, and I wasn't ready to tell him that I was risking myself and my livelihood to tell my girlfriend that she might very well be targeted by witches.

If she even believed me and didn't just laugh in my face over all this.

"Oh fuck," I said, "This is such a bad idea."

But I kept driving. I couldn't be the reason Rias got hurt. Whether she believed me or not, I couldn't let anything happen to her.

The mountains that could only be seen in the distance from Calgary or Edmonton loomed high through my windshield as I passed the sign welcoming me to the small town. Terabend boasted a population of a couple thousand. The first thing to see was the trees that lined the highway for several kilometers before they thinned out to show the first signs of settlement. I saw the sign for the diner before I saw the actual building, and as soon as my mind interpreted what I'd seen, my stomach made a growling noise that could be heard around the world. The yawn that followed almost had me driving off the road, and I set my sights on the diner on the right-hand side of the highway.

I read the sign for the Tooth and Claw Diner as I pulled into the parking lot. I shook my head at the appalling parking job of some random person who'd decided to park horizontally across three spaces, and then I slipped into a spot beside a Jeep. "What the hell kind of name is that for a diner? Sounds like someone does a lot of hunting or something. If the place doesn't look rustic as hell, it just won't live up to its name."

Bells rang as I stepped through the doorway and drew the attention of a handful of people who were sitting down to breakfast. The diner was relatively plain, with a long counter with bar stools along one wall that had doors that led to what I assumed to be the kitchen. Against the other wall, full-paned windows shone sunlight down on booths that lined the entire wall to the back of the place. And in between was a scattering of tables that could be moved and pushed together for larger parties, I supposed. The booths had seats of plush, deep red fabric and the tables were all a dark oak. What walls weren't windows were also a dark color, almost—but not quite—giving it that rustic look the name really pushed.

A couple of the booths by the window were full, and there was a small group of three people clustered around the far end of the bar, but besides that, the diner was empty. I glanced at the clock on the wall behind the counter. This should be prime mealtime, I figured. Why was it so empty in here?

One of the three from the end of the bar, a shorter brunette with a wide smile and sparkling blue eyes, caught my eye and moved toward me.

"Hi! Welcome to the Tooth and Claw. Sit anywhere you'd like."

I nodded and took a seat at the bar near the door. I still wasn't even comfortable being here, but I had to make sure Rias was okay. And for that I needed to get some coffee and food in me before I collapsed from exhaustion.

"I'm Heather. Is there anything I can get you this morning?"

"Coffee, please," I replied. "And a menu."

She smiled even wider, if that was possible, and moved around the back of the bar to grab a hot coffee pot. She poured coffee into the mug in front of me and placed a menu on the bar too. It wasn't a double-sided, single page like I was expecting. No, this thing was a small book, showing quite a diverse selection of meals. I was impressed. Whoever the cook was had quite the repertoire.

I glanced down the bar at the other two people, one of whom was watching me with interested eyes. She moved slightly and I saw a heavily distended belly. Heather seemed to follow my gaze and laughed. I blinked.

"Oh, that's Wren. She owns the place, but she won't stay home even though she's hugely pregnant. The other one is V, my beau, my reason for being." She wore a sloppy smile as she described the tall piece of meat who had an air about them of not caring what other people thought. I liked that. I respected that.

"It's…emptier than I expected it to be today."

She nodded sagely. "It is. Like there's something in the air or something. It's been pretty quiet all night and morning."

"You've been here all night?"

"Yeah, there was an emergency, so I'm pulling a double until Wren's wife gets back." As if on cue she covered up a wide yawn. "So, what brings you into our little slice of paradise?"

I stared at Wren for a long moment as realization hit me. Wife. She'd said wife. And it had been so easy to say and listen to. Like there was nothing different about it. And why should there be? It was normal, wasn't it? It deserved to be normal. Was that something I could have with Rias?

I blinked, shaking my head a little at that thought. Was that even something I wanted? That she wanted? This was my first real relationship, after all, and it really hadn't been awesome so far. I mean, Rias had been awesome, and I loved spending time with her and being around her and I wanted it more, but something like marriage? Being together for…well, for a long time? Was that something that I wanted?

Something inside me was answering every one of those questions with a great big nod, screaming yes into the void that was somehow where my heart was supposed to be. Was my reticence because of my parents, because of my upbringing? I wanted a relationship with her. A *real* relationship with her, not this long-distance bullshit we'd barely been pulling off. I wanted to get to see her every day, to tell her that I loved her every day. I imagined us sharing the same bed more often than one or two nights every few months, going to breakfast in a diner just like this one and then going about our day together—or separately, if that was what was needed. But I just wanted her near me, with me. To give me a chance.

"Oh, I know that look. Boy trouble," Heather said, laughing.

I stuck out my tongue and shook my head.

"No? Girl trouble, then."

"Is it that obvious?"

"My dear, you look like you haven't slept in a day or two and you're here in a small town drinking awesome coffee and acting like you have no idea what you're doing. Am I close?"

"Yeah, yeah, you're not far off. I came here to be with the woman I've been dating for a while…but I don't even know if she wants me here. And—" I shut my mouth, not about to tell this random stranger that Rias might be in trouble because of me. I shook my head again. "And I just don't know what I'm doing here."

"Well, right now you're enjoying a cup of coffee, and I'll get you some food. Better to think about these kinds of things on a full stomach."

I glanced at the almost-forgotten menu and scanned it quickly. "I'll get a cheeseburger and fries," I said, selecting something that hopefully couldn't be screwed up. "No tomatoes or onions, please."

Heather gave me a funny look that I couldn't quite place, then smiled. "One Natalie special, coming right up." She punched a few buttons on the computer and nodded, then wandered back to where Wren and V were sitting at the far end of the bar.

I wrapped my hands around my mug, taking a sip of the now not quite as scalding coffee. I grimaced at the taste—I'd never managed to grow accustomed to it, but I knew I needed the energy it offered. I wondered who Natalie was and why she had a particular burger named after her but didn't want to get into a talk about diner lingo with Heather. I needed to focus on what I came here to do.

The door opened and the bells chimed again. I glanced over to see the newcomer, and my jaw dropped as my mind almost screamed in panic. There in the doorway, staring at me, I could swear, was my mother!

I took a breath, then a second, and focused my eyes on the slight differences between this woman and my mom. The much more copper colored hair as opposed to my mother's lighter, more blond hair. The lack of lines on the face, the heftier body and even the choice of a soft halter-topped sundress that she was wearing proved that this wasn't who I thought it was. I managed to calm my nerves enough to take a sip of the coffee in front of me, taking my eyes off the newcomer for a second.

"Ashly?"

I froze with the cup millimeters from my lips. That voice. My *name*. I knew that voice, and the way she said it…it sounded so familiar. There was something about it, about her, that I couldn't place. I put the cup down slowly, ready to reach for the gun at the small of my back. I had to remember why I was here. There were witches in this town, and they were after me and my girlfriend. Everyone was a potential threat. I let out a soft breath, then turned toward the woman.

"I'm sorry," I said, "have we met?"

"You're Ashly Mercer."

In a second, I was off the stool and my gun was out, pointing at the woman. There was commotion from the other end of the bar, but I kept my aim on the newcomer.

"Witch," I snapped.

"What the hell is going on?" a voice behind me asked. I shot a quick glance over my shoulder, noting that Wren was on her feet, but V's hand was on her shoulder, holding her back. Heather was looking between me and the newcomer like she had no idea what was going on.

"It's all right," the woman said, holding her hands up in the air. Her eyes were on me, not the weapon between us. "She won't hurt me."

"That's assuming a lot."

"She won't hurt me because that's not how she was trained."

I glared at her. "You know nothing about my life."

"Err on the side of caution when using firearms, wasn't it?"

A quote directly from my father, from when I was young.

I shook my head. "You think you know me? Who the hell are you?"

"I know your dad's name is Allan. Your mom's name is Meredith. I know you had a brother who ran away when you were barely a teen."

"Fucking witch!"

She shook her head. "I'm not a witch."

"Then how the hell do you know so much?"

"Because I lived it—same as you."

"You're lying. You're no hunter."

"A hunter? I never said I was a hunter." She finally looked down and away from me, and I was glad for the respite from her piercing gaze. "Damn. He really didn't tell you why, did he?"

"I'm going to shoot you if you don't start making sense right now."

"Ashly, I'm—" Something moved behind the woman, and I snapped my aim toward it. My finger pulled the trigger before I could think better of it. The pistol jumped in my grip, and I saw the woman flinch backward, clutching her arm. It allowed me to see who was behind her and my eyes went wide.

"Rias?"

"Ashly?"

Rias stood staring at me for all of a second before something hard hit me in the back of the head. The gun slipped from my hand as I fell to the ground, blackness creeping into the edges of my vision. I could just make out Rias running toward me before the world went dark.

CHAPTER SEVENTEEN

Rias

"Ashly?" I cried, as she fell like a brick with her eyes blinking unsteadily. "No!"

I ran forward, but Natalie was in my way, on the ground, her hand on her shoulder. I faltered, not sure who to go to.

"I'm okay," Nat groaned, as if she knew that I was hesitating.

I knelt by Ashly, taking her hand and quickly checking for a pulse. It was there, strong and sure. I glared up at V.

"What the hell did you do that for?"

V answered my glare with their own. "She shot my Lupa." They put a dented napkin dispenser back on the bar before hurrying to Natalie's side.

"I said I'm okay." Nat grumbled as V helped her sit up. She was still holding her shoulder, blood pouring out from behind her hand. "It's not silver. I'm okay."

"What the hell is going on?" Wren demanded. "Who the hell is she and why did she pull a gun?"

"She's…" I hesitated. "She's my girlfriend."

"She's my sister," Natalie said at the same time.

I stared at her. "Wait, what?"

"Your sister?" Wren asked.

"You can talk about this later," V said, their voice offering no other option. "We need Dr. Maru here. And someone should check to make sure I didn't kill the woman."

"You didn't—" I said, still staring at Nat. Why the hell didn't she tell me I was dating her sister? Then again, how would she have known? Even knowing the name didn't mean it was the same Ashly

Mercer that she'd grown up with. And knew so much about. And had been estranged from for a little over a decade. I shook my head. "Why didn't you tell me?"

I didn't mean to sound so accusatory, but the tone definitely came out with my words.

"I didn't know it was her until I walked in and saw her sitting there." Nat's words were laced with pain, but she was still breathing, and damn it, I wanted answers.

"You could have told me there was a chance."

"I didn't want you to overthink it. The relationship was doing you a lot of good."

Wren held up her hands. "Okay, wait a moment. Since when the hell did you come from a family of hunters, Nat?" She turned to me. "And since when were you dating one of them?"

"I didn't know they were hunters," Nat said, "I just thought what we went through as kids was pretty average. When I realized it wasn't, I figured my parents were just…militia fanatics or doomsday preppers or something."

"She said she was a private investigator," I added. "She never mentioned anything about the supernatural to me."

"Does she know?"

"Know what?"

"That you're a witch. That we're werewolves."

I shook my head. "I don't think so. I never gave her any reason to suspect it."

"Well, she's here for a reason. And she sure seemed to think that Natalie is a witch."

"Um…" Heather raised her hand from the other side of the bar. "She said she was here to be with the woman she was dating…" She gave me a pointed look. "If that helps at all."

"Shit!" I slapped my hand against my forehead. "She must've come back to the hotel. I left it such a mess, she probably figured something happened to me. Goddess, I'm such an idiot."

"Well, either way," Wren said, "I can't have an unconscious hunter on my floor all day. Someone call Zeke and get him here so we can take her to the sheriff's station and throw her in one of the cells. Then call Hikaru and get her to make sure the hunter is still alive and well after that blow to the head. We need to talk to her before we figure out how to deal with this situation."

"We're not killing her," Natalie snapped, harsher than I think I'd ever heard her voice before.

"I'm not saying we kill her. Just whether or not she can be trusted to leave town and not come back, or if she'll continue to be a threat."

"Wren…" Natalie began.

"Don't you *Wren* me," her mate growled. "I'm pissed off at you."

"Why?"

"Because you let her shoot you! *Oh don't worry, Wren, she won't hurt me*. That's what you said!"

"I didn't think she'd shoot me."

"Well, clearly you were fucking wrong! What if the bullet had been silver?"

"Then I think getting Dr. Maru here might take precedence over you yelling at me? And over calling Zeke."

I shook my head and tuned out the bickering between the loving couple. I cradled Ashly in my arms as best I could, unsure if I should try moving her with the injury or if I should keep her on the floor. Luckily, the bells on the door started ringing and I glanced over my shoulder at Dr. Maru, our resident doctor and vampire, as she looked around at the scene before her. She hefted a bag almost as big as she was and twice as heavy but carried it like it was nothing.

"I'm okay," Natalie said again. "Check on Ashly."

"Who's Ashly?" Dr. Maru's voice was always low and sultry, like she was actively trying to seduce someone. Maybe that was just a vampire thing, but it seemed like something that came naturally to her.

I nodded to the woman in my arms. "I need to know if we can move her."

"What happened?"

I gave her the short version, and she shook her head.

"Are you sure the bullet wasn't silver?"

"I think I'd be in a lot more pain if it was," Natalie said.

Dr. Maru knelt down beside me, examining the place on Ashly's skull where V had hit her. Her hand came away with blood, and I felt panic rise in my throat. And my magic with it. Ashly was hurt. Because she came here for me. This wasn't what I wanted. Wasn't the way I wanted to introduce her to life in Terabend. Into my life.

Dr. Maru pushed a gauze pad into my hands and pulled out some bandages. "Apply pressure here. I'll wrap it up, we'll stop the bleeding."

I did as she said, and she swiftly wrapped a layer of bandages around Ashly's head. We were just finishing up when the bells tinkled again and a tall, lanky man wearing a sheriff's uniform burst into the diner.

"What the hell is going on? A gunshot, Wren, really?" Zeke demanded, looking around at the small crowd.

"It wasn't my fault this time."

Once again, the story was told, and Zeke knelt by me as Dr. Maru went to Natalie and started poking at her shoulder.

"Why is the hunter still alive?" he asked.

"I'm not letting you kill her."

"It would solve a lot of problems."

"You aren't killing her."

He grunted and together we lifted her into a modified princess carry, with me desperately trying to make sure her head was supported and didn't start to bleed again.

"Well she's going into one of the cells. The doctor can check on her again there."

"That's fine. We have a lot to talk about anyway."

"This isn't a time for you to work on your relationship skills," he said.

"That's not what this is."

It's totally what it was.

He snorted and left the diner with Ashly, heading for the squad car he'd driven up in. I followed him and helped him put her gently in the back seat, then we drove across the two lanes of highway to the sheriff's station. He pulled me aside before I could work on getting her out of the car and pushed me against the vehicle.

"You've been here for a long time, Rias. We've never had any issues with you, not like with the wolves. Tell me that isn't changing."

I shook my head. "I don't know. I don't know what this is. I need to know why she followed me back here."

"If this goes wrong, or anyone else gets hurt, it's on you. You understand that, don't you?"

Zeke had always been a gruff son of a bitch, but this was something else. There was something harsher than normal in his tone, and for the first time I worried what he might do if this situation was to turn sour.

"I won't let anyone get hurt."

"You'd better not. You promised to use your magic to help the town, now's your chance to prove it."

I swallowed hard. He had no idea that when I made that promise so many years ago, I was planning to never use my magic again. Everything that had happened in the last year or so could easily be traced back to one simple decision—freeing Heather's wolf. I'd decided to play hero, and now I was reaping the whirlwind.

"She's innocent," I said softly. "She doesn't deserve your ire. I know hunters aren't your favorite people, but she hasn't hurt anyone that I know of."

"I can smell blood on her," he said, "and not just her own. It's faint, but it's there. She killed or was around someone who died in the last day at least."

His words made me pause for a moment. I felt shocked by a thought. Had she been there when Brigid was killed? Had she pulled the trigger? I looked at Ashly through the window, needing answers from her now more than ever.

"I won't let anyone get hurt," I said again.

He grunted and pulled away from me, giving me space again. Together we got Ashly out of the car and into one of the cells in the station. The lock clicked shut on the door of her cell and echoed in my chest as I pressed myself against the bars, leaning my forehead against their coolness.

"C'mon," Zeke said, waving to me from the door to the front room. "Vadi is on their way here. They're going to want to hear what happened from you."

I sighed and turned away from my girlfriend. I didn't want to leave her, but there wasn't much choice. I didn't look forward to explaining it all over again, especially to someone like Vadi, the Genius Loci who watched over the town. I just wanted to stay with Ashly until she woke up.

But first, I had things to explain and a relationship to figure out, quickly, before it all fell down around me.

Chapter Eighteen

Ashly

I awoke to nimble fingers prodding around the back of my head. I opened my eyes slowly as I relished the almost massage-like feeling of those digits as they worked their way through my hair. Until they touched a spot that made pain shoot through me, and I sat bolt upright, pushing the woman who'd been leaning over me backward. She fell on her ass, and her purple-tinted glasses fell to the concrete floor. She stared at me with blood-red irises.

"Get the hell away from me," I yelled at the vampire as I pressed myself back against the concrete wall of what looked like an old-fashioned jail cell. "I'm not a fucking snack."

"I have no intention of snacking on you," she said, as she brushed herself off and picked up her glasses. "If I wanted a meal, I have plenty who enjoy spending the time with me."

"Fucking vampire."

"Brainwashed hunter."

"What the hell were you doing to me?"

She sighed. "At another's request, I was making sure you didn't need stitches for the wound in your head." She flashed a smile that showed her fangs. "I am a doctor, after all."

"And?"

"And what?"

"Do I need stitches?" The thought of letting her near my head again almost made me gag. I couldn't believe I'd let a vampire that close to me at all, never mind allowing it again just for something simple like stitching up a wound.

"Wouldn't you like to know." She laughed and walked away, heading for the wall of bars at the front of the cell. A tall, lanky man in a sheriff's uniform stood there, staring at me with an undisguised malevolence that almost made me wither away on the spot. He opened the door for the vampire, then closed it with a loud clang that reverberated through my head and made my ears ring for a good couple moments.

I reached up to the bandage around my head, following it to the back where the thicker padding was. Just touching it sent a flare of pain through me, and I pulled my hands away.

"I wouldn't play with that," a voice said from outside the bars. I looked up and saw the red-haired woman from the diner standing there, watching me. "V hit you harder than they probably had to."

"Is that what happened?" I couldn't remember much after the gun went off in my hand. I stared at her, noting the new dress she was wearing and the bandage wrapped around her shoulder. "What the hell did they hit me with?"

"Napkin dispenser."

"Yup, that'll do it." I put my head in my hands, leaning over with my elbows on my knees. What the hell was I doing, having a simple conversation with whoever the hell this was? At best, she was someone who knew far too much about my family for comfort. At worst, she was a witch, and she was after me and Rias. Maybe it was the wound in my head, maybe it was something she was doing, but I still couldn't bring myself to see her as an enemy. My father would be so damned disappointed in me. "So who the hell are you? How the hell do you know so much about me and my family?"

"I'm Natalie Donovan. And like I said before, I lived it, same as you."

I shook my head. "But I don't know you. You aren't a hunter."

"No, I wasn't there long enough to find out what all the training was for. I mentioned that you had a brother…"

"So what? He ran away. He's gone."

"Well, he is gone, in a way."

I stared at her. "You know my brother?"

She sighed. "It's right in front of your face and you still can't figure it out? Dad never told you what I said to him?"

"What are you talking about?"

"Ashly, I'm your sister."

I laughed. I couldn't help it. It just burst out of me. I didn't care how much this woman looked like family. Didn't care how much she knew about my family. There was no way I was going to believe this bullshit.

"I told him at the top of the incline during our weekly hike," she said, ignoring the laughter. "I told him that I wasn't a boy, that I was transgender. That I'd always felt like a girl. I told him I wanted to transition."

I shook my head, knowing I shouldn't be listening to these lies. Her words were taking me back to that day so many years ago.

"He hit me, slapped me hard across my face. I lost my balance and fell down the incline to you and Mom. He told you not to touch the little shit," she said, and I could see on her face that she was reliving the moment just as I was. "You started to move toward me, but he shouted again. Mom just watched me bleed. He told me to get up, called me a shithead. Swore to kill me if I said anything like that again."

"Y-you can't know all this," I whispered.

"I was there, Ashly. It happened to me."

"B-but you…but you're…"

"I lived. I ran away, changed my life." She shook her head again. "I didn't know why he did everything he did, or what the end result would be. I didn't know it was to hunt the supernatural. He never told me that much before I ran."

"You ran away."

"I did."

"You ran away from all of us. You ran away from me."

"Ashly…"

"Don't even try to apologize right now."

"I did what I had to do."

"But you ran from me!" I shouted. "You know I would have accepted you! I would have stood with you!"

"I couldn't be there with him. I wouldn't have survived it."

"And that means running away from your sister? I looked up to you. I loved you! And you left me all alone with that family?"

"If I could have brought you with me, I would've. Believe me, there wasn't a day that I didn't miss you, Ashly."

"So why didn't you come find me? After the fact. After your transition, after everything. Why didn't you find me and tell me that you were okay?"

"I wanted to. I intended to. But I kept pushing it back. First it was after I finished high school, then college, then when I was established in a career, when you could be proud of who I was. I wanted to see you again. But I was afraid. I was so afraid that you'd be like them, that you'd hate me. I couldn't stand knowing that you hated me. It was better not to know how you'd react, almost." She shook her head sadly. "And then…then I almost died."

"What are you talking about?"

"I found my mate."

"Your mate? What…do you mean?"

She sighed. She stepped away from the bars and I stood up, wanting to keep her in sight. As much as what she was saying just wasn't making any sense, I couldn't argue anymore. I had to accept that she was my sister. My sister.

She took a deep breath, and then I saw dark, midnight black fur begin to grow up her arms, on her bare legs. Claws jutted out from her fingertips, and her copper hair turned black and grew into something of a mane around her face and head. Her ears shifted and moved to the top of her head, and she stood there as if this was entirely normal. I couldn't take my eyes off her.

My sister…was a werewolf.

"This isn't happening," I told myself. "I'm dreaming. I have to be dreaming."

"It's not a dream."

"You're a fucking werewolf!"

"Yes, I am. I—"

"I don't give a shit. Look, being my sister I could handle. No problem. That's you being you. But a fucking werewolf? You're a fucking monster!"

"I'm not—"

"You don't get it! I kill monsters like you." I slammed my hands against the bars. "And now I find out my brother—I mean, sister, is a fucking werewolf!"

"Ashly, I—"

"No! I don't care what fucking excuse you have! You are a fucking monster!"

"I'm not a monster!"

I bared my teeth at her. "Sure look like one to me."

That shut her up. And hurt her. I saw the look that flickered across her face and felt that pang of regret in my chest, but I kept up my angry glare.

"I'm done talking to you."

"Ashly, I'm not—"

"I said I'm done! Get the hell away from me!"

I pretended I couldn't see her lip beginning to quiver before she took a deep breath and held her head high. She didn't try and talk to me again, instead she turned and headed for the door that I assumed led to the front room. The moment I saw that door swing shut, I backed away from the bars and sat back down on the thin cot on the side of the cell. There was so much going on in my head I couldn't think straight.

I was so mad at him—her. Not because she was my sister now. That was cool, really. That was interesting. I'd always kind of wanted a sister, and having my sibling back was something I had wanted ever since she disappeared.

But a werewolf? I shook my head. I couldn't accept that. I couldn't let her be a monster like that. I remembered the bandage on her shoulder, where I'd shot her back in the diner. I hadn't known I'd be up against werewolves and hadn't packed the silver bullets. But was that a good thing or a bad thing? If I'd killed her already, would I even be in this cell? Would they have killed me?

I was still alive, so they didn't see me as a threat. They would regret that. I went over what I had in the trunk of the car. There were silver bullets there. I could do some damage with them.

But could I bring myself to kill my sister?

I couldn't say. I just didn't know.

CHAPTER NINETEEN

Rias

"I had no idea that she was going to follow me here."

It was the third time I'd said it, and each time it seemed to go in one ear and right out the other. Zeke stared at me like I had a third head, and Wren, lounging on the only couch in the office, was giving me a dirty look.

"There's no way I could have known that she was a hunter."

"There had to be signs," Wren insisted. "These people aren't exactly subtle. Hell, even I know that much about them."

Zeke glanced her way then turned back to me. "She's not wrong. Hunters aren't trained to be subtle. They sense a monster, and they go after it. It's one of the reasons we've been so careful not to draw them here. And now we find out you've been dating one?"

"I told you I didn't know! Yes, she carried a gun around, but she said it was because her father made her do it for their job. She said she was a PI, and that people sometimes came after them for whatever. I didn't question her much."

Zeke snorted. "You didn't question her because you wanted to get in her pants."

"Hey!" I snapped.

"Zeke!" Wren shouted at the same time.

He held up a hand. "I'll admit, that was crass, but it's not untrue, is it? You didn't ask questions because you wanted to be with her."

"Isn't that how relationships work? At least at first? You don't just gush to someone on the very first date about all the small little things about your life that you hate or are going through. No one sticks around if you do that."

"Surely there was some hint of who she was."

I shook my head. "I told you there wasn't. It's not like I met her parents. Not like she took me on a hunt with her." I thought about the last night we were together, when we were both sitting on things we wanted to talk about. I wondered if that was her secret, about being a hunter. I was glad now that I hadn't told her I was a witch. How would she have dealt with it?

"Tell us what happened in Calgary," Wren said.

"I've been over it twice already."

"Not with me." A deep, rough voice interrupted our conversation, and I spun around. In the entranceway stood Vadi. I felt myself tense up under their stony gaze as it swept through the room, taking in everything. They reached up and adjusted the red tie around their neck, their black three-piece suit sharp and neat, as if they had just walked off a magazine page.

"V-Vadi," I stammered. "W-what are you doing here?"

Coal-black eyes settled on me without a flicker of emotion. In all my time in Terabend, it was only Vadi that I never really felt comfortable with. They were a force of nature, coming and going as they pleased, and protecting the people of this sanctuary. The last time I remember them taking an interest in what was going on was the summer Natalie came to town. The summer the werewolves attacked.

Hopefully this wasn't going to be as bad.

"Why is there a hunter in my town?" they asked, their voice soft and the words said without inflection.

"I didn't know she was a hunter."

They entered the sheriff's office, walking past Wren and offering her a polite nod as they did. Wren nodded stiffly back, looking like she was about to bolt. As much as Vadi was one of us, I don't think any of us really knew how to act around them. They came to a stop next to Zeke, who inclined his head in a sort of bow and took several steps backward. That left Vadi and me, standing and facing each other, between the two desks in the room.

"Tell me everything, please."

Maybe it was their commanding presence, maybe it was the *please*, but I told them everything. Everything that had happened since I went to Calgary, from the awkward dinner to skipping the rest of date night to head for the hotel, to waking up to find Ashly gone. I stumbled over the phone call from Brigid and losing control of my magic in the hotel room, and I faltered when I got to Natalie helping me with my magic. I had to look away from them when I tried to explain that part of it. I didn't want to admit to having troubles with my magic, especially not to Vadi.

"I didn't know she followed me here. Not until I saw her in the diner. She spooked and shot Natalie—with a regular bullet, no silver."

"Is Natalie all right?"

I started to reply when the door to the cells slammed open and Natalie appeared, partially shifted and with huge tears streaming down her face. In a second, she was across the room and almost launching herself at Wren, who pulled her in close and held her tight.

"Oh, darling," Wren crooned. "Are you okay?"

"S-she called me a monster. She said that she kills monsters like me." Natalie's words were sullen and cold, and I swear I could feel the pain radiating from her. Wren stared at the door that led to the cells, looking like she was about to bust through them to give Ashly a piece of her mind.

"Wren," Vadi said. "It's not worth it."

"She hurt my mate," Wren growled.

I shook my head. "She doesn't understand. She's a hunter. She hunts werewolves and witches and everything. I'm sure she doesn't mean it personally."

"Oh, she meant it," Natalie said. "She said it was fine that I was trans, but apparently being a werewolf is crossing some kind of line."

"Nat…I'm so sorry."

She shook her head against Wren's shoulder. "Don't apologize for her, Rias. It's not your fault she's being a bitch."

"It's not really her fault either. If you want to blame someone, blame your parents. They control her life." I couldn't say why, but I felt compelled to defend Ashly. I knew who she really was. I knew that given time, she would be okay with having a werewolf for a sister—hell, she might even embrace it. And I hoped she'd be okay with having a witch for a girlfriend. She didn't want to live in her father's shadow. She didn't want to be a hunter, not like the rest of them. I was certain of it.

"Why are you defending her?" Wren asked.

"Because she's not a bad person!"

"She shot my wife!"

"She was scared!"

"Enough." Vadi's voice rose just enough to be louder than the both of us. "Whether she is a bad person or not is irrelevant right now. I am sorry, Natalie, that she hurt you. As of this moment, we cannot do anything that would risk having more hunters come to our town, so she cannot just...disappear."

My breath hitched in my throat at the idea. I was not going to be part of Ashly disappearing. I didn't care what the others might think of me.

"We need to know more about her, more about what brought her here this morning. If this is all a misunderstanding, then it's very possible we can let her go on her way. She hasn't seen too much, and if she is as Danaan claims, she will keep our sanctuary a secret." Vadi looked around at the four of us, as if waiting for arguments.

I could see Wren grinding her teeth as if she wanted to say something. It made sense. She would do anything for Natalie, even turning her into a werewolf to save her life. Zeke stood to the side silently, his eyes on Vadi. He would follow their orders to the letter, without question, as always.

Natalie had dried her eyes and returned to her fully human form. She looked like she was going to be sick, probably wondering if they were going to have to kill her sister just when it looked like she might get her back. I wouldn't let that happen. I would let Ashly go before I let them hurt her. Right now I didn't care about the safety of the town. There were enough werewolves and ghouls and other supernatural people here to fight off any group of hunters that came. I wanted no part of harming the woman I loved.

"I'll talk to her," I said, breaking the silence. "I'll find out why she's here and what's going on."

"Does she know you are a witch?"

I shook my head. "I don't think so. I've never revealed myself to her like that." Wren opened her mouth and I held up a hand. "Don't even think about saying it!"

Wren snarled at me. "You have no idea what I was about to say."

"Something pithy, I'm sure."

"I was going to suggest we take her out to the woods and make her find her own way home."

"Wren!" Natalie cried.

"What?"

"You know that wouldn't end well."

"Beautiful, I don't care. All I care about is that they hurt you. Your family has done nothing but hurt you your entire life. They don't deserve to get to know you now. They don't deserve to see what a wonderful person you are. They don't deserve a second chance."

"Ashly does," Nat said softly. "It wasn't her fault. It was my dad. Ashly was just a kid, younger than I was. She couldn't argue against my father. She had no idea what was going on that day."

"But she hurt you today. She shot you, she yelled at you, called you a monster. She didn't even get to know you first." Wren shook her head. "She doesn't deserve a sister like you."

"I can't abandon her again. I just can't do it."

"Neither can I," I added.

Vadi turned to me. "Are you in control of your magic enough to handle this?"

I nodded. "I'll manage. I promise. I won't let her hurt anyone else."

They looked to Wren and Natalie. "Come, I will take you back to the diner. You can drive home from there." They looked especially hard at Wren. "The health and well-being of that baby is your first priority right now, do you understand?"

"I understand," Wren said. She pulled Natalie to the door with her, following in Vadi's wake. "But if that girl hurts my mate again, I can't promise anything."

I watched them leave, then looked to Zeke, who nodded toward the door that led to the cells. I pushed through the doorway and looked in the first cell where Ashly was lying on the cot, her eyes closed, her breathing even. I let her rest, going into the cell next to hers and lying down on that cot. I tried to think of what I would say when she awoke—when we both awoke. What I could tell her to make her come to our side, to forget that she hunted supernatural folk like us. Would I have to tell her that I was a witch? How would she take it?

Can she accept me for who I am?

"Goddess, please," I said softly. "Please, let her understand. Don't take her away from me now that I finally have her."

Chapter Twenty

Ashly

The door Natalie had left through opened once more and I slit my eyes open the barest amount to watch Rias come into the hallway. She stopped by the bars to my cell for a long moment, and I fought my urge to get up and talk to her. I didn't want to do that right now. I didn't want to talk to anyone.

After a moment, she moved on, shaking her head like she was disappointed. So was I. But I couldn't talk to her yet. Not when I felt this heavy weight in my heart. A weight that had been there since I yelled at Natalie.

The day in the ravine played in my head on repeat. I'd watched my sibling fall down that embankment again and again, and always wondered what was said that had earned my father's ire. I'd thought about it a lot during those years that I was pushed harder than before. As soon as Natalie was gone, it was like my father was worried about losing me too. My freedoms were cut. I was expected to be stronger, faster, better than I already was. Better than I could be, I felt often. All for some obscure goal that never seemed to make sense.

I remembered the hospital where Natalie had been taken after the fall. Neither of us had been injured in our training like that before. She was bedridden for almost a month, and even then the training—for me—continued. Dad used the hospital as a learning experience, expecting me to follow his every order or wind up like my sibling. I remembered hating it, hating the restrictions he put on me, hating my sibling for doing whatever she'd done to anger him. I couldn't remember when that hatred had turned to blind servitude. Or why.

And then Natalie was gone. One night at the hospital, a few days away from discharge, the hunter assigned to watch her had fallen asleep on duty. The next morning I didn't have a sibling any longer, and Marcus had fallen in my father's estimation—at least for a while. Mom and Dad both acted like Natalie never existed. They got mad whenever I tried to talk about her, tried to question what had happened.

No one told me anything. No one explained anything. I went from having a sibling to being an only child in a single night.

What were the odds that I would ever get to see her again? Never mind that she transitioned. Never mind that she was a werewolf now. What were the chances that we'd meet, and I'd get a second chance with the closest family I'd ever had?

I'd looked up to her. Loved her. Idolized her. Before I even knew she was a her. Was I really going to let something like her being a werewolf stop me from getting a chance to know her again?

There was a huge part of me that said yes. She was a monster now, after all. I couldn't admit to being able to overlook that. I had been trained to kill monsters, to stop them from preying on innocent people. And now my own sister was one of them.

I couldn't see Natalie hurting an innocent. I couldn't see her hurting anyone. Wasn't that supposed to be a part of it? That we stop the monsters from preying on innocents? But what if that monster didn't hurt anyone? What if they just wanted to be left alone?

It wasn't something Dad talked about, but it was something that had always been on my mind. Even the other night, with the witch. She claimed that she hadn't hurt anyone, and I believed her. How many innocent monsters had been killed just because they had the bad luck to be born, well, a monster? Were the hunters just as bad as the monsters?

Why couldn't I have been born to a normal family? Not a family that decided it had to play judge, jury, and executioner to the types of creatures that no one else believed in. Not a family that couldn't handle one of its children being transgender. Not a family that couldn't handle their other child being a lesbian.

It wasn't fair.

I shifted slightly and swore when pain shot through my head like lightning. I shoved myself into a sitting position and rubbed my face, resisting the urge to tear the bandage off and take my chances with bleeding all over the place.

Why the hell was I still alive? I was a hunter, they were monsters. I should be dead. V should've killed me, not just knocked me out. It's ridiculous how bad they were at their jobs of being monsters.

"A-are you okay?" a timid voice said from beyond the cell bars. I glanced up to see Rias standing there, looking massively unsure about something.

"Oh, just peachy," I said. "I've got a fucking hole in my head, and I'm being held captive by a bunch of werewolves. Whether or not they're going to actually kill me is still on the damned table, and I'm pretty sure your awesome sheriff guy out there is a fucking ghoul. Oh! And the town doctor is a vampire. Think that sums it up?"

"I think there are a couple other doctors around that are human, so she isn't the only doctor in town."

"Really? That's the part you take away from my rant?"

She shrugged. "It seemed the part that needed the most correcting."

I scoffed. "I'm sitting here pretty much on death row and you're making jokes?"

"Don't be such a drama queen. You're not going to die."

"Clearly you don't know your friends as well as you think you do. They're monsters. They kill people. It's what they do. And I'm their next victim."

"Well, if that's what you really think, then there's no hope for you, and I should just go away. And I do know my friends. And they are not monsters."

She turned away from the bars and started to head for the other room. There was a pain in my chest when I thought about her walking away. I didn't want her to go. I couldn't stand to see her walk away, not now. I came here for her. I needed *her*. And a sudden sinking in my gut made me realize that out of everyone in this little town, Rias was probably the only one who had anything good to say about me. If there was anyone I wanted on my side, it was her.

"Wait," I said, getting up from the cot, "don't go, please."

"And why not? You've obviously made up your mind about my town and my friends. You're so certain you're going to die, I might as well save my breath."

I shook my head. "No, please, I mean…okay, fine, they haven't killed me yet, so there's a chance I'll live through this."

"See? Have a little faith. You'll get through this."

I gave her my best smile. "I'll get through this faster if you let me out."

She frowned, biting her bottom lip as her eyes flicked to the other door. "I would if I could, Ashly. You know that, right? I'm a deputy sheriff and Zeke is my boss. And you shot Natalie."

I started to shake my head again but stopped as pain flared. I put a hand to the bandage. "I don't understand. Why am I even still alive? They should have killed me the moment the gun went off, if not earlier."

"They aren't monsters, you know. They don't kill everyone that comes through town or whatever. There'd be a lot more missing people around here if they did."

"But they *are* monsters, Rias. They live to prey on humans. It's what they do."

"Who told you that? It's not true. Have you never considered that maybe they just want to live their lives? The way *humans* get to?"

"My father always said that no matter how peaceful the monster seems, they will always fall back into their bloodthirsty ways."

She snorted. "Wow, they really have you brainwashed, don't they?"

"What are you talking about?"

"Your parents. The hunters. You really have it stuck in your head that just because they're different, they're a threat."

"No, I mean, that's not…" I faltered, trying to find the right words to explain it all to her. "They're monsters, Rias. All of them."

She laughed and gave me a look that screamed pity. "I've seen a lot worse from people who don't turn into wolves once in a while."

I leaned my forehead against the bars, closing my eyes for a moment at the coolness of the metal against my head. My hands wrapped around the bars, holding me steady. A second later, another pair of hands wrapped around mine and I opened my eyes to see Rias in front of me. She held my hands tightly, looking at me in a way that made me feel like it was okay that I was in this cell, because she was here with me.

"It will be okay, Ashly. I promise you that."

I wanted to believe her. I really did. I tried to tell her that, but when I opened my mouth, different words came out. "What can you do against the monsters? You're only human. Are you even safe with them?"

She glanced away, but I saw the look of sadness that crossed her face first.

"I can help you," I insisted, pressing closer to her against the bars. "I can protect you, Rias, but not from in here. I want to help you."

She shook her head slowly. "They aren't as bad as you think."

"They're monsters, Rias. They're all monsters."

She glared at me. "Did you ever give them a chance?"

I opened my mouth, then closed it again. I knew I had no good answer for her. And something told me she knew it too. She let me go, stepping away from the bars. I didn't want her to let me go. I didn't want her to leave.

"Please," I said softly, "please don't go."

She shook her head. "Get some rest. Think about what I said."

"Please."

She headed for the door, pausing only after she was touching the handle. "I'm sorry, Ashly."

She left the room and I tried to fight back the tears that threatened to fall. I didn't want to be in here alone anymore. Being alone meant I had to think about things. That meant trying to figure out what was right and what was wrong. And my head didn't want to do that. The dull ache was threatening to become something worse as I returned to the cot and lay down, trying to find a comfortable position for my head.

Did I ever give them a chance?

The easy answer was no. The harder answer was I wanted to.

CHAPTER TWENTY-ONE

Rias

Be quick, my dear Danaan.

"Fuck!" I shouted, rolling off the couch and landing on the hardwood floor of the sheriff's office. I blinked against the rays of the morning sun, peeking through the big picture window at the front of the office, and groaned, rubbing my face.

Be quick, my dear Danaan.

I gave a little gasp as those words echoed in my head. Brigid's voice was soft but panicked and I knew, knew that I had to get to her before something happened. But I didn't. I couldn't. I was too late. She was already gone.

So why the hell was her voice haunting me with the last words she said to me?

I got up off the floor and headed for the bathroom. I did my business and splashed water on my face, trying to chase away the demons that were hovering in my thoughts. It was just that Brigid was gone, my oldest friend, the one who'd seemed untouchable, the one I turned to whenever I had a problem. She was gone now, and I hadn't had a chance to try and cope with it. But now, now there was an even worse thought circling my brain, one I didn't want to even consider.

How would Ashly react to me being a witch?

If she was already so adamant about hating her own sister being a werewolf, was there any way she could allow herself to be with a witch like me? Would she still look at me the same way or want to be with me? She said she came here for me. To protect me from the monsters. What would happen when she found out I was one of them?

I wiped at my eyes, pretending like I was rubbing sleep from them when really it was to stop the stupid tears from starting to flow. I loved her. I loved Ashly and wanted to be with her, even with knowing that she was a hunter. I was certain I wasn't wrong about her, that she wasn't like her parents. She could be different. She could be mine.

If she could bring herself to love someone like me.

More questions clouded my head, and I shook it to try and clear out the jumble. There was so much more going on here than I understood, and I had to admit that I didn't care. The only thing on my mind was Ashly, and making sure the wolves didn't take her out to the forest and not bring her back. I had to be sure that she didn't deserve to make a trip like that.

I shook my head and went back out to the office. I needed something to eat and drink before I could keep going on these lines of thought. Of course my brain was a traitor and kept trying to bring it up, but I staunchly pushed back, refusing to consider anything until I had proof of what she thought of me. And the source of that proof was sleeping on a cot in the other room. Behind a wall of bars.

I went to the door and grabbed the handle but didn't push my way through. I hesitated, unsure of what I was going to say if she was awake. I still needed to know why she was even here—I couldn't bring myself to ask her the night before. I went through the door and headed for the cell.

"Good morning, sunshine," Ashly's voice came through the bars as I stopped in front of her cell. She was sitting on the cot, fiddling with a thin gold chain necklace that I recalled her always wearing. There was a small green stone hanging from the pendant, something that looked vaguely familiar, like I'd seen a stone like it before. She let it twist in her fingers as I leaned against the bars, trying to find the right words to say…well, anything, to my girlfriend who was currently in a jail cell.

"Did you sleep okay?" I asked.

"Oh, just peachy. You know, between this cot and the hole in my head I got a good hour or two. Great for being able to make rational decisions, being sleep-deprived is."

"You're the one who shot your sister."

"I shot a werewolf. Anywhere else I'd be getting a medal."

"You really think so?"

"No, maybe not, but the hunters would congratulate me."

"I'm sure your parents would be so happy if you killed your sister," I snapped. That seemed to take the wind out of her bitchy sails.

"I'm sorry," she said, and she sounded actually contrite. "I didn't sleep well and I'm starving. I barely know what I'm saying anymore."

I watched her carefully. Her movements were more sluggish, less precise than usual. She looked exhausted. "If it makes you feel better, I didn't sleep that great either."

"At least you got a bed."

I shook my head. "Nah, I slept on the couch in the other room."

She glanced up at me, taking her eyes off her necklace and meeting my gaze for the first time. "Why would you do that?"

I bit my lip. "I didn't want you to be completely alone."

"Damn it, Rias," she said, barely loud enough for me to hear it.

"What?"

"You make it really hard to want to hate you."

"Is that what you're trying to do, Ashly? Hate me?"

"It'd be easier. It'd be so much easier than…than whatever this feeling is inside me."

"Why would it be easier?"

"Because then I wouldn't have any reason to be here. I came here for you, you know. I came here to protect you, to make sure you were safe. I wanted to save you. Because I…because I like you. I like you too damned much, and it's killing me that you're out there and you won't let me go when I didn't do anything wrong!"

I stared at her, long and hard. "Wow, there's a lot to unpack there."

"What are you talking about?"

I shook my head. "What do you mean, make sure I was safe? That you wanted to save me? Do you think I can't take care of myself?"

"No—that's not what I mean."

"No, you just seem to think I'm absolutely inept and need a big, strong hunter like you to come and save me from the scary monsters that roam this town."

"I didn't know you knew what they were! I thought a witch was after you! Because you were dating me."

"Because I'm dating you? You thought a witch was after me for that? What the hell gave you that idea?" I thought about that night when she left me. About Brigid's phone call, telling me hunters were after her.

Be quick, my dear Danaan.

"Where did you go that night?" I asked her.

"What night?"

"The other night, before you came here."

"You mean at the hotel?"

I nodded.

"My father…he called me. Wanted me to help him with a hunt."

"He couldn't have called someone else?"

She chuckled softly. "That's exactly what I asked. But no, he needed me. And honestly, I never thought I'd get the chance to help him, so I went."

"What were you hunting?"

She looked down at her hands, stiff on her knees. "Why do you want to know?"

"Because I want to know everything, Ashly. I want to know what was so important that you had to leave me in the middle of the night, then follow me back home."

"I told you—I'm trying to protect you."

"From what?"

"From the witches! From the werewolves and the ghouls and all the other monsters you've surrounded yourself with."

"What made you think I was in danger?"

She made a face. "I went back to the hotel after…after I was done with my father. It was trashed. I found your phone, smashed up on the ground. I thought something had happened, that you'd—I don't know. I hoped you'd gotten away and come back home or something. I needed to know you were safe, Rias."

I took a deep breath and repeated the question I didn't want to ask. "What were you hunting that night, Ashly?"

"It doesn't matter. The monster is dead. She can't hurt anyone again," Ashly muttered, refusing to look at me.

"Tell me what you were hunting, please."

She let out a long sigh. "We were hunting a witch. My father got a lead on her and needed me for backup."

My fingers tightened on the bars of her cage until they ached. "Did you kill her?"

She shook her head. "No. My father did. Shot her in the back."

"I-in the back?" I said, shaking my head. I couldn't believe it. My girlfriend had a role in the killing of my mentor and dear friend. "How could this happen?"

"Why all the questions? Why do you care about some witch?"

I gripped the bars hard enough that I could hear my knuckles pop, but I didn't get a chance to reply as Zeke poked his head through the doorway.

"Rias," was all he said. I was immediately grateful for a reason to turn and walk away from Ashly. I really wasn't sure what I was going to say or do about this new revelation, but it probably wouldn't have been anything good. I headed back into the office where Zeke was waiting with a couple bags that I recognized from the diner.

"What's up, boss?"

"Natalie left these for you and the girl." He nodded to the bags with a look that screamed he wanted to let Ashly starve. "I wanted to let you know before I headed out for a bit."

"Thanks, Zeke." I focused on the bags, not wanting to look at him. He could probably see that I was avoiding talking to him right now, as he gave a little huff, then headed for the outside door.

"I'll be back in an hour or so. Don't get into trouble."

I wanted to say something pithy or smart, but I just didn't have it in me. I couldn't stop thinking about Ashly and her role in the death of Brigid. I didn't want to be the one who brought her food. I didn't really want to see her again right at that moment.

But I had a job to do, and damn it, I was going to do it. She said she came here for me, but what if there was more to it than that? A hunter just happening to show up in Terabend, chasing her girlfriend? Was she telling the truth? What if it was the beginning of something else, an attack maybe, something against the good people of this town? I couldn't let it happen, not after losing Brigid already.

I grabbed the bags and headed back into the cells, glancing through the bars at Ashly. She was lying on the ground, unmoving. A trickle of blood seeped from underneath her bandage at the back of her head, and I froze, dropped the bags on the floor, and raced for the keys to unlock the cell.

I'd promised nothing would happen to her. I'd promised she'd be okay. What the hell had happened? I hurried to get the door open and slid it out of the way as I ran into the cell and knelt beside my lover.

I wasn't ready for the elbow in my gut. As I doubled over from the pain a knee came up and smashed into my cheek. I fell to the ground and Ashly stepped over me and out the door.

"I'm sorry, Rias." I heard her words as I shook my head and tried to regain my senses. "I never meant to hurt you."

Then she was gone.

Chapter Twenty-Two

Ashly

I only looked back once. I saw Rias on the floor of the cell, shaking her head, and I felt a pang of regret for what I'd done. But I had to do it. I needed to get out of here—or at least warn someone. There were monsters here in Terabend, and the humans were at risk.

Right?

I ran into the office area, ready to throw down with whoever might be in there, but the place was empty. I almost cheered but kept my mouth shut and my mind on the job. I searched the larger desk in the room, quickly coming up with the bag that had my effects—and my car keys. I grabbed the whole thing and pulled out the keys, then burst out the front door before anyone could catch up to me.

I squinted against the brightness of the morning sun as I raced across the two lanes of highway, earning a honk from a rather large semi truck on the way, and dashed for the diner parking lot. I mashed the button on the fob to open the trunk, knowing exactly what I was going for.

The trunk popped open as I approached, so far undetected in my efforts. I knew it was only a matter of time before Rias came to her senses, though. Would she follow me or send someone else? I didn't have time to think about it. I lifted the trunk lid all the way, then the false bottom that we'd installed in case someone wanted to look in the trunk. I needed a weapon. I needed to be able to defend myself from the werewolves here. That meant I needed silver.

I grabbed one of our pistols, strapped down so it wouldn't shift. It was larger than the one I normally used, a little heavier, but I'd practiced with nearly all of our weapons since I was a child. The differences wouldn't bother me for long. On the underside of the false bottom, magazines and ammo were strapped to make sure they didn't shift during a drive. I grabbed a full clip of silver ammo and loaded the pistol, chambering a round before I could forget to.

I kept the gun in one hand and searched the bag of my effects with the other. I pulled out my phone, thankful that there was still a charge. I didn't have time for a phone call, and I hesitated to try and message my parents. Would they call in the cavalry to come get me?

Instead I went with the next best alternative—I found Marcus's number and started typing furiously.

"Excuse me," a familiar voice said, "I don't believe you're supposed to be out here."

I spun at the words and dropped the phone to take my pistol in a steady, two-handed grip. Natalie stared at me from a couple feet away, a small smile flickering over her face. She was wearing a different dress today, but the bandage from yesterday was gone. I didn't know a werewolf could heal wounds *that* quickly.

"Are you going to shoot me again, Ashly?"

"I should."

"So why don't you?"

"Move one step closer and I swear I will."

She shuffled half a step forward, that damned smile never leaving her face.

"I'm warning you."

"Why?"

"Why what?" I said, gripping the weapon tight.

"Why are you warning me? I'm a monster. A werewolf. It's your job to kill me." She sniffed the air and looked pointedly at the gun. "And you have silver bullets this time, so why not do it?"

I pretty much growled at her, but I couldn't think of a good enough answer. Why the hell wasn't I shooting her? She was right—she was a monster and I killed monsters. My father trained me to kill monsters.

But was I just like my father?

"Please," I whispered.

"Please what?"

"Please don't make me do this."

She shook her head. "You don't have to do it if you don't want to."

"You don't understand!" I shouted. "This is who I am!"

"Is it? Is it really who you are? Because if it is, then why haven't you shot me yet?"

"Damn it, Natalie. Why are you making me do this?"

"I'm showing you that you aren't him, Ashly. You are your own person. You can make your own decisions."

"He trained me to kill things like you!"

"He trained me too—at least for a while. But I'm my own person. I became my own person."

"You ran away! You left me behind!"

"I know, and it's the greatest regret I've lived with ever since."

My hands wavered, my arms shaking. "I…I'm not as strong as you."

She took another step toward me, only a foot now from the barrel of the gun. "No, Ashly. You're stronger than me."

My finger twitched on the trigger, but I couldn't do it. I told myself to do it, but it didn't happen. The werewolf—my sister, stood right in front of me and I couldn't pull the trigger. She took one more step forward and her hands came forward to wrap around mine.

"You're so much stronger than me," she said as she gently pushed my hands down. I allowed it. My grip on the weapon loosened as it pointed at the ground. "You lasted years with them, even after I was gone. But you can still be your own person. You deserve to be your own person."

Her grip tightened on the pistol, and for a second, I panicked. She was taking the weapon away from me. Everything in my training refused to let that happen, and I clutched tight to the pistol and started to bring it up again.

"It's okay," Natalie murmured softly, and I did my best to focus on her voice. "No one here is going to hurt you."

"Ashly!" Rias's voice rang out over the parking lot, and I shook off Natalie's hands, bringing the weapon back up, then took a step away from the werewolf.

"Stay back!" I shouted, furious with myself that I was so weak that I let Natalie try to talk me down. Real hunters didn't get distracted like that.

"Ashly! What the hell?" Rias approached slowly, cautiously, as she noticed the gun pointing once again at Natalie. She rubbed her head. "If you needed something, you could have asked."

"Like you would have given it to me." I shook my head. "I'm not stupid, Rias. You work for these monsters, there's no way you'd side with me against them."

"Why does there have to be sides?" Natalie asked. "Put the gun down. We can talk it out."

I shook my head. "There's no sense talking to a damned monster!"

"Ashly, please. Put the gun away," Rias said.

I looked to the phone with my unsent message, still on the ground. It was too close to Natalie to pick up without risking her getting to me again. I couldn't let that happen.

Damn it, I did want to believe her! I wanted to listen to her! But I was a hunter, like my father wanted me to be.

She was right about one thing, though. I was stronger than her.

"What's going on over there?" someone behind me yelled, and I jumped and pulled the trigger.

Natalie grunted and fell, the same way she had before. I stared at my sister's body, the blood pooling around her abdomen. There was a neat hole in her dress that was soaked with red, and more and more just kept pumping out of her. I dropped the gun, letting it fall to the ground, and ran to Natalie's side.

"Shit! Shit!" I shouted. "What the hell? What did I do?"

"Nat!" Rias yelled and fell to her knees on Natalie's other side. "Is it silver?"

I nodded. I felt the presence of someone else behind me and craned my head back to see who was there. Heather, the woman from the diner, came up behind me, staring down at Natalie.

"Don't just gawk, call your vampire doctor!"

She stared at me with a fierce kind of hatred for only a second before she ran back into the diner. I heard the bells tinkling as I got up and started digging through the trunk again.

"What the hell are you doing?" Rias demanded.

I found the first aid kit that my dad and I had put together and pulled out swathes of bandages and whatever else I could find to help staunch the wound.

"I'm sorry, Natalie," I said as I pressed the bandages to the wound. There was too much blood coming out, and I could see the effects of the silver on her skin as if it were almost being eaten away. "Shit, shit, shit!"

I leaned down, trying to see if there was a wound on her back too. I used full metal jacket rounds when it came to silver bullets, so there was a chance that the bullet had gone through her instead of sitting inside and releasing silver into her system.

"I need to roll her over a little," I told Rias.

"Why?"

"I need to see if there's an exit wound."

I had her hold Natalie at the shoulders and lift her sideways so I could see the underside. I almost missed it, a little hole in the dress and in her skin where the bullet had exited. I breathed a sigh of relief. Hopefully that meant things would be easier to heal. But it didn't negate the fact that I'd just shot my sister with a silver fucking bullet.

I packed the wound as best I could with some more of the gauze and bandages before I let Rias put her back down. I pressed more to the front wound, putting pressure on it. I didn't know what else to do.

"I'm sorry, Natalie, I'm so sorry," I kept whispering over and over again.

"What the hell happened?" I heard Wren's voice before she appeared, an ominous shadow standing over me as I pressed hard down onto Natalie's abdomen.

"What does it look like?" I said. "I shot her."

"You what?" Wren snapped. "Get the hell away from her!"

Strong hands landed on my shoulders, and I tried to shake them off, refusing to allow anyone to move me away from my sister. Rias stood up and moved behind me as I glanced over my shoulder at Wren, who had a death grip on me.

"I'm trying to save her life."

"You shot her! Why would you do anything good for her?"

I gritted my teeth as the grip on my shoulders tightened. "Because I'm not a monster." I slipped out of her grasp with Rias's help and she stepped between me and Wren as if to protect me. "Now get your vampire doctor here!"

"Heather already called—Hikaru is on her way. Now get the hell away from her!"

I shook my head. "Not until she gets here."

"You're going to make it worse!"

"I'm really trying not to here."

"Get the hell away from my mate!"

I blinked, losing focus for a moment as I glanced back at Wren. Mate? This was Natalie's mate? And she was pregnant? The full weight of what I had just done slammed into me.

"You're her mate? B-but that means…that means I'm going to be an aunt?" I whispered. "What have I done?" How the hell hadn't I put it together before? I'd been so all over the damned place since coming here, I didn't know what was up and down or black and white. I had no idea what the hell I was doing. And honestly, it showed. I'd fired my weapon twice in as many days, both times by being startled. I couldn't be trusted around guns, and I clearly couldn't be trusted around my sister. I had practically killed her twice now. I couldn't let her die. Right now, all I knew was that I couldn't let that little wolf grow up without both its mothers. And an aunt, if they'd have me. "Damn it, Dad."

"What does your dad have to do with this?"

"Brainwashing," I said offhandedly, then focused back down on Natalie. "Rias, keep Wren off me, please, she looks like she wants to eat me."

"What?"

"I'm the only person trying to keep Natalie alive right now, I'd appreciate you preventing a werewolf from ripping my head off because of it."

"Wren…" I heard Rias say.

"I'm fine. I won't kill her—yet," Wren said and moved to Natalie's other side, took her hand, and clutched it as if it were a lifeline. She looked up at me and growled. "If you make one wrong move, I will end you. I don't care if Rias is so damned smitten with you."

"I'm trying to help," I said, but the words were woefully inadequate, even to me.

Natalie shifted slightly, her eyes opening, and she gave her mate a look with something in it that I didn't have the words to describe.

"I'm sorry, Wren," she said softly.

I gave the wolves their moment as I continued to put as much pressure as I could manage on the wound.

Wren shook her head. "Don't be sorry. Just don't go anywhere."

"Don't blame Ashly. She deserves a new life, just like I did."

I had to grit my teeth to stop myself from saying something stupid and ruining the moment. Instead I just whispered: "Stay with us, Natalie."

I could feel Wren glaring at me, but I kept my focus down on my sister. Where the hell was that vampire?

As if answering my unasked question, what I assumed was the

town's only ambulance pulled up to the scene. The vampire got out of the driver's side, squinting in the morning sun, and hurried toward us with a large kit on her hip. She knelt down beside me, far closer for comfort than I would have liked, but I gritted my teeth again and dealt with it.

"What happened?"

I filled her in, making sure she knew that the bullet was silver this time. She listened intently while moving around me and checking the wounds.

I was reluctant to let the doctor take over, but I wasn't given much of a choice as strong hands grabbed me and pulled me back and away from my sister. I struggled against them before realizing they were supernaturally strong, then let myself get pulled away.

"All right, all right!" I snapped. "I get it. Let me go."

Surprisingly, the hands did, and I turned to find V and Heather behind me, furious, but watching Wren and Natalie with rapt attention. Wren glanced up at me, then to her wolves.

"Kill her."

"No!" Rias shouted. She moved to my side and roughly grabbed my arm.

"Step aside," V said quietly, like they didn't want to say it but didn't have a lot of choice. I looked at them, then at Rias, and lowered my head. It was the least I deserved.

"You can't kill her!"

"Like hell we can't," Wren snarled, glaring at Rias. "V, you know what to do."

"Rias, please," V said, looking uncomfortably between Rias and Wren.

"Vadi says she stays alive," Rias said. She pulled me by the arm. "She's going to come quietly, aren't you?"

I didn't respond. I only stared at the ground, wondering how everything had gone so damned wrong so quickly. My gaze fell on the fallen phone, the message only half typed out.

I pointed the phone out to Rias. "You should probably destroy that thing," I said softly, "otherwise the hunters might trace it."

She looked at me, alarm across her face, before repeating my words to V. They seemed more than happy to have the chance to crush something, as my phone was smashed underneath their heel. It surprised me when I let out a sigh of relief. I let Rias lead me away from the scene, feeling several sets of eyes more focused on me than on the wounded werewolf.

I didn't blame them, I decided, as I walked back toward the sheriff's station with my head hung low. I had no idea what the hell I was doing either. All I knew was that I'd almost killed my sister, twice, and I never wanted to be in that situation again.

Chapter Twenty-Three

Rias

"But how the hell did she get out of her cell?" Zeke roared, and I cringed.

"I told you already. She feigned an injury and hit me when I went in to check on her."

"And you let that happen?"

"I was worried about her!"

He shook his head. "I knew I shouldn't have left her alone with you. You're too involved with her."

"Considering I'm the only one around here who doesn't want to kill her, you're damned right that I'm too involved. I still care about her, no matter what happens."

"How could you stand up for a hunter against your own people?"

"She is my people. She's a good person, Zeke. You weren't there, you didn't see what she did."

"She shot her own damned sister!"

"Yeah, she did, and she stuck around and tried to help her too. Any other hunter would've just put more bullets into Natalie."

"I'm not talking about any other hunter. I'm talking about the one we have in our cells right now."

"She's not a threat to us," I insisted. I turned to Wren, who was sitting on the couch next to me. "Back me up here! You know she worked her ass off to keep Natalie alive."

We were back in the sheriff's office. Wren and I sat on the couch, while Zeke was pacing between the two desks. Ashly had returned to her cell peacefully, and apparently, I was not allowed to have a key to the cells for the time being.

"I don't know what I saw, exactly," Wren said softly, "but she did try to help Natalie after the gunshot went off. I don't understand why. But hearing you two arguing isn't exactly my idea of a good time. Where's Hikaru? She said she was on her way."

It was clear Wren didn't want to be here, and I didn't blame her. Dr. Maru—Hikaru—had insisted that she stay away from the doctor's office until she could be sure that Natalie would be okay. I wouldn't want the pregnant wolf underfoot while I worked on her mate, either. But it had to be hard for the werewolf not to go wild with worry about whether her mate was okay or not.

Zeke looked like he wanted to argue further but kept casting glances at Wren like he was afraid of upsetting her. For all that he was quick to admonish people, he had a particular love for the people of his town that made him a good sheriff, and a good friend when he wasn't angry about something. I owed him a lot, and not just because I worked under him.

"I'm sorry, Wren," I said softly. I knew the apology was too little, too late, and probably the last thing she wanted to hear right now.

"I don't care, Rias. I don't care how in love with this hunter you are, what she means to you, or what she did to help Natalie. She's a danger to all of us and needs to be dealt with."

"But, Wren—"

"But most of all, I blame you for this. I blame you for bringing her here and causing all of this. If Nat doesn't make it, it'll be your fault, Rias." She didn't look at me as she said the words that felt like a knife piercing my heart.

Nat was my best friend, Wren a close friend too. And those words were enough to bring my panic and anxiety to the forefront and I felt my magic start to roil. I pushed it down, because I didn't have a way to safely let it out right now. I fought to hold back the tears that threatened to fall. My fault. It was all my fault.

There was nothing I could say to her to make her feel some other way. I did feel responsible. Maybe if Wren knew that Nat would be okay, and given enough time, she'd forgive me, but right now I didn't want to make things worse, so I kept my mouth shut and sniffled quietly as I tried not to cry.

She had to be okay. Natalie had to pull through this. She had to.

The door to the office opened and Dr. Maru walked in, followed by Vadi. The vampire took a look around before her eyes settled on Wren, and she gave a soft smile.

"Natalie will be fine. She's in good shape and will be up and about again in a couple days."

I saw Wren all but physically deflate, as if she'd been preparing herself for the worst. "I want to see her."

"I'll take you when we're done here."

Wren tried to get up but had troubles. I stood and offered my hand, but she only stared at me with cold eyes until I backed away, once again rejected. She managed to lever herself off the couch and headed for Dr. Maru, but the doctor shook her head.

"I need to see the hunter. Check on her injury."

Wren opened her mouth, probably to argue, but Vadi was quicker. "While she lives as our captive, she will be treated well. That means checking on the wound that was given her."

Wren only nodded and pulled up a chair to sit in, something not as deep as the couch. She wouldn't argue with Vadi. No one argued with Vadi.

"Rias," Vadi said, as Dr. Maru disappeared with Zeke into the cells. "Come, talk with me."

They opened the door to the outside and waited patiently. I gave Wren one last look, but she refused to meet it. She kept her focus solely on the door to the cells and waited impatiently for Dr. Maru to return. I exited the building and felt Vadi right behind me.

"I am told that you fell for a very obvious ruse," they said, as the door behind them swung shut.

The afternoon sun was strong today, with few clouds in the sky to give some sort of relief from the heat of it. I denied my body's wish to just stare into the sun until it blinded me, in penance for what I'd done today, and turned to Vadi. I took in their crisp suit and immaculate appearance. They seemed unaffected by the heat of the day.

"It felt like the right thing to do at the time."

"And it led to Natalie getting shot and nearly killed."

I shook my head. "There's no way I could have known that would happen. I went into the cell to check on her. I didn't want her to be hurt from her wound."

"So you should have called the doctor instead of attempting to deal with it yourself."

I put my hands on my hips and glared at them. "Did you drag me out here just to blame me? Because I'm feeling pretty shitty about it all already, thanks."

"I do not mean to admonish, only to understand why this happened. It is my duty to protect the people of this town from the outside world. That goes for humans and supernatural folk. This sanctuary has been threatened before, but I have not had to step in overmuch. But if more hunters come, then that may change. I can only do so much. If danger comes, it will take all of us to push it back."

"I don't want that to happen, and neither does Ashly."

"Doesn't she? She did harm her own sister."

"She got spooked. She didn't mean to. Why can't anyone understand that?"

Vadi held up their hand in a placating gesture. "I did not bring you out here to argue with you. I merely want to warn you. You are too close with this hunter, and it is blinding you to the possibilities of what might happen. Imagine if it had been Wren, and not Natalie, who had been shot today. Do you think the puppy would have survived a silver bullet?"

My jaw dropped open. I had no words to argue with that. Hell, I hadn't even considered such a situation.

"She wouldn't have done that."

"No? How can you be so sure?"

There was nothing I could say to convince them. If Ashly could shoot her own sister, what would have stopped her from shooting a random werewolf, whether they were pregnant or not?

"I'll make sure she doesn't hurt anyone else." I moved to go back into the office, but Vadi moved in front of the door.

"No. You will go home. Take some time to think of where your loyalty lies—and if you can tear yourself away from this hunter."

Again my magic roiled inside, and I pushed it back down before it could burst out and embarrass me in front of Vadi. What the hell were they saying? That I had to either pick the town or Ashly?

Which would I choose?

But I didn't try to argue with them. Instead I headed for my car, which was still in the parking lot of the diner across the street. I shook my head as I got in. So much had happened in the past two days, I could barely keep track of it all. Maybe spending some time alone was a good idea. Get my priorities straight, figure out whose side I was on. And maybe, just maybe, figure out a way to appease everyone—without it ending in Ashly's death.

Chapter Twenty-Four

Ashly

I was about to consider eating the corner of the mattress when Zeke opened the door between the office and the cells, and the vampire doctor walked in. I sat primly on the cot with my hands on my lap, my feet flat on the floor, and did my best to show I was no threat to them. I'd made a mistake earlier, thinking that pulling that maneuver on Rias was a good idea. It only led to more confusion, more questions, and me nearly killing my sister.

But I'd found out I was going to be an aunt, so that was interesting. More interesting than a part of me wanted to admit. The part of me that still called Natalie a raving monster and insisted that she needed to be put down. That part of me that sounded exactly like my father, telling me what to do, demanding that I listen to him, and be exactly the person he wanted me to be. That voice seemed to be getting more frantic and more insistent the longer I was away from my father. But also easier to push aside.

And I wanted to push it aside. Like I did this morning, when I ran to help Natalie after shooting her. I hated myself for shooting her, even if I didn't completely mean to. I'd done what I could to save her, and hopefully she was going to be okay. But I couldn't quite forgive myself, and I could feel the anger and disgust for my father growing.

I was broken from my reverie by the sheriff unlocking my cell. He glared at me, a hand on his sidearm, like he was warning me without words that he would be more than happy to put me down if I made any wrong moves. Instead I stayed seated on the cot, even as the vampire came closer to me.

"I need to check your head wound," she said, her tone businesslike.

If I'd managed to impress her at all this morning, she didn't seem affected by it now.

"Is my sister all right?" The words tumbled out of my mouth before I could really think about them. My dad's voice in my head screamed that I shouldn't care, but it was being bullied to the side by my own thoughts and worries, and I needed to know if Natalie was okay.

"She'll live," was the cryptic answer. I supposed it was the best I was going to get from her.

"I…I didn't mean to shoot her."

"I find that hard to believe. You escaped from your cell by deceiving your girlfriend. And you went immediately to get a weapon loaded with silver bullets."

"I thought I needed to defend myself. To defend Rias." I shook my head. "I was raised to kill people like you."

"And how's that working out for you?"

"I don't know what I'm doing," I said, already feeling the tears start to come as the doctor gave me a skeptical look.

"You tried to kill one of the beloved daughters of this town. Twice now. You're lucky to be alive."

I sat still as she carefully removed the bandage and started poking around my head. I hissed in pain when her fingers touched the welt that was still swollen under my hair at the back of my head.

"It's healing well," she said softly, "the cut is almost scabbed over, so you shouldn't have to worry about blood too much. There doesn't seem to be any internal damage. How do you feel?"

"How do I feel?" I echoed. "I feel like I found out I had a sister, shot her, shot her again, tried to keep her alive despite her being a werewolf, and then found out I'm going to be an aunt in the space of like five minutes."

"I guess it's a time for self-reflection, huh?" she said dryly.

My chuckle was a little wet with tears, and I fell silent as she continued to poke and prod. I was used to care like this. When my mother would check on wounds when we were children, we stayed still or earned a smack upside the head. I didn't think the vampire would go that far, considering the head was where my wound was in the first place, but I didn't want to give her reason to even consider it.

"What did you mean yesterday when you called me a brainwashed hunter?" I asked cautiously.

She paused for a long moment. "You are not the first hunter I have met, but you certainly act the same as all of the others."

"I don't understand."

"He spouted the same rhetoric as you did. *All monsters are bad. Kill all the monsters. Wipe them out before they wipe out humanity.*"

"But there are monsters out there that hurt humans."

"There are also a lot of humans out there who hurt other humans. Where are the hunters then?"

"Well, that's what police are for."

"And when the police are the ones hurting others?"

I…had nothing to say to that. Even living under a rock like I did, I knew enough about the bullshit happening all over the place with so-called police officers making piss-poor decisions and getting away with murders. It was disgusting, pure and simple. But we hunters weren't the same as that—were we?

"We help protect humans," I said in a small voice, but there was no conviction in my tone.

"True, some of you do. Some of you have. But most of the time, you're killing innocent folk who are just trying to survive in this unhinged world, same as you."

"B-but my father said…" I trailed off. I should have known better than to listen to my father. I should have known he'd say anything he had to in order to make me feel like I had to be the person he wanted me to be. "Oh, I feel sick."

"Sick from your head or from your heart?" the vampire asked.

"Both? Neither? From my stomach, I think." I shook my head. "I don't know anymore. I don't know if I should listen to you or my father or nobody."

"What does your gut tell you?"

I stared at her, for the first time not avoiding those red eyes behind the purple glasses. "That I've been living a lie for years, and my father is to blame."

"We aren't all so bad, you know," she said softly. "I mean, look, I haven't even tried to bite you once."

The joke made me laugh—something I never thought would happen.

The vampire stepped back, seemingly satisfied with my health. "You'll be all right."

"And Natalie?" I asked again, hoping that she might give me something more than she had before.

She smiled at me. "You probably helped save her life. She'll be up and about in a couple of days. The bullet going through her was a blessing, otherwise the silver would have had more time to do a lot more damage."

I nodded. "I didn't mean to hurt her. I really didn't."

"You don't need to convince me of that."

I glanced to the sheriff. "Who do I need to convince?"

"That would be Wren. She wants to let you run free in the forest and run you down herself—which would be bad, because she isn't allowed to shift right now."

I looked down. "I don't blame her."

She headed for the door, but I heard her stop as the door slid open. "For what it's worth, a piece of advice: Stop blaming everything on your father."

I glanced up at her. "What?"

"It's time for you to step up and take direction of your own life. You can't do things and be blaming your parents anymore. You're not a child. Grow up."

I stayed seated on the cot as the vampire left, Zeke closing and locking the cell behind her. He gave me one parting glare before disappearing into the other room with her, and I was left alone once more. My stomach growled, reminding me that I'd kind of ruined my chance of eating something this morning. I did my best to push the hunger aside and closed my eyes.

The doctor was right. I had to stop blaming my father. Yes, he had a hand in…creating who I was, but I was the one who allowed it. I was the one who performed the actions, and I had to live with that. I'd shot Natalie—twice—and almost killed her. That was on me. Now I was done being that person. I was done being the tool of my parents.

It's not easy to change the way you think, especially after years of indoctrination. Sometimes it takes months of work to change one little thing. Other times, it can be as simple as one grand event that shocks the system and makes you realize that you've been wrong about things your entire life, no matter what you were taught. That's what happened this morning after I shot Natalie. That voice that told me she was a monster and deserved to be killed was now getting quieter and quieter. It no longer had the power to override what I really wanted to do. Maybe it was the idea of having a sister. Maybe it was the idea of being an aunt. Maybe it was just the idea of getting away from my parents. I couldn't say. All I knew was that I was starting to see my life in a different light—and I wasn't sure who I was anymore.

I thought about Rias too. I could see a bit better how she could let herself be surrounded by these monst—no, these people. It was going to be work to look past the fact that they weren't human. Maybe Rias had the right idea, being able to live around these people like they were just people. Good and bad. I shook my head slightly. I had to stop thinking of them as other. It wasn't fair to them. They had lives. Jobs. Wren ran a diner. The vampire was a doctor, of all things. A ghoul was their sheriff. And despite my actions, most of them had treated me with a certain amount of respect.

I didn't know what brought Rias to this town, but it was clear she was regarded highly by the supernatural community here. And with the way I felt about her, I didn't blame them. I'd come here to protect her, but she didn't need it. She was perfectly capable of defending herself—and if she couldn't, she had a damned army of werewolves that seemed to be pretty close to her.

At least she did before I showed up. I sighed. How much else was I going to ruin for her? Maybe they'd let me go if I promised not to breathe a word about them to the other hunters. I could tell my parents that I went after a girl, but it didn't work out. They'd probably be happy, tell me to go settle down with Marcus or one of the other hunters. The mere thought of that made me almost puke.

I didn't even want to return to my parents. Not now. Not when I knew they'd been lying to me. Their dogmatic bullshit determined everything they did, everything they believed. There was no way that anything different would ever be considered fair or good. No wonder my father did what he did to my sister. No wonder she felt her only choice was to run away. Now more than ever I wish she had found a way to take me with her. But that would have been worse for them. They probably figured losing one child was fine when they had a backup. Losing both their children at once? They'd never give up their chance to have some sort of legacy. That's what the hunters cared about. Leaving a legacy, making more hunters to kill innocent nonhumans.

"Damn it!" I snarled out loud, unable to hold the anger in any longer. Too long I followed my parents without question. Too long I let them dictate my life. No more. I was done with it.

And Rias? That was a question I couldn't answer. I still wanted her. I still wanted to be with her. She knew my secret now. Was it going to be too much for her, or would she be able to accept me as I was? A broken hunter?

I lay down on the cot and fought to find a comfortable way of lying that didn't hurt my head too much. I let Rias dance into my mind again and again, with the overarching question: Did she still want me? I couldn't even fathom a guess.

❖

I woke to a loud metallic clanging and grumbled something unintelligible under my breath. I tried my best to ignore the noise, but whoever was doing it was rather insistent.

"Go away, Sheriff," I said loudly.

"Is that any way to speak to someone who brings you breakfast?" Rias's voice filled the cell, and I all but jumped off the cot and spun around to see her. I hadn't seen her for three—no, four days now. Not since I broke out. I hadn't seen anyone but Zeke, and the odd visit from Dr. Maru, in that time, and I swear I had been starting to forget what Rias even looked like. Yeah, right.

I stared at her through the bars. She looked good. She was wearing her deputy uniform, dark shirt and dark pants, with an empty holster on her hip, plus the bulletproof vest. She wore it well. Very well. I realized then that I had a thing for women in uniform. Or at least for Rias in uniform. I won't deny that I leered for a good moment before I noticed she had a bag from the diner in her hands. She bent over and slipped it through the bars. My stomach growled but I largely ignored it, more focused on my girlfriend. Was she still my girlfriend?

"You look spiffy," I said. "What's the occasion?"

She shook her head. "I needed to get back to work. Just because there's a hunter in town shooting up werewolves doesn't mean I get to take an extra-long vacation."

Her tone was teasing but her mentioning what I'd done still touched a nerve. I did my best to shake it off, though. I'd spent the last few days getting used to the idea of having a sister—family—that were werewolves. I wondered over and over again if I could be welcomed after all I had done—if that was even a possibility. Most of all, I knew that I couldn't go back to my parents. Or at least, I didn't want to.

But I knew eventually they would come looking for me. If Ritten hadn't already told them where I was going, they'd find out sooner or later. Then the hunters would come and people would get hurt. Innocent people. I didn't want that. I didn't want Rias getting hurt, or Natalie, or even Wren or the vampire doctor, or any of the people I'd met here.

Except maybe Zeke. He could probably stand to be knocked down a peg or two.

"I'm sorry, Rias," I said, realizing the silence between us had become kind of awkward.

"Don't, Ashly."

"Why not? I am sorry for what I did. I never wanted to hurt you. And honestly, I feel terrible for what I did to Natalie."

"It's not entirely your fault. But there's a lot you need to work through."

"I know. And I am. I promise." I stepped closer to the bars, reaching out to touch Rias's fingers, curled around the bars. But she stepped back, away from me.

I tried not to let the pain of rejection show on my face, but I don't think I did a good job of it.

"It's not enough, Ashly. Natalie and Wren are beloved around here. Nat's my best friend, for fuck's sake. And you shot her. You hurt me and earned Wren's anger."

"I know, but there's nothing I can do but say sorry."

"It's not good enough. Because I stuck up for you. I spoke up for you, spoke up against killing you. I risked my neck for you because I trusted you, and you did nothing but break that trust."

"I thought I was doing the right thing. I thought you were…I don't know, trapped here or something. Being kept against your will, a pet human for the monst—nonhumans. I thought it was best to contact the hunters and tell them where I was."

"And did you?"

I shook my head. "No. Natalie interrupted me while I was typing the text."

"Why didn't you call?"

"I thought it would take longer to call than to text."

She chuckled and I smiled, wrapping my hands around the bars. I wanted her to come closer, so I could touch her, feel her, make sure I wasn't imagining things after being trapped in this cell for days. But most of all I just wanted the closeness that I missed from the last time we were together—when our secrets were a barrier between us. Now the secrets were out, but the barrier was still there.

"So, you know my secret now."

She gave me a small smile. "I guess I do. Why didn't you tell me before?"

"Oh, you have no idea how much I wanted to. I was desperate

to tell you, honestly. But I was afraid that you'd think I was out of touch with reality, telling you that there were such things as shifters and vampires and ghouls. I had no idea that you already knew about them."

"Looking at it from that perspective, I kind of understand why you didn't say anything."

"I was going to tell you when I got back to the hotel room. My father would've been pissed about it, but I don't even care anymore. I don't care about what he wants anymore. I know what I want. I know *who* I want."

I thought that would do it, have her running into my arms—as much as we could with the bars between us. Instead she took a step further away, her eyebrows furrowed, her smile turned into a frown.

"But you barely know me."

"We've spent the last year talking," I said. "I know you better than I know myself. Especially of late."

"You don't understand."

"What do I need to understand? I really like you, Rias. I want to make this work between us. And I don't mean keeping with this long-distance stuff. I want to be with you. For real."

She rubbed her hands over her face, looking almost panicked by my admission. Shouldn't she be happy? Did she not feel the same way?

"What were you hunting that night?" she asked suddenly.

"That night?" I echoed. "I told you the other day. My father and I were after a witch."

"And you said your father killed her. Right?"

I nodded slowly, unsure of where this was going. "I was talking to her, threatening her. My father shot her in the back."

She made a sound that could have been something like a sob. When she looked back at me, there were tears in her eyes.

"Did she tell you her name?"

"I…no. No, she didn't."

"It was Brigid."

"What?"

"Her name. Was Brigid. She was a friend of mine."

My heart sank and I went with it, falling to my knees on the cold concrete. "I didn't know," I said softly. "I swear, I had no idea."

"Would it have mattered to you?"

I started to say, of course, but stopped. She deserved the truth. Always the truth. "That night? Not as much as I'd like. Now? Yes, very much."

She squatted down in front of the bars until she could look me in the eye. She still had unshed tears pooling around her lower lids, but her voice was strong with conviction.

"And I'm supposed to trust you now? When you hunted my friends? Killed one in another city, and then came here and almost killed another? And you think I can just…what? Wipe the slate clean and go running into your arms?"

My mouth dropped open as I sputtered, trying to find something redeeming to say. She was right again. After everything I had done, had I really expected her to just fall into my arms like a lovesick puppy? I needed to prove to her that I'd changed.

"I'm sorry, Rias. I'm working on changing, I truly am. I want a different life. Not the one my father has planned for me, but one of my own. That I choose. With the woman that I love."

"Ashly…"

"I'm sorry, Rias. I'm sorry for what I've done since I came here. But I'm not sorry for coming here. I'm not sorry, because it meant that I got to be with you—more or less."

She stood up and stepped back away from the bars again. and I watched her, and wondered what was going through her mind. She wrapped her arms around herself as if she needed the comfort. Damn, I wanted to be the one to hold her instead.

"You…you love me?"

I nodded, almost frantically, as I stood up and pressed myself to the bars. "I do. I have for a while—I just didn't want to admit it."

"But you don't know who I am."

"I don't care. It can't be worse than being a werewolf, could it?"

She was quiet for a long moment.

"It's not worse than shifting into an animal once in a while, right?"

She turned toward me with a stern look on her face, and I swallowed hard, wondering what exactly I was in for. Then she raised her hand, palm up, and suddenly a floating ball of light appeared, hovering over her palm. I stared at the light for a long moment, then looked to her face, which showed signs of her fear.

"You're a witch…" I murmured. And then things started clicking into place. Why Brigid had Rias's number, why she fit in with all these nonhumans. I stared at the ball of light for a long moment before she closed her hand and the light disappeared. Before she could pull away, I reached out between the bars and took her hand, pulling it and her closer to me, until I could kiss her fingers gently.

"But I'm a witch," she said softly, like she was uncomfortable with the idea.

I kissed her fingers again and again, trying to show my love for her with every touch. I didn't care that she was a witch. Hell, it made things more interesting. I was done being scared of the supernatural. I wanted to learn more about them. Have a life with them instead of hunting them down. A life with Rias, in particular.

I smiled. "I think, given time, this is still a hand I would love to fuck myself on."

The way the blush crept up her cheeks was beautiful to see, and she gently took her hand back from me. I wanted to reach out and keep it, but I gave her the distance I felt she needed.

"I…I love you too, you know." She hugged herself again, as if ready for an argument or something from me. Instead I gave her the biggest smile I could manage, trying to convey all my feelings for her into something as simple as that.

"I do now."

She shook her head as if to clear it. "But I can't let you out just because you profess your love for me."

"I know."

"Then why do it now?"

"Because I want to show you that I'm changed. I'm not the person my parents want me to be. Not anymore. I'm done with them. Done with all of that. I want to stay here. Be with you. Be an aunt—if Natalie and Wren can ever forgive me." I pushed away from the bars to pace the cell a little. Yes, I wanted out of the damned thing, but I could be patient. Especially if it meant I got to stay with Rias.

"Really? This isn't another ruse?"

"I promise."

She bit her lip in the cutest way possible. "Then I need you to answer a question for me."

"Anything, beautiful."

"How did your dad know that Brigid was in Calgary? She was there to meet me."

I raised an eyebrow and tried to remember back to what my father had told me. "We got a tip from another witch that we work with from time to time. He helps the hunters, and in return we don't hunt him." I laughed lightly. "Hell, he was the one who told me to come here for you."

She froze, and I wanted to wipe the look of anguish off her face with soft kisses.

"What's this witch's name?"

"Ritten. Eric Ritten."

"Son of a bitch!" The words exploded out of her, and I swear the building shook. Without even looking at me, she was gone through the door to the office.

"Hey!" I called out, confused. "Hey! What's going on? Hey, come on! Talk to me!"

But no one came back in, so I grabbed the almost forgotten sack of diner food, sat back down on my cot, and tried to be patient again. She'd come back. I hoped she'd come back.

I needed her to.

CHAPTER TWENTY-FIVE

Rias

“I’m telling you, this isn’t over,” I said, slamming a hand down on the desk.

“There haven’t been any newcomers to town in the four days we’ve held the hunter. They’re not coming for her,” Zeke said, reclining in his chair.

Vadi put a hand on his shoulder, shushing him. “What makes you think that there is more to come?”

“This isn’t just about the hunters,” I said, “it involves a witch too. It’s Eric Ritten.”

Natalie and Wren looked at each other, alarmed. Both wolves looked exhausted but present, sitting on the couch together. Dr. Maru sat in a chair beside the couch, keeping an eye on both wolves. Her expression didn’t change with my proclamation. Zeke snorted, arms over his chest like he didn’t believe me, while Vadi, standing beside Zeke, looked at me quizzically.

“Who is Eric Ritten?”

“He’s a powerful witch that’s working with the hunters in Calgary. He came after me last year when I went to the convention. He wants my magic, to make himself even more powerful.”

“That’s a thing that can happen?” Natalie asked.

I nodded. “It’s a forbidden magic, but it’s possible. The covens outlawed it, but something tells me that Ritten doesn’t care.”

“That may explain an attempted incursion some months ago,” Vadi said, and we all turned to look at them. “Someone powerful attempted to gain entrance into our territory. I was able to repel them, but it was difficult. They were quite strong.”

"That has to be Ritten. I knew he wouldn't just give up after the convention, but I haven't seen him since."

"Maybe he just thought of a different way to get to you," Natalie offered.

I shrugged. "If he couldn't get through Vadi, I wouldn't be surprised if he sent his pet hunters here."

"Does that have anything to do with your girlfriend in the cells?" Zeke demanded.

"No. No way. Ashly wouldn't work for a witch. She knew him enough to know that the hunters worked with him, but…" I trailed off, remembering what she said. That he'd told her to come here to find me. What was his game plan, doing that?

"If Ritten is on his way here, we need to protect my pack," Wren said, her eyes boring into me with a mixture of anger and frustration. I wanted to tell her this wasn't my fault, but more and more it was kind of feeling like it was. "I won't let any of my wolves be hurt by him again."

Vadi started to say something, then froze. They straightened up and turned their head to the side, as if they were looking at something that no one else could see. They seemed to shake it off after a few seconds, then looked at us like nothing had happened.

"Zeke, bring the hunter in here. We will talk with her."

"I don't like this idea," he said, but he got out of his chair and went into the cells.

"Thank you, Vadi," I said, grateful that someone was listening to me.

"Do not thank me. A large group of people have entered the territory. I worry that these are the hunters that you warn us about."

Genius Loci, the words echoed in my head. A guardian spirit, powerful enough to feel when people enter and exit their territory. To have that kind of power seemed entirely unreal.

"Did you feel Ritten with them?"

They shook their head. "There is no one with power amongst them that I can sense."

Zeke returned with Ashly in tow, her wrists bound with handcuffs and his hand clamped down on her shoulder. The moment she saw me, she tried to come straight toward me, but Zeke forced her to sit in the chair in front of his desk.

"Get up from that chair for any reason and Wren will eat you," Zeke said, nodding to Wren, who bared her teeth at Ashly. I shook my head at the theatrics. There was no way Wren would eat Ashly. At least, not right now. She wouldn't endanger the baby by shifting like that.

"I'm not going anywhere," Ashly replied with more confidence than I expected. If the tension of the room bothered her, she didn't let it show. "What do you need from me?"

"Tell us what you know about Eric Ritten and the rest of your hunters," Zeke said.

She nodded. "I don't know a lot about Ritten really. He's a witch, and he works with the hunters. He lets them know about witches and other supernatural people to hunt, and in return they let him help. At least that what he says. My parents don't really trust him, but I think my dad views him as a necessary evil." She paused for a moment, then added, "He's also the one who told me to come here after Rias when I thought she was in trouble."

"Why send a single hunter here?"

"Your guess is as good as mine. Maybe to test your defenses, to cause confusion regarding my relationship with Rias. I don't know. But I do know I name-dropped Rias before I left to come here. He must've known who I was talking about."

"Why did you tell him that?" I asked.

"I needed to talk to someone about it, and he was there. And he was being overly nice. I didn't consider it might be for less than savory reasons." She raised her hands, cuffed together, and brushed a strand of hair off her face.

"What about the other hunters?" Zeke demanded.

"What do you want to know about them? I mean, there's Marcus, who is kind of a dipshit, but he's basically the next in line to lead the hunters after my father retires. He likes long walks on the beach and getting caught in the rain."

Natalie snorted and I had to fight to keep the laughter inside as Zeke looked like he was going to have a fit.

"You said you'd be helpful."

"I am being helpful. What do you want me to say about the hunters? Most of them are trained from youth to fight and shoot and survive. Those who come into it later are sometimes even stronger in their convictions, having lost a loved one or found out about the supernatural in some terrible way. They will kill anyone who they think is not human, or they will try their damnedest to do so. And more often than not, they succeed." She looked around the room, her eyes finding each and every one of us until they landed on me. "I used to think it was because they were just that good. But now I think the reason is because the person they're hunting doesn't want to hurt anyone and avoids using their abilities."

"She's not wrong," Dr. Maru said. "If they really are coming here, we're going to have to kill them all. Otherwise they will keep coming. They won't quit."

"I'll call in the pack," Wren said, reaching for her phone. Natalie straightened up and turned toward me.

"Can we count on you and your magic?" The words were said softly, but it still caused all eyes in the room to turn to me. I paled under their stares, unsure even of what I should say.

Should I tell them the truth? That I'm not sure how effective I'll be? Or pretend that nothing is wrong, and tell them I could handle all the hunters if I wanted to? Which was not a reality, really. It wasn't like I didn't know how to use my magic to fight. I learned basics in combat back in the covens. It was that I'd never really had the need to do it—save for when Ritten attacked me in the parking garage. Even then, I was surprised that I got out of there alive.

"I don't know," I replied, my eyes on the floor. "I don't know if I have enough control, if I'm strong enough."

"When you first came here you swore to use your magic to protect the people of this town," Vadi said. "Is that still something you are willing to do?"

"Y-yes, of course I'm willing to. I just…I don't know how effective I'll be."

"You got this, beautiful," Ashly said with a smile. I looked at her, and for a second it was like there was no one else in the room, just the two of us. I wanted this moment to last forever.

It didn't.

A second later someone's phone started blaring incessantly. We all turned toward Wren, who had just tucked her phone away. It was ringing loudly, and she looked almost embarrassed as she fumbled it back out of her pocket and tapped the screen.

"It's a video call," she muttered. "From Heather at the diner."

"Answer it," Vadi said.

Wren tapped on the screen again.

"Hey, Wren, you there?" Heather's voice came through the connection.

"Yeah, Heather, you've got all of us. What's up?"

"There's some people in the parking lot that I don't think are going to be loyal customers."

"What do you mean?"

"I mean they're really interested in that hunter's car—and they're badly hiding some rather large guns."

"Yeah, that sounds like Marcus and his crew," Ashly said.

"What? Who's that?"

"Never mind, Heather," Wren said, shooting Ashly a dirty look. "Just stay calm, play human, and keep your head down. Tell V to be ready for anything. I already called Cale, and he's getting the pack together. We'll be there soon to deal with them."

"Should I lock up the diner?"

Wren looked to Vadi, who nodded.

"If you can do it without drawing attention to yourself, then do it. Get anyone else in the diner to the kitchen and keep them safe."

"And V?"

Wren hesitated. "Tell them to wait until someone else makes the first move, then do what they do best."

"Got it, Alpha."

The phone went dead, and Wren started to stand but lost her balance and fell back on the couch. "We need to get out there."

"You are not going anywhere," Vadi said. "I will make sure this battle does not boil over to the others in this town. We will keep it contained here and at the diner. Send your wolves in when first contact is made."

"Who's going to confront them?" Wren demanded.

"I'll go," I said. "Me and Zeke. At least we look all official-like in our uniforms. Maybe we can get them to leave peacefully."

"I'm not going to let my wolves get killed while I sit here twiddling my damned thumbs."

"Love," Natalie said softly, "you can't shift so close to your due date. You would be in such danger out there, and the puppy too. I don't think either of us would be much help to the others."

"But I can't just sit here."

"They understand. They want to see this puppy as much as we do. They will understand."

"Neither of you are in a condition for this battle," Vadi said. "Hikaru, scout the situation without being seen." Dr. Maru nodded, then shed her white coat and glasses, leaving her in a black tank top and dark jeans. I'd never really noticed it before, but damn, was the doctor ripped. I almost swooned over her arms. "The rest of you, wait for the fog."

"What?" I said. "The fog?"

Vadi didn't answer. Instead they turned and headed for the back door that led to the private lot where our couple of squad cars were parked. Dr. Maru slipped out the front door and all but disappeared, and Zeke and I kind of looked at each other.

"Shall we?" Zeke said, nodding to the door. I took a deep breath and tried to calm myself enough to stay casual, then nodded. I stopped by the door, realizing that Ashly was still sitting primly in her chair.

"What about Ashly?"

"We'll be fine," Natalie said quickly, before Wren could snarl something. "She'll stay in the chair until you get back. Won't you, Ashly?"

Ashly gave a sloppy salute, raising both hands. "Yes, ma'am."

Zeke's gaze lingered on Ashly for a long moment, but he opened the door and gestured to me. I didn't keep him waiting.

"Are you ready for this?" he asked softly as we headed for the highway.

"Nope."

"Then you should stay behind."

"Not a chance."

We crossed the highway and idly made our way toward the diner, acting as if we were heading there for lunch or something. I felt the eyes of the newcomers on us as soon as we started across the parking lot. There were at least ten of them, wearing heavy coats that must've been sweltering in the springtime sun. Most of them were hanging around the vehicles parked a couple lanes back from the diner entrance, but four of them seemed really interested in Ashly's car.

"Good morning, gentlemen," Zeke said loudly. "Is there something we can help you with? I believe the diner is closed today—private party."

One of the men stepped forward, a shorter man with dark hair buzzed close to his head. His coat bulged awkwardly, like he was wearing a shoulder holster and hadn't bought a jacket that could hide it well.

"We're looking for a friend of ours," he said calmly, hands in his jacket pockets. I clenched my hands at the word *friend* coming out of his mouth. "This is her car, but we can't seem to locate her."

"The owner of this car is currently in one of our jail cells. She was arrested for shooting one of our diner staff." I had no idea how Zeke was remaining so damned calm in the face of this asshole.

The hunter looked back at his friends, as if sharing a silent conversation of some sort. They started to spread out, almost as if they were going to surround us. I tried my best to keep my eyes on them.

And then the fog rolled in.

Anyone with sense could see it wasn't something natural. It covered the diner and created something like a barrier that blocked off the rest of the town, leaving only the parking lot, part of the highway, and the sheriff's office from what I could see. Everything else was covered in a thick, gray fog.

The hunters were not oblivious. The leader turned back to us with a snarl on his lips, pulling a small pistol out of his jacket pocket. I reached for my magic, but I wasn't quick enough. The gun went off and Zeke fell backward.

"It's a trap!" the hunter shouted and I swung my arms sideways, kicking up enough force to throw all four of them back into the parking lot and toward their friends.

A scream from that crowd drew my eye, and I saw a shadowy figure latch itself onto one of the hunters and bury its face into their neck. He went down like a brick and the figure disappeared into the shadows as the hunters turned, drawing their weapons.

The hunters I hit with my magic got to their feet, pulling out whatever weapons they had on them. Mostly a collection of pistols and shotguns, and a couple with long rifles. Nothing of the assault variety, thankfully. Two of them turned my way and hefted their weapons, and I pushed power into the air in front of me, forcing it to essentially harden until it could stop bullets. They roared their inadequacies into the wind just in time for the first wolf howl to echo out of the fog.

Several larger-than-life wolves burst from the fog, sprinting toward the hunters. Weapons swung toward the newcomers, and I pushed power into the air again, forming another shield low enough to protect the werewolves until they could reach the hunters, who couldn't seem to understand why their weapons seemed ineffective. The leader turned to me, noticing my hand movements and the fact that I hadn't drawn my gun yet, and twisted his pistol to point at me.

"Witch!" he screamed, then fired the weapon, and I hit the ground. I felt a burning sensation on my upper arm. My uniform was ripped, and blood was staining the fabric as I scrambled back toward Ashly's car, using it for cover.

I tried to take a deep breath as more bullets pinged around the vehicle and more gunshots echoed through the air. I heard a wolf whine and another hunter scream as shouts of "Vampire!" meant that Dr. Maru was getting in on the action. Panic started to overcome me when I heard another whine, and I began to fear that it wouldn't be enough. Maybe we couldn't stand against the hunters. What if they killed all of us?

"No, damn it!" I tried to shake those thoughts out of my head. We'd make it through this. There were more of us than them, and as I tried to think of what to do next, I saw Zeke sit up, eyes glowing red and mouth opening wider than a human mouth had any right to. He let a guttural screech out into the sky and leapt to his feet, tearing into the hunters.

Well, then, I couldn't let him show me up.

I stood up from my hiding spot and drew forth more magic, weaving together a ball of power just above the hunters. As I poured more and more power and will into it, the silvery ball of magic began to pulsate. The hunters nearest the sphere suddenly lost their grip on their weapons as they were drawn upward into my magnetic spell. I poured a bit more power into it, shifting their vehicles and even toppling one over onto one of the hunters that Dr. Maru had knocked down.

Their leader focused on me again, seeing what was happening to his hunters, and he fired again. I ducked and cut off my magic from the sphere, instead taking what I could and weaving it into a new shape, like a shovel. With one massive swipe of my hands, a blast of air and force picked him up like a child's shovel picks up sand. He screamed as he was tossed into the air and thrown across the parking lot, across the highway, and toward the sheriff's station. I heard the glass shatter and felt my heart stutter. I'd just tossed a hunter into a building with an ex-hunter, a wounded werewolf, and a pregnant werewolf.

I started to head across the street but stopped when I saw a couple of wolves on the pavement. The remaining hunters had retrieved their weapons and formed something of a phalanx to prevent even Zeke and Dr. Maru from getting at them. I snarled as one of them took a potshot in my direction and called forth more power, kneeling and pushing the magic into the ground at my feet and envisioning the asphalt splitting in a massive crack. What happened in my mind happened in real life as a small crack appeared in the parking lot, becoming larger and larger as it reached for the hunters and their vehicles. By the time it reached them, it was large enough that three of the hunters fell into the crack with terrified screams and the others were scattered, giving the wolves and everyone else time to push back against them.

I stayed kneeling on the ground as I pulled as much power back into myself as I could, trying not to waste too much, and surveyed the destruction. The crack slammed closed, cutting off the screams of the hunters that had fallen, and I swallowed the bile that rose in my throat. There'd be time to think about what I'd done later. Right now, I had to make sure Ashly was okay. I got up and stumbled my way across the parking lot, confident now that the wolves et al had the hunters dead to rights.

I was halfway across the highway when someone new stepped into my path. I didn't even bother to look at them, I just swiped my hand and used far too much force to bat them out of the way. I didn't care. I needed to get to Ashly. I needed to know she was okay.

It was my turn to take care of her.

Chapter Twenty-Six

Ashly

I turned to Wren and Natalie the moment Zeke was out the door. I held up my hands. "I don't suppose you'd be kind enough to take these off?" I nodded to the handcuffs still adorning my beautifully dainty—yeah, right—wrists.

"Not a chance," Wren snarled. From the way she was looking at me, I was certain that Zeke's warnings about her eating me weren't without merit.

"Love," Natalie said soothingly, "she's not going to hurt us."

"That's what you said before. Twice. And both times she shot you!"

I shook my head. "For one, I don't have a gun. Secondly, I'm never going to live that down, am I?"

"I will never let you forget it."

I wasn't sure if that was a warning or the beginnings of a fun family anecdote for us to tell at the holidays. I was hoping for the latter. I started to say something else when the gunfire began, and I had to resist the urge to get out of the chair and head for the window to keep an eye on Rias. Yes, she was wearing a vest. Yes, she was a witch. But she was mine. My love. I wanted to protect her, and I couldn't do that from here.

"This fucking sucks," I snarled, and for the first time I think Wren actually agreed with me. Especially when the wolves started howling and Wren's face went cold. She jerked a couple times, as if she could feel whatever was happening to her wolves out there, and Natalie pulled her in closer, wrapping strong arms around her as if to keep her safe.

Screams and shouts were punctuated by gunshots and other noises that made it feel like someone in the next room was watching an action movie at full volume. I started to get up from the chair, but Wren turned toward me and growled, and I sat back down. I was not in the mood to anger her. At least not yet.

Then something came flying through the front window, showering us in glass. I brought my arms up to protect my face and hissed at the small cuts the broken glass caused. Something in the debris groaned and I did stand up this time, if only to see who was over there. I recognized Marcus in an instant as he turned his head and looked at me. His eyes lit up with recognition through the bloody mask that was his face after going through the window, but he managed to push himself to his feet and I watched as he started to draw his pistol from a shoulder holster inside his jacket.

"Traitor!" he roared, pointing the gun toward me. I was already moving, though, as I bent over and grabbed the chair I'd been sitting in and swung it into the air, tossing it at him. It smashed him into the wall, and I launched myself over the desk hands first to tackle him back to the ground. His gun went spinning away as I rained two-handed blows to his upper body, but he managed to get his hands between him and me and push me off him. I slipped on the debris and went down with him on top of me, his hands going for my throat.

I tore at his fingers, digging my nails into his nail beds and doing everything I could think of to loosen his grip, but he managed to keep it tight enough that I couldn't get him off me. I almost hoped that Wren or Natalie would intervene, but I wasn't even sure they knew what was going on. I scrabbled my hands across the ground, searching for some sort of weapon. I grabbed a long shard of glass and felt it bite into my palm as I gripped it tight and shoved it as hard as I could into Marcus's side. He reared back with a ferocious cry as I took the glass in a two-handed grip and shoved it farther into him. I took a deep, gulping breath and bucked him the rest of the way off me and scrambled backward, ignoring the line of blood on the ground from my hands. Marcus stared at me with cold, hard eyes before he teetered and then fell backward, going still upon the ground.

I reached out for the desk and used it to climb to my feet. I was panting heavily, blood all over my hands and arms, as I turned to Wren.

"Sorry I got out of the chair," I said.

She stared at Marcus, her eyes flickering from the body to the gun still on the ground. "I think in this case you're forgiven."

I opened my arms—awkwardly, as my wrists were still cuffed—

and invited her in for a hug, but she just gave me a blank look. I guess we weren't that far in our relationship yet, but I could be patient.

More cries sounded from outside, louder now with the window gone, and I turned, watching a figure dart across the highway toward the station.

"Rias!" I shouted, waving to her through the window. I didn't have a clue if she heard me, but she didn't stop until she reached the door and almost pulled the damned thing off its hinges. She charged into the room ready for war, blood dripping from a wound on her arm, but she stopped dead when she saw Marcus bleeding out on the floor and me standing by the door.

"Ashly? Are you okay?"

I nodded and ran forward, not caring that I was covered in blood, both my own and Marcus's. I lifted my arms over her head and put them around her neck, pulling her into an awkward hug. She dug into her pockets and pulled out a handcuff key, laughing as I tried to untangle the metal chain from her hair. She unlocked the handcuff on one wrist, and we got to hold each other properly, clutching each other like we never wanted to let go. And I didn't. I wanted to hold her forever, to apologize for all of this and just be with her forever. I wanted my Rias. Witch or not. Hunter or not. This was where I was meant to be. In her arms.

Suddenly Rias was ripped from my arms and thrown across the room. I spun, looking around for what was going on, and saw a newcomer in the doorway.

"Ritten!" I shouted, freezing at the sight of the witch. He was wearing that stupid leather trench coat and had the widest grin on his face, showing off that stupid gold tooth of his. "What the fuck are you doing here?"

"What do you mean, Ashly? I'm just here to rescue you." He laughed. "Or am I here for your little friend instead?"

Natalie snarled and pulled a partial shift. Fur erupted on parts of her body and the wound on her stomach started trickling blood. She leapt at Ritten, claws out, but he waved a hand, and she halted in midair, unable to move. He spared her a glance.

"I would have thought your wolf friends would've warned you that I have a certain…expertise when it comes to shifters." He shook his head, then flicked his fingers. Natalie went flying into the far wall, hard enough to crack the drywall and a couple of the studs. Wren growled at Ritten but looked to her mate, then down at her own hands. Fur was starting to sprout on them.

"Wren, no!" I shouted, throwing myself at Ritten like I had at Marcus. Ritten waved a hand as if trying to smack me down like he'd done to Rias. I felt a wave of force flow over me, but I cut through it like a wing cuts through air currents and tackled Ritten to the ground. I smashed my fist into his face, then wrapped the hanging handcuff around my other hand and used it as a makeshift brass knuckle, bashing him in the nose and chin before he managed to push me off.

He got up as quickly as I did and stared at me for a long moment, eyes searching mine as if questioning why his magic didn't work on me.

"Leechstone," he growled. "I should have known."

He waved a hand again and the chair I'd thrown at Marcus lifted into the air and launched itself at me. I threw myself to the side and rolled to my feet, picking up Marcus's fallen gun in the process. I stood and fired three times at Ritten, but he waved his hand again and the bullets seemed to hit some sort of invisible shield in front of him.

"Shit," I said, throwing myself to the ground again as he found more debris to launch at me. I took a piece of glass to the leg and hissed sharply against the pain, but it would take a lot more than that to keep me down.

The same seemed to go for Rias, who finally shook off the initial attack and got up, waving her hands in a fluid motion and unleashing something I could only sense as it passed over me and hit Ritten squarely in the chest, throwing him back out the window.

"Wren!" I ran to the werewolf and took her hands. "You can't shift like this, remember?"

"B-but Natalie."

I shook my head. "Take care of her. We'll take care of Ritten."

It took her a moment, but slowly she seemed to come back to herself, and she nodded. "Kill him, or I *will* eat you."

"Promises, promises."

Rias was already at the door by the time I joined her, holding the pistol from Marcus. She looked to me for a moment and opened her mouth, but I shook my head at her.

"I'm coming with you. I've got some payback to deliver for using me like this."

"Keep your necklace on."

"I plan to."

I followed her out of the station, finger on the trigger and ready to fire. I had her back. I would protect her as best I could and let her do her thing. Even if I didn't fully understand it.

Ritten was outside in the parking lot around the station, standing on the asphalt as if he didn't have a care in the world.

"What the hell do you expect to gain from this, Ritten?" I said, aiming the pistol at him.

He shook his head. "You really don't get it, do you? You think you're the important one here? You've been nothing but a pawn to me since the moment we met."

"What are you talking about?"

"Who do you think led the hunters here? Who told you to come here and cause chaos? I was kind of hoping they'd kill you because then I wouldn't have to do it myself, but c'est la vie."

"But why are you here?"

"For her." He pointed at Rias, who was watching Ritten closely, her hands moving as if preparing an attack or defense, I couldn't tell. "She's the only one who matters to me. And you were so kind to help prepare my arrival."

"How?"

"By making sure the hunters would come looking for you. By causing chaos and taking out most of the defenses this town had. But most of all, because you and the hunters have kept that pesky guardian spirit of this town busy enough that they're not going to be an issue for me." He laughed aloud. "I should really thank you. I don't think it would have gone so well if it wasn't for you."

I glared at him. "The hunters are dead. You failed."

He shrugged. "They were expendable. Like I said, your girlfriend is the only one I want."

"Then come and get me," Rias snapped. She suddenly wound up and threw something like she was a major league pitcher. Whatever it was burst into flames the moment it left her hand and flew at Ritten. He twisted, flaring the trench coat and using the heavy leather to take the splash of flame. It died almost immediately, and Ritten only laughed.

"Is that all you've got, little one? I've felt your power. I know you have so much more in you."

"Shut up!" Rias screamed. She wound up and threw another fire-ball, but this time Ritten moved his hands in a similar motion, catching the ball and throwing it back at us. I threw myself to the ground and rolled, coming up with the pistol in a strong grip. I fired again, trying to keep track of how many rounds were left in the weapon as I did. The bullet hit his trench coat but seemed to have the same amount of effect as it would hitting a bulletproof vest. I swore and tried to find a better angle to aim at something more vital—and stay out of Rias's way.

The witches continued flinging magic at each other and I punctuated their attacks with the odd gunshot, trying to take Ritten in the leg or the arm or even the head. A bullet grazed his hand and his attention turned to me. He snarled and lifted a hand, his magic working not against me but on one of the concrete parking curbs. It lifted into the air and swung toward me, and I ducked underneath, then fired at his outstretched hand.

A second swing of the curb caught me hard in the back and I cried out, thrown across the asphalt. I heard something small hit the ground and I put a hand to my neck—the necklace had broken in the fall.

The moment I noticed it, Ritten did too. He grinned that savage grin of his and waved a hand and suddenly I couldn't move, I couldn't control myself. I was lifted into the air, unable to even bring the gun up to shoot the fucker in the face, and brought closer to him.

"No!" Rias shouted. "This is between us, leave her alone!"

He flexed his fingers, and I cried out in pain as my limbs started bending the wrong direction, slowly, painfully, and I screamed and screamed.

"Fuck…you…Ritten," I snarled through gritted teeth. He answered by forcing my limbs back further, and I cried out.

"Stop!" Rias screamed.

"Only if you give me what I came for."

"Don't…" I managed to say before the pain was too much and I cried out again.

"Okay!" Rias said. "Okay. It's yours. It's all yours."

A second later I collapsed to the ground, barely able to move. I ached everywhere, the pain lingering especially in the tortured joints that were forced to bend in ways they weren't supposed to. I flopped around on the ground for a second before I could see what was happening.

Rias was on her knees before Ritten, who had his hand on her face. I could see whatever power was inside her flickering across her body, slowly being siphoned up by Ritten.

"No!" I shouted, but it came out as a hoarse whisper as my throat constricted on the word.

"Not this time, my dear. Be good until I'm done, yeah? Then I'll deal with you myself."

"R-Rias!"

I saw her head twitch, like she was trying to look at me. "It's okay, Ashly. It's okay. I promise."

"F-f-fuck that!" I fought through the pain and grabbed the gun that had fallen when he'd picked me up. I rolled onto my stomach, my arms out in front of me, taking careful aim. Then I fired.

The gun clicked empty.

I screamed my frustration to the sky. Then there was a blur of movement behind Ritten and Dr. Maru emerged from a nearby shadow, her eyes blood-red with red ink-like stains spreading across her face. She moved too quickly to see. One moment she was in the shadows, the next she was on Ritten's back, her face nestled in the crook of his neck, as she rode him down to the ground.

He was quick, though, and with a wave of his hand Dr. Maru was ripped from him and tossed bodily through the window of the sheriff's station and into the back wall. It wasn't much of a distraction, but it was enough.

As Rias started to get to her feet, Ritten was right beside her, his back to me, getting ready to continue his siphon. I got to my feet slowly—partly to do it silently and partly because my body wasn't moving entirely well. I wrapped the one handcuff around my hand once more and pushed myself harder than I'd ever pushed myself before, taking the last few steps toward them at a run and leaping onto Ritten's back. I slammed my fist into the back of his head over and over again, taking him down over top of Rias.

"No!" he shouted, struggling to get his hands free from underneath him as I kept up my assault. It wasn't long before I was flung off him like the vampire had been, only he used his magic to slam me back down on the asphalt. I cried out and coughed up something warm and metallic, my body going suddenly numb.

"Ashly!" Rias screamed, and I watched her get to her feet, swaying as if a little woozy. She stared at Ritten with a dangerous gleam in her eyes. "You want power, Ritten? I'll give you power!"

I don't know what kind of well of magic she drew the power from, but even with the magic Ritten had siphoned from her, she started throwing spell after spell at him until he was hard-pressed to defend himself. Something caught him off balance and he fell with a terrible scream. His leg had been neatly severed at the knee.

Rias caught him by the lapels of that stupid coat and hoisted him to his good knee, shouting incoherently in his face. She wrapped her hands over his face, and suddenly the world around them turned dark. The only light source was the magic that I could see being drawn out of Ritten and into Rias.

"You wanted power," she said, "but you couldn't hope to deal with how much I'd give you. You don't deserve your strength. You use it for evil, for selfish gains. Never again."

The corners of my vision started going black as the light between the witches grew brighter and brighter until all I could see was whiteness. Then there was nothing but darkness.

Chapter Twenty-Seven

Rias

I felt the last breath leave Ritten's body and let him fall to the ground. I stumbled back, my body thrumming with energy. It was almost too much to take, having renewed everything I'd used during the fights with the hunters and the witch and then some. I fell to my knees, placing my palms on the ground.

"Ground the power," I panted, "find somewhere to put it."

I looked out past the parking lot to the grassy area that separated the forests that surrounded the town from the sheriff's station. I focused on that patch of grass and shoved my magic into the ground and let it feed anything that might be living in there.

Suddenly, what had been a nicely shorn, if a little unkempt, patch of grass almost a kilometer square was filled with shrubs and bushes and sprouted trees and wildflowers galore, as if nature had taken it back. I pushed the magic into the goodness of nature, ignoring everything else around me, until I could breathe again. I let myself fall to the side, rolling slightly until I came to a rest beside another body.

"Ashly," I said softly, reaching out and brushing a strand of strawberry-blond hair out of her face. Her eyes were closed, her breathing heavy and punctuated by a harsh rattle. Blood covered her almost from head to toe, a dozen small and large cuts and wounds everywhere. Her fingers were stained red, and I could see more blood trickling from deep wounds in the palms of her hands. "Maru," I called out hoarsely. "Maru!"

Hands grabbed me and pulled me away from Ashly, and I struggled against them. "No!" I shouted.

"Rias, calm down," Zeke said, pulling me away from my lover.

"No! Ashly!"

"She's okay, Rias. She'll be okay."

"G-get Dr. Maru. She's bleeding."

He looked like he was about to argue, then just shook his head and headed for the station. I crawled my way back to Ashly, putting a hand against her cheek.

"It's okay, lovely," I purred. "It's okay. You can wake up now. Everything will be okay."

She didn't wake up, no matter how much I wanted her to. I could still feel the magic flooding through me, sated but not emptied by my little stunt with the wild space. I took her hand, not having a clue what I was doing but knowing that if there was something I could do, then by the Goddess I was going to try.

I focused on my magic, focused on that pool inside me, the one that seemed to become still and calm every time I was around this woman. She was my soulmate. I knew she was. But there was still the idea that someday, I'd lose her. She wouldn't live as long as me.

But I was the strongest witch in the country—hell, probably the world now, thanks to Ritten's power inside me. If that wasn't good for breaking some rules, I didn't know what it was good for.

"Goddess, let me have this," I whispered as I wove my magic around the love of my life. "Goddess, please let me have her. I need her. She needs me. We will forever be indebted to you. Please, Goddess, let this feed and nourish her as it does me."

For a long moment, Ashly's body seemed to reject the weave, refusing to let it in. Then as I laid it gently around her, the magic sank into her skin. I could see the thin golden thread in my mind's eye, just under her skin, covering her entire body. It pulsated with her breathing, with her heartbeat, and suddenly she gasped, and her eyes opened wide.

"Rias!" she cried, and I'd never heard my name said so beautifully in my entire life.

"Hi there, lover," I murmured, running a hand across her cheek.

"W-what happened? I was…it was dark and then there was a light and I feel…different."

I shook my head. "I don't know, exactly. I prayed to the Goddess. I used my magic." I looked at her hands, still covered in blood, but the wounds seemed to have sealed themselves. "I think it healed you."

"And you? Are you okay?"

I smiled and clutched her to me, ignoring the fact that we were still lying on the asphalt of the station's parking lot. "I'm perfect now."

❖

"Okay, this is getting old now," Ashly said, raising her hands that were once again handcuffed together. She sat in the same chair she'd been in before—cleaned up of blood and debris, of course, and now near the back of the room, while the rest of the survivors of the fight stood around Zeke's desk.

"Patience, love," I said softly, standing beside the chair and putting a hand on her shoulder. "Patience, please."

She sighed. "Anything for you."

The fight had been hard-won, even with my help. Two wolves had been overwhelmed by the silver bullets of the hunters, and Zeke was in worse shape than he let on. Thankfully silver didn't affect ghouls like it did the shifters, so he was putting on a brave front currently—but he had taken enough bullets to kill anything less than he was.

Natalie had been knocked out by Ritten but came to with Wren at her side. Neither wolf had said much in the aftermath, but I noticed the dried salt tracks of the tears on Wren's face. She would take the deaths of the two wolves hard. I know I did. They'd died for me. Because of me. Because I had brought the hunters here. Me and Ashly. But I felt guiltier that I was elated that it was over now, and I had Ashly at my side.

"The bodies are taken care of," Dr. Maru was saying. She'd come through the battle with little more than a broken leg from that last big hit from Ritten. She had healed already and was standing beside Vadi, who looked paler than usual, and their face was a little gaunt. Whatever they had done to call in that localized fog must've taken a lot of their strength. They looked about ready to collapse. "Zeke's family are handling the disposal. We've got the wounded wolves at the clinic, working on getting rid of the silver sickness from those who were hit."

"I'd like to go see them," Wren said quickly.

"I'll take you when we're done here."

"The parking lot at the diner will need to be repaved," Vadi added, giving me a look that I couldn't read. I blushed and looked away. "But that is a small price to pay for the part Rias played in this."

I shook my head. "I didn't do much. It was already my fault that they were even here in the first place."

"Take the praise, Rias," Zeke said, "you deserve it."

"And the hunters were not your fault," Ashly said. "If anyone is to blame, it's me. I came here and upended all of your lives. I got your wolves killed and people hurt. I'm so, so sorry that this happened."

Vadi raised their hand. "It was bound to happen sometime, hunters finding out about us. I can only hope that we will not be bothered by them anymore, at least for a while. This is supposed to be a safe place for all of us, human and supernatural alike."

"I think it will be quiet for a while," I said. "With Ritten no longer around to pull the strings, whatever is left of the hunters have no reason to come here."

"She's right," Ashly said. "Ritten was leading these hunters. Whoever is left—like my father—probably has no idea what even happened here. I don't think Ritten would have trusted him to be part of his plan."

"That leaves us with one last problem," Vadi said, turning to Ashly. "We still have a hunter in our midst."

She held up her hands in a placating gesture. "Ex-hunter. I'm not doing that shit anymore."

"I still don't trust her," Zeke said, not even looking at her.

"I say give her a chance," Dr. Maru said. "She did help protect Natalie and Wren."

"And herself," Zeke pointed out.

"Be that as it may, she was still willing to risk herself for some of us. Look at what happened in the fight against Ritten."

Zeke had missed most of that part of the fight, but Dr. Maru hadn't. I swear I could've kissed the vampire for standing up for my Ashly.

Wren took a deep breath, looking between me and Ashly. "I still don't like it," she said. "But she did help us. She stopped me from shifting and risking the baby. She protected me and Natalie and the puppy. She deserves a chance." She glared at Ashly. "*One* chance."

Natalie chucked Wren on the shoulder. "And it will make Rias happy."

"Yes," Wren agreed through gritted teeth. "And it will make Rias happy."

I resisted the urge to bound over to the couch and hug the both of them—I didn't think they'd be in the mood for that. I turned to Ashly, who was watching me with such a look in her eyes that I couldn't even describe.

"Very well," Vadi said. "The hunter—"

"Ex-hunter."

"The ex-hunter can stay. Provisionally."

I did a little cheer on the spot and reached for the handcuffs with the key I'd been clutching since we put the cuffs back on her. A hand on my shoulder caught me before I could unlock them.

"Be safe with her," Vadi said quietly. "You both deserve to be happy."

"Thank you," I said as I unlocked Ashly and pulled her into a tight hug. I kissed her hard and long and ignored the rest of the room as Wren and Natalie exited the station with Dr. Maru. Vadi disappeared again and Zeke pried himself out of his chair with only a sound of disgust at our display.

"Come on," I said to Ashly. "Let's get you home."

She shook her head. "I am home. I'm with you."

Chapter Twenty-Eight

Ashly

One week later

"Are you sure you want to do this?" Rias asked, looking at me from the driver's seat. I gave her what I hoped was a brave smile.

"No," I replied honestly. "but I should do it anyways. There's things here I'd rather not leave behind. And a full week of my being gone is enough to make them absolutely irrational. More so than usual."

"Besides," Natalie piped up from the back seat, "I'm here too! It's going to go so damned well."

"You didn't have to come," I told her.

"Yeah, but I figured I should do this someday or I'd probably live to regret it. And according to Wren, I'm going to live a long time now."

I wanted to tell her that I had a feeling I was right there with her, but I didn't. Since Rias had healed me with her magic I'd felt a little… different than before, and I wondered still if something about her magic had done something inside me. But that was a conversation for another day. Right now we were sitting outside my father's house, the car I took from him—which wasn't actually mine—now rightly returned. The three of us were sitting in Rias's car as I stared at the house with nerves eating at my gut.

"You know they won't accept you," I told Natalie softly. "And it'll only be worse if they find out you're a werewolf."

"I know. But I need to show them what they missed out on. What they gave up." She shook her head. "I don't know. I have no idea if this is a good idea or not."

"Well, I'm going in. I need to."

She smiled at me. "I said you were stronger than me."

I chuckled and started to get out of the car, then hesitated. I turned and pulled Rias in for one more kiss before I had to go and face the music—as it were. I closed the car door behind me and started the dreaded walk up the path toward my parents' front door.

The door opened as I went up the first step and I found myself staring at my mother. She was looking over my shoulder at the car I'd just come out of, frowning.

"Where have you been?" she demanded.

I cocked my head at her. "I'm not a child anymore, Mother. I can go where I please, thank you."

"Your father's been worried sick."

I snorted. "Horseshit."

"Get in here."

I paused, waving until I caught her proper attention. "Only for a moment, Mother. Then I'm leaving. And I'm not coming back."

She let out an honest-to-goodness growl that was nothing compared to the ones Wren had been giving me, so it didn't really bother me much. "We'll discuss this inside."

"We can discuss it all you like," I said as I pushed past her. "That's not going to stop me from leaving."

She closed the door behind me, and I heard the deadbolt lock with a loud click. I gritted my teeth to keep from saying something. If they thought they could keep me here by merely locking a fucking door, they had another think coming.

My father was sitting in the living room, and he looked up as I walked in. "It's about time you showed your face."

"Hi, Dad!" I said, faux-cheerfully. "I missed you too! What've you been up to while I was gone?"

He glared at me. "You think you're funny."

"I think I'm hilarious."

"Do not talk back to your father," my mother said.

"Then don't treat me like a child."

"I will treat you as a child as long as you continue to act like one."

I shook my head and walked away from both of them, heading for the stairs.

"Where do you think you're going?" my father demanded.

"I'm getting my things and then I'm leaving."

"What are you talking about?"

I turned back to him. "Exactly which of my words do you not understand? I am getting my things and leaving." I repeated myself slower this time, wondering if he'd even try to understand it or just ask another stupid question.

"You aren't going anywhere. You've missed a week of training already, and I need you to assist on some of our hunts."

"Aw, what's the matter, none of the other hunters answering your calls?"

He looked at me sharply. "No. No they have not."

I laughed. "Maybe they're as tired of you as I am."

He started to say something else when there was a knock at the door. I took the opportunity afforded to me to head up the stairs and go to my room, grabbing a duffel bag and starting to pack it with everything I could think of needing.

"Um, hi." I heard Natalie's voice from downstairs and froze. She was giving me time to do my thing and get out of here, but she was also putting herself in harm's way. I was torn between finishing up and heading down to support her. "Hi, Mom."

"Mom?" My mother's voice was incredulous. "Who are you?"

"I'm Natalie Donovan."

"I don't know that name. Why are you calling me mom?"

I raced around the room, pulling mementos off the wall and grabbing clothes I didn't want to leave behind. I was kind of tired of wearing the same pants and shirt I'd been wearing for a damned week—but hadn't had a lot of choice.

"Remember what you told me in the hospital after Dad knocked me down the embankment? That one moment where I thought you might understand who I really was? You told me that Natalie was on the short list for names if I'd been a girl." There was a long moment of silence. "I never forgot that moment."

Oh, shit. She was pulling the memory lane shit with Mom, same as she had with me. I quickly zipped up the bag and hefted it onto my shoulder, then ran to the stairs.

"D-d-d—" I heard my mother stammer.

"That's not my name anymore." Natalie's words came out harshly, and I didn't blame her. I bet she hadn't heard her deadname in a very long time now. "My name is Natalie."

"But you—"

"Are my sister," I said as I came down the stairs. I glared at my father as I walked through the living room. "I told you I would find my sibling someday, and I did."

He stood up and came toward me, close enough that I could see the angry pulsing veins in his forehead.

"What nonsense is this?" he demanded, staring at Natalie. She looked so unsure of herself, but when she saw Dad, she straightened up in a way that I remembered her doing when she was a kid. Always wanting to impress him.

"This is Natalie," I said, "your eldest child and my sister."

"You don't have a sister."

"Yes, she does," Natalie said. "And you have a second daughter."

Dad's face started going purple in his anger and he stormed forward, raising his hand. "Get out of my house this instant! I have one child. One! And she is not going anywhere with you!"

"Yeah, I figured you'd act that way," she said, shaking her head. She looked to me. "Are you ready to go?"

I nodded. "I'm done with this place."

Dad looked between the two of us. "What are you talking about? I told you you're not going anywhere with this…charlatan!"

Nat and I looked at each other and burst out laughing.

"Charlatan? Really?" Nat said.

"Yeah, he really talks like that, don't you remember?"

"Oh, Goddess, it's been so long I almost forgot."

Dad clenched his raised hand, and I knew what was going to happen next. I moved to intervene, but Nat was faster. As his fist came toward her in a hammer blow, she caught him by the wrist and twisted in a maneuver he had taught us when we were young. She spun him around and pinned his wrist to his back, then pulled up, causing him to gasp in pain.

"Not so much fun when you're on the receiving end, is it?" she said softly.

A clicking noise echoed through the room, and I looked at my mother, wondering where she had pulled the small semi-automatic pistol out of. She had the gun aimed steadily at Natalie.

"Are you really going to shoot me, Mother?" Nat asked.

"I'm not your mother, you freak."

Dad yelped as Natalie's smile was wiped from her face and she stared at Mom with the deadest eyes I'd ever seen on her. I slipped in beside my mom, knocking her hands up and pulling the gun out of her grip in a single motion. I unloaded the gun and cleared the chamber before tossing all the pieces into the living room.

"If you ever call her that again, I'll kill you myself," I told her softly, pushing her back against the wall. She stared at me like she'd never seen me before. I turned to Natalie. "Let him go. They aren't worth it."

She did, pushing Dad away from her, probably a little harder than she had to. She turned on her heel and started back down the pathway toward the car as I headed for the door.

"Y-you're not going anywhere," Dad snapped.

I looked at him and shook my head. "Good luck, Dad. I honestly hope you realize how your actions brought all this on."

"You're my child. You're my responsibility."

"I'm not a child anymore. And I haven't been your responsibility for a long time."

He seemed more confused than hurt as I exited the house and slammed the door behind me. I met Natalie back at the car and gave her the biggest hug I could manage with the heavy duffel on my shoulder.

"I tried to warn you," I said soothingly.

"I know." Her voice was cold and distant, but I could hear the sadness underneath. "I-I thought Mom might be different."

"They don't deserve you."

"You either."

"C'mon," I said, "let's go home."

She nodded and got in the back seat. I tossed my duffel in after her and reclaimed the passenger seat. If Rias had pressing questions for either of us she didn't pry, instead just pulling out onto the street and heading back to Terabend.

It was odd, thinking of the small town as my new home. I was leaving the only home I'd ever known, really, and now I had something brand new. I had a sister, a lover, and soon enough would have a little niece or nephew to dote upon. Well, little werewolf anyway. And all I had to do was get rid of a couple of controlling parents and make a promise not to try and hurt any of the supernatural folk of the town. It was a trade I made gladly.

Chapter Twenty-Nine

Rias

One month later

Having another human in my living space took some getting used to. As someone who had lived alone for the past four decades or so, I'd become somewhat set in my ways. But it was kind of nice to make room for someone else. Someone who was irreplaceable. Someone who fit with me almost perfectly.

I was honest with her about my age. I think it took a bit of time for her to get used to the idea that I was actually in my sixties, but I think it took even longer for her to figure out that she might look as good as she did now when she was in her sixties and past that too. Whatever my magic had done to her hadn't made her a witch per se, but I could feel the energy that still permeated her skin, her very essence, almost like she could use magic. But no matter how much I tried to teach her, she couldn't seem to cast any sort of spell, not even conjuring witchlight.

Which was okay. The town seemed happy having only one witch in it, and Ashly seemed happy not to have to worry about being overly supernatural. A lifetime of being told to hate nonhumans was a hard habit to break, but she worked hard at it every day and I wanted to say she was doing really well—most of the time.

She had to learn, because she took a job as deputy to the sheriff when I quit. That's right, I quit my job. I had never found it fulfilling, really just something I did for money and to help people. But I realized I could help people more with my magic than I could as a sheriff's deputy. But Ashly's skills were uniquely suited to the profession, and she seemed happy to replace me, even if Zeke wasn't so keen on it. But even he had to admit that she was working out well.

We never talked about Ashly's parents. Whatever had been said to her and Natalie stayed between them. But there were times when I really wondered what had happened that had brought a bit of sadness into Natalie's eyes whenever anyone spoke about their family. She seemed really happy to have her sister in Terabend, however, and Ashly was just as happy to have family that actually cared about her and didn't just see her as a tool.

And I loved having her here too, because I got to wake up every morning staring at the most beautiful woman I'd ever seen. Someone who knew me, fully and completely, and loved me for who I was. I used my magic more and more now, helping people, growing things, finding things, sometimes just being there for people when they needed it.

It was a month after the fight with the hunters, and things were starting to get back to normal. We'd attended funerals for the two wolves that had given their lives for us, and I promised to always remember Liam and Autumn for their sacrifice. Even Wren had decided that their names would live on in the pack hierarchy and would never be forgotten. Wren also got grumpier and grumpier as her due date approached and then passed and the baby seemed to have no intention of actually leaving the womb.

We laughed about it a lot while Wren growled at Ashly—as was the norm these days. Still, the Alpha werewolf was warming up to her new sister-in-law. She had even stopped threatening to eat her—as often.

As the evening approached, we were all together in my backyard. I sat at the table with a glass of whiskey in front of me. Nat had her usual can of Coke and Ashly had opted for a beer, while Wren was relegated to water. She sat slouched down in her chair, clearly disgruntled with the baby.

"They seriously need to get out of me," she growled during a lull in the conversation. This earned laughs from the sisters, but I only nodded.

"What does Dr. Maru say?" I asked.

"Says they'll come out when they come out."

We laughed together and enjoyed each other's company. The sisters told stories of their childhood and Natalie caught up on getting to know her long-lost sibling. I zoned out for a while, staring at the concrete where only a couple of years ago I had helped a wolf break free of shackles put on it by an evil witch.

I had to wonder, if I had the option to do it all over again, would I?

Of course I would. I helped Heather because it was the right thing to do. Even if I'd known it would lead to all this, I'd still do it. Because I was richer for having done it, not just in that I could use my magic without being afraid now, but because I had Ashly too.

I was broken from my thoughts by a slight commotion as Wren stood up as suddenly as she could manage. I glanced at her, confused.

"What is it?"

"Um…I think I made a mess."

I looked down at the ground where there was a puddle of water. I glanced at her glass, still full. My mind was slow to put two and two together.

"Oh shit!" I said. "Someone call Dr. Maru!"

Natalie already had her phone out and the others laughed at me as they called the doctor. It looked like that puppy had just been waiting for the right time to come out, I thought, as I escorted Wren around the house and out to the front where the doctor was pulling up. We loaded Natalie and Wren up in the ambulance and they pulled away with a promise that they would let us know the moment we could come and see them.

Ashly and I held each other as the ambulance disappeared into the night, and I looked up at the stars. I remembered the bones I had thrown that night after I freed Heather's wolf, what they had shown me. Things had been rough, but it had all worked out for the best.

And I had my soulmate. My lover. My Ashly.

I kissed her tenderly, pulling her in close.

"What was that for?" she asked as she pressed her forehead against mine and our lips parted.

"I love you," I told her.

She smiled. "I love you too."

About the Author

Elena is a trans woman, a parent, and wife to her amazing Goddess. She loves to write and read everything from paranormal romance to sci-fi and fantasy books with sapphic characters. She enjoys playing video games and watching cooking shows, hoping to learn to cook purely through osmosis. She lives in Edmonton, Alberta, with her wonderful spouse and amazing offspring. Elena uses she/her pronouns. Connect with her on Twitter @WriterElenaA or through email at writerprincess8@gmail.com.

Books Available From Bold Strokes Books

Back to Belfast by Emma L. McGeown. Two colleagues are asked to trade jobs. Claire moves to Vancouver and Stacie moves to Belfast, and though they've never met in person, they can't seem to escape a growing attraction from afar. (978-1-63679-731-1)

The Breakdown by Ronica Black. Vaughn and Natalie have chemistry, but the outside world keeps knocking at the door, threatening more trouble, making the love and the life they want together impossible. (978-1-63679-675-8)

The Curse by Alexandra Riley. Can Diana Dillon and her daughter, Ryder, survive the cursed farm with the help of Deputy Mel Defoe? Or will the land choose them to be to the next victims? (978-1-63679-611-6)

Exposure by Nicole Disney & Kimberly Cooper Griffin. For photographer Jax Bailey and delivery driver Trace Logan, keeping it casual is a matter of perspective. (978-1-63679-697-0)

Hunt of Her Own by Elena Abbott. Finding forever won't be easy, but together Danaan's and Ashly's paths lead back to the supernatural sanctuary of Terabend. (978-1-63679-685-7)

Perfect by Kris Bryant. They say opposites attract, but Alix and Marianna have totally different dreams. No Hollywood love story is perfect, right? (978-1-63679-601-7)

Royal Expectations by Jenny Frame. When childhood sweethearts Princess Teddy Buckingham and Summer Fisher reunite, their feelings resurface and so does the public scrutiny that tore them apart. (978-1-63679-591-1)

Shadow Rider by Gina L. Dartt. In the Shadows, one can easily find death, but can Shay and Keagan find love as they fight to save the Five Nations? (978-1-63679-691-8)

Tribute by L.M. Rose. To save her people, Fiona will be the tribute in a treaty marriage to the Tipruii princess, Simaala, and spend the rest of her days on the other side of the wall between their races. (978-1-63679-693-2)

Wild Wales by Patricia Evans. When Finn and Aisling fall in love, they must decide whether to return to the safety of the lives they had, or take a chance on wild love in windswept Wales. (978-1-63679-771-7)

Can't Buy Me Love by Georgia Beers. London and Kayla are perfect for one another, but if London reveals she's in a fake relationship with Kayla's ex, she risks not only the opportunity of her career, but Kayla's trust as well. (978-1-63679-665-9)

Chance Encounter by Renee Roman. Little did Sky Roberts know when she bought the raffle ticket for charity that she would also be taking a chance on love with the egotistical Drew Mitchell. (978-1-63679-619-2)

Comes in Waves by Ana Hartnett. For Tanya Brees, love in small-town Coral Bay comes in waves, but can she make it stay for good this time? (978-1-63679-597-3)

Dancing With Dahlia by Julia Underwood. How is Piper Fernley supposed to survive six weeks with the most controlling, uptight boss on earth? Because sometimes when you stop looking, your heart finds exactly what it needs. (978-1-63679-663-5)

The Heart Wants by Krystina Rivers. Fifteen years after they first meet, Army Major Reagan Jennings realizes she has one last chance to win the heart of the woman she's always loved. If only she can make Sydney see she's worth risking everything for. (978-1-63679-595-9)

Skyscraper by Gun Brooke. Attempting to save the life of an injured boy brings Rayne and Kaelyn together. As they strive for justice against corrupt Celestial authorities, they're unable to foresee how intertwined their fates will become. (978-1-63679-657-4)

Untethered by Shelley Thrasher. Helen Rogers, in her eighties, meets much younger Grace on a lengthy cruise to Bali, and their intense relationship yields surprising insights and unexpected growth. (978-1-63679-636-9)

You Can't Go Home Again by Jeanette Bears. After their military career ends abruptly, Raegan Holcolm is forced back to their hometown to confront their past and discover where the road to recovery will lead them, or if it already led them home. (978-1-636790644-4)

A Wolf in Stone by Jane Fletcher. Though Cassilania is an experienced player in the dirty, dangerous game of imperial Kavillian politics, even she is caught out when a murderer raises the stakes. (978-1-63679-640-6)

The Devil You Know by Ali Vali. As threats come at the Casey family from both the feds and enemies set to destroy them, Cain Casey does whatever is necessary with Emma at her side to bury every single one. (978-1-63679-471-6)

The Meaning of Liberty by Sage Donnell. When TJ and Bailey get caught in the political crossfire of the ultraconservative Crusade of the Redeemer Church, escape is the only plan. On the run and fighting for their lives is not the time to be falling for each other. (978-1-63679-624-6)

One Last Summer by Kristin Keppler. Emerson Fields didn't think anything could keep her from her dream of interning at Bardot Design Studio in Paris, until an unexpected choice at a North Carolina beach has her questioning what it is she really wants. (978-1-63679-638-3)

StreamLine by Lauren Melissa Ellzey. When Lune crosses paths with the legendary girl gamer Nocht, she may have found the key that will boost her to the upper echelon of streamers and unravel all Lune thought she knew about gaming, friendship, and love. (978-1-63679-655-0)

Undercurrent by Patricia Evans. Can Tala and Wilder catch a serial killer in Salem before another body washes up on the shore? (978-1-636790669-7)

Milton Keynes UK
Ingram Content Group UK Ltd.
UKHW021531050924
447875UK00001B/51